Without You

a novel by

Yesenia Vargas

Cover by Yesenia Vargas
Proofread by the Eclectic Editor

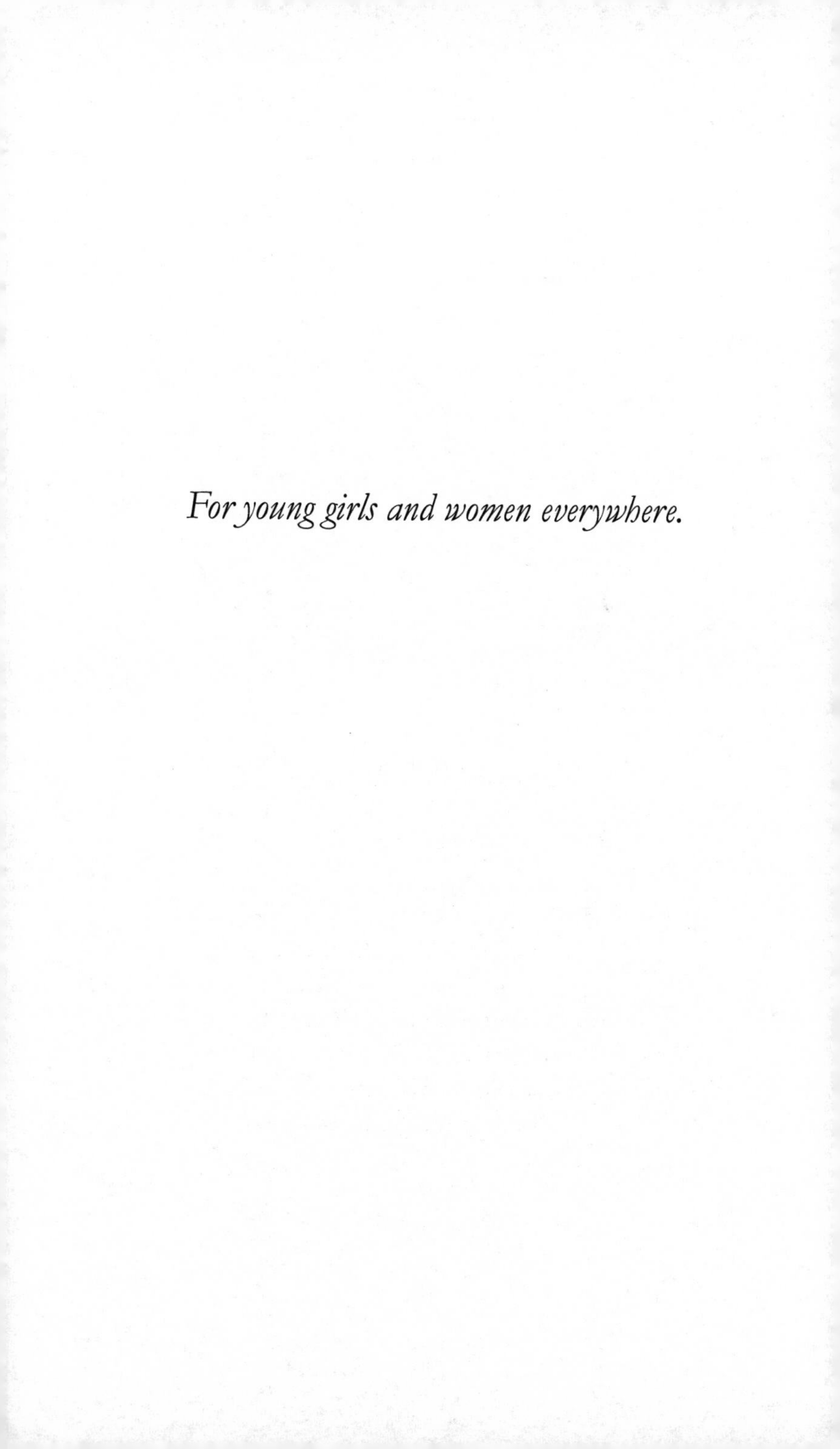

For young girls and women everywhere.

Without You

chapter one

"I wish you'd just go to school here," Mayra said. "I feel like I can't even fully appreciate the awesomeness that is senior year if you're leaving at the end of it."

Ariana gave her best friend a smile from her desk.

"Well, it's just an idea." Ariana's stomach did a flip just thinking about it, but at the same time, she thought it would be amazing to have a fresh start. "We'll see if I can even get in."

She browsed around UGA's site some more and looked at pictures of the campus, including the famous arch. Legend said if you walked under it before graduation, you'd never actually graduate. Next, there were pictures of the gigantic football stadium. She imagined being surrounded by entirely new people.

"Oh, you'll get in. No question about it, with your grades." Mayra shut her laptop.

Ariana smiled and bookmarked the UGA application link. The computer's fan sounded angry. The early decision deadlines were in about two months. She had plenty of time to fill out the applications and decide where she wanted to go. So far, she was set on UGA.

"What do you think you're going to major in?" she asked Mayra.

"I have no idea." She lay back on the bed. "Maybe nursing."

"You'd make a good nurse. You helped nurse Jimmy back to health after…you know."

Mayra threw a pillow at her. Thank goodness. She had not wanted to say it out loud. It had been about eight months since the whole thing with her ex, but she still didn't like to talk about it too much.

"It was the least I could do," she said. "He helped both of us out at that party, and then…" She shook her head, and Ariana could tell it was time for a subject change. Hey, that would be another good reason to move away. To make sure she was far away from him.

"Do you still think about him?" Mayra asked quietly.

She sighed. "Sometimes, in the beginning," she admitted. It felt good saying that out loud, even though her throat felt funny. "But I hardly ever think about him now."

"That's good," Mayra said, sitting up.

"Let's go get some air," Ariana said. They could hear Jimmy and Ryan dribbling a basketball outside.

They walked outside. Her parents were getting rid of weeds in the garden. Jimmy and Ryan were playing one-on-one basketball in the driveway. Their dad had gotten Jimmy that basketball hoop in fifth grade, and he had never stopped playing since. She could still hear him begging for it like it was yesterday.

Jimmy dribbled the ball as Ryan tried to guard

him. He was well over six feet tall now. He had grown four more inches over the summer. He was the tallest sophomore in school. Not only that, he had taken on weight training, and he definitely did not look like a freshman anymore. She watched Mayra stare at him as he exploded towards the hoop, past Ryan, and dunked the ball.

"Can we play?" Mayra asked.

Jimmy looked at them. "Sure."

"Go easy on them," their dad said with a smile.

Jimmy and Ryan smiled. She didn't know how Ryan understood the Spanish. Maybe he was starting to pick it up from hanging around all summer.

"Me and Ryan against you and Ariana," Mayra said.

"Yeah." Ariana agreed with her hands on her hips.

"Fine," Jimmy said.

"Sounds good to me," said Ryan as he threw the ball at Mayra.

She and Ryan began the game. Mayra quickly passed the ball to Ryan, who shot but missed. Jimmy grabbed the rebound, and Ariana ran around, trying to get open in case he decided to pass to her. She wasn't that good at basketball, but she tried.

Jimmy did pass to her, and Ariana shot the ball, aiming for the square on the backboard. It went in. She gave a fist pump.

"Nice," Jimmy said as he gave her a high five.

She smiled and got ready as Mayra took the ball out again. Ryan ran behind her, and she moved to cover him. Jimmy was closer to Mayra anyway. Mayra dribbled the ball and tried to get past Jimmy. He was behind her, a little too close, not giving her any room to pass, move, or shoot.

Mayra kept dribbling, and Ryan pretended to go one way and then another. Ariana couldn't keep up. Mayra managed to pass to him, and this time, Ryan's shot went in.

It went on like this for a while. When both teams were still tied at ten points, Ryan spoke up. "Let's go to twenty." Everyone else nodded and continued, too out of breath to reply. Ariana wiped sweat from her brow. Her parents finished weeding and sat down to watch the game with a drink in hand.

A few minutes later, Ariana was completely out of breath, but Jimmy was just getting into his groove. They got ahead by a couple of points. Ryan and Mayra still gave it their all, weaving in and around the court, making passes and shooting.

But it wasn't enough. Jimmy and Ariana's team had nineteen points, and Mayra and Ryan had seventeen. Jimmy threw the ball at the hoop from down the court, and it rebounded. Ryan quickly grabbed it and put it in himself.

"That's eighteen," he said, breathing heavily. Jimmy grabbed the ball, bounced it to Ariana, and she bounced it back. Then he ran like hell down the right side of the court.

"Shield!" he yelled at Ariana.

Ariana stood like a brick wall in front of Ryan as he tried to follow Jimmy. He ran into her, but she stood firm. He didn't get by quickly enough. Jimmy dunked the ball as Mayra jumped in an attempt to block him.

Jimmy ran back to the end of the driveway,

laughing.

Ariana began laughing too. Not because they had won, but at Jimmy. His energy. It was more than contagious. She walked over to Mayra. "Good game."

She smiled. "It was a good game."

"You're tough to guard."

Ryan went over. "You're not bad, Mayra. Maybe you should try out for the girls' team at school."

"Thanks." She smiled. "But I hate the drama that comes with extracurricular activities involving girls."

"Are you guys hungry?" her mom asked. "I have dinner almost ready upstairs."

"Yes!" Jimmy ran up to her and hugged her. She looked tiny next to him. Even her dad, who was tall by Hispanic standards, looked short next to him. Jimmy picked their mom up, and she screamed. Jimmy laughed and put her down.

They all walked over to head inside, but Ryan hung back.

"Can you believe this big boy was inside my belly at one time?" she heard her mom say.

"I should head home," Ryan said as he began walking down the driveway toward the street.

"Where do you think you're going, man?" Jimmy went over and put his arm around him.

"I don't want to, like, impose."

"Nonsense," Ariana said.

"Yeah," Jimmy said. "I don't even know what impose means."

She told her parents what Ryan had said.

"Tell him he's welcome at our house any time, and he'll offend us if he doesn't come in and have dinner with us," her mom said. Her dad nodded and motioned for him to follow them. They began heading inside.

Mayra looked at Ryan. "They'll be offended if you don't come in and eat. It's part of our culture. The Mexican way," she said with a smile.

"Well, I'd hate to offend anyone," Ryan said with a smile.

###

A couple of days later, Mayra and Ariana headed to their next class, Spanish for Native Speakers. It was their favorite class because they were both in it, and the teacher, Mrs. Randolph, was awesome. She was white, but everyone had been surprised at the fact that she could speak and write Spanish better than any of them.

They walked in. It had been a couple of weeks since school started, so everyone had a seat they always sat in. To ruin that order was unthinkable. She and Mayra went in with their books and headed towards the back, where their seats were. Ariana sat behind the only empty seat in the room, so she was surprised when a tallish guy came in and sat in it a few seconds later.

She looked at Mayra, who looked at him and back at her. Mayra was to Ariana's left. Tallish guy put his books on his desk, took a note out of his binder, and walked over to Mrs. Randolph, who was still at her desk. The bell hadn't rung yet, but most of the class was already in their seats, chatting with one another.

Ariana and Mayra went back to talking about their weekend plans even though it was only Monday. After having a boyfriend behind her parents' back last year, Ariana had been grounded for a couple of months. Jimmy too, since he had helped keep her secret. But she had worked hard to prove to her parents that she wanted to earn back some privileges, and over the summer, her parents had loosened up a bit. She, Mayra, Jimmy, and Ryan were allowed to go out to the movies or the mall on Friday or Saturday night as long as they were back by eleven and check in every so often. And those were the only places they had gone. After what had happened last year, they'd decided to stay away from parties.

Mrs. Randolph nodded and smiled at tallish guy as he headed back to his new seat.

He caught Ariana's eye as he sat down. She didn't realize her mouth was open until he had already sat down. She closed it and cleared her throat.

Mrs. Randolph got up from her desk and walked to the front of the class. "Buenas tardes a todos."

Some people replied good afternoon back in Spanish.

She smiled. "Today, we have a new student in our class." She continued in Spanish. She glanced at and smiled at the guy in front of Ariana. "His name is Lucas, and he'll be with us this semester. Some of you might already know him."

A couple of guys wolf whistled at him or shouted hi. Lucas smiled back.

So he wasn't new new, Ariana thought. She thought she'd seen him a couple of times before. Her high school was huge, and she wasn't that popular, so she didn't really know a good part of her class.

Mrs. Randolph turned on the projector and began the day's lesson on Spanish art.

Ariana found it hard to focus, though. She kept

staring at Lucas's hand on top of his books. He had strong hands, and a couple of veins down his arm popped out. She wondered why he had switched classes. That normally only happened the first week of school. Maybe the second. But this was the third week.

A while later, the projector was turned off, and it was time for lunch. She grabbed money for a soda and headed out the door with Mayra. They headed to the bathroom.

As she came out of the stall, Mayra was already washing her hands.

"He's cute, right?"

"Who?" Ariana turned on the faucet and watched the cool water wash over her hands.

Mayra stared at her and rolled her eyes. "You know who. Lucas." She said his name slowly.

"Yeah, he's cute, I guess." She focused on rubbing soap in between her fingers.

Mayra scoffed. "Please. I saw you staring at him the whole time."

Ariana shook her head but smiled. "No comment."

They dried their hands and walked to the lunchroom, stopping for a soda from the machines on the way there.

Lucas was in line already, and they joined the line behind him.

Ariana saw him grab a slice of pizza, some corn, and an apple. He already had a water bottle. She went through the line herself and grabbed a chicken sandwich and some fruit.

As they paid for their lunch, they saw him walk

towards their usual table.

A large group of people from their class sat together most of the time. They always had a blast. Much better than last year when they had to sit with some other girls.

She punched in her student number and handed over a crumpled five dollar bill to the lunch lady sitting at the register.

She heard someone talk to her. "Excuse me, young lady," the lady asked. "Do you want change back or not?

"Uh, no. Just add it to the account."

The lunch lady punched some numbers in and shook her head.

"Thanks," Ariana said as she grabbed some napkins and headed towards the table.

She sat down next to Lucas. The only two empty seats at the table were right next to him, and everybody else was already seated.

Mayra joined them just a few seconds later, putting down her tray.

Ariana tried to focus on eating her chicken sandwich. She squirted some mayo on the bun, opened her soda, and took a bite of her sandwich. She listened to the conversation around them, laughing when someone said they'd gotten in trouble for wrecking their car. She felt someone looking at her. She wiped her mouth with her napkin and looked to her right.

Lucas was looking right at her, a slight smile on his face. His eyes met hers for a brief microsecond before turning back to his food.

She stared a bit too long before getting back to

her sandwich, wondering why he had looked at her. Did she have an ugly laugh or something? She made a mental note to make sure her laughs weren't dorky.

She finished eating her sandwich, ate most of her fruit, and looked at the clock over her shoulder. Their lunch was almost halfway over. As she turned her head back to the table, she saw Jimmy come into the cafeteria. He smiled and waved as he got in line and grabbed two chicken sandwiches and a slice of pizza.

"Oh my gosh," she said with a smile.

"What?" Mayra asked, looking to where Ariana was turned.

"Jimmy," she said.

"Oh wow," Mayra said, looking at Jimmy's tray, piled high with food. Lucas turned in the same direction and smiled. "Is that your brother?"

She hesitated for a second before answering. "Yeah, he's a sophomore."

"Maybe you know him," said Mayra. "He's on the varsity basketball team."

Lucas looked at her again before looking back at Jimmy. "Oh yeah. I recognize him. I went to some of the basketball games last year. He's good."

Lucas flashed her a smile.

They rejoined the conversation at their table. All the while, she kept reimagining Lucas looking at her with that smile.

chapter two

Ariana walked out of her last class and to her locker, which was around the corner. Mayra was already there, twisting the dial to unlock her own locker.

Ariana began doing the same, holding her books in one hand.

"So…" Mayra said with a smile in her direction.

"So," she said as she got the locker open and threw in her books. She took out her math book and a novel she was reading for her advanced literature class.

"I saw the way you were looking at Lucas today during lunch." Mayra put in all of her books and took out her science textbook and binder.

"Please," she said.

"Why are you in denial about it?"

"I'm not. I just met the guy, remember?" She looked at Mayra, who stood still.

"You're right. He's cute, though, you have to admit."

"Yeah, he's cute. But that's it." They began walking towards Ariana's car. It was hot outside, too hot for fall.

They passed Ryan, who was running to the bus all the way at the end of the parking lot. He waved. They waved back.

"Does it scare you?" Mayra asked.

"What?" She looked somewhere else, anywhere else.

"What happened with Carlos? Do you think it'll happen again?" They climbed the steep steps towards the student parking lot.

"I don't know." They passed people walking down.

A few minutes later, they were at her car.

"Not every guy is Carlos, Ariana," Mayra said as she got into the car. "It's been a long time since that happened."

Ariana turned on the radio and closed her eyes as they waited for Jimmy so they could go home.

Mayra began reading a magazine. The silence began to annoy Ariana.

"So when are you going to go out with somebody? I haven't heard you go on and on about any guys lately." She thought about it. "Or for a while, actually."

Mayra shrugged. "Eh. Pretty much all the guys at our school are dumb, too short, jerks, been there done that, or just not boyfriend material at all." She flipped another page.

Arian squinted her eyes at her. "You said pretty much. Not all. Who is he?"

Mayra rolled her eyes. "There is no 'he'."

"Whatever. You've taught me too much. I know you like someone." She looked over at her. "Is it someone I know or what?"

Mayra began to open her mouth. Then Jimmy opened the door and got in. "What's up, guys? Did y'all miss me?" He messed up their hair.

No way Mayra would say it now. They each brushed their hair out of their faces. Mayra put her magazine away and put on her seatbelt.

Ariana started the car, and they headed home.

"How was school, Jimmy? Did you learn anything today?" Ariana asked.

"No. It sucked. I can't wait until basketball season starts." He looked out the window.

"Are you passing your classes, though? Remember you need to be keeping your grades up."

"Yeah, I know. I'm passing. I have Bs. It's just boring. I'd much rather be playing basketball."

She nodded. "Of course."

###

Ariana was walking to Spanish class on Thursday when Lucas fell into step with her.

"Where's Mayra?" he asked.

So he was interested in Mayra? She made her mind shut up before answering the question.

"She's out sick." She stared at his hands out of the corner of her eye and noticed the way they gripped his books and notebook. He nodded.

"Tell her I said to feel better."

"Sure."

They walked into Spanish class. She went right to her seat, but Lucas went over to a group of guys. She was a bit bummed. Maybe he *was* interested in Mayra then.

She had no one to talk to today since Mayra was home sick with a nasty stomach virus, and she didn't really talk to anyone else as much anymore. They used to have a couple of other good friends, but those friendships had died away last year. Now she only talked to Mayra, Ryan, or the people in her DECA class. And she preferred things that way.

She still hadn't forgotten those few weeks of school last year. It had been torture for a little while, but everyone seemed to have forgotten about what had happened. There was one other girl in this class, Megan, that Ariana talked to sometimes, but she was busy talking to Francisco at the moment. She grabbed a library book from her stack of books and opened it.

She was just getting into the story a minute later when someone said, "Watcha reading?" It was Lucas, and he was right in front of her. She hadn't even noticed him sit down.

"Oh. Just a book." She closed it, and he laughed.

"Well, that much was obvious," he said. He twirled a pencil in his hand. It reminded her of Carlos and the way he would put a pencil behind his ear. She made her eyes go back to her book briefly before meeting Lucas's eyes.

"It's about a girl who has to fight to the death against twenty three other teens," she said. "And she finds out one of the guys has been in love with her forever."

"Wow," he said. "I think I saw the movie."

"Trust me. The book's way better. It's actually the second time I've read it." She tried not to internally groan because of how nerdy she just sounded.

He grabbed it from her desk and looked at the cover. He turned it over and flipped some pages.

He put it back.

"Do you like to read?" she asked.

He looked away. "Sometimes." He looked back at her. "Not really. I like drawing and art better."

She nodded. "Well, you should give this one a try. It's really good."

He nodded but kind of pursed his lips. Ariana tried not to cringe. She wanted to ask him about the drawing, but the bell rang. Mrs. Randolph shut the door and walked around the room.

"Buenas tardes, amigos." She began in Spanish. "Today, we'll be continuing our unit on Hispanic art. So we're going to go to the library to conduct some research on an artist you'd like to know more about. You'll end up doing a presentation and a paper on the artist." Some people groaned.

"In Spanish." More groans. "With correct Spanish grammar and spelling."

"Mejor mátenos ahorita," one guy said.

"I do think death would be a better option," muttered Lucas. Ariana laughed quietly. He looked back at her and smiled quickly before turning back around. Her stomach fluttered, and her mouth fell open for a second before she snapped it shut.

"You don't have to choose an artist today, but browse around. And think about who you want to be in a group with. We'll have groups of three. You'll need to let me know by the end of class on Monday who you'll be working with and who you'll be researching. We'll be in the library working on this project this week and next. It'll be twenty percent of your grade for this nine weeks. Let's line up."

Everybody got up at a snail's pace and headed to

the library. They were more of a huge blob than a line as they went there, but the great thing about Mrs. Randolph was that she didn't mind as long as they didn't get too loud.

Lucas and Ariana headed straight to the computers against the wall.

"There are plenty of books over there too." Mrs. Randolph indicated some tables stacked with books, but no one took her up on her offer except one group. And only because there weren't any computers left.

Ariana sat down, with Lucas right next to her. She knew Mayra would be in her group, but she didn't know who else could be in it. She said it before she could doubt herself. "So you wanna be in my group? Mayra and I will need one more person."

Lucas turned to her. He was leaning back in his chair.

"You're smart, right?"

She rolled her eyes.

"Just kidding," he said with a laugh. "Yeah, I'll join your group."

What a relief, she thought. It would have been mortifying if he had said no.

And it meant that she'd spend more time with him for the next week and a half. Inside, she pretended she didn't know why that idea appealed to her.

###

Mayra was pale and up to her neck in blankets when Ariana arrived at her house to see her. She had a sports drink on her nightstand that she drank out of every few minutes.

"We have to do a presentation and a paper together on the artist," she finished explaining to Mayra.

Mayra groaned rather loudly.

"Lucas said he'd be in our group," Ariana said while playing around on her phone.

Mayra sat up. "Interesting," she said. "So he asked to be in the group?"

"Yeah," she said quickly. "He didn't have one."

"Hm." she said. And then she smiled.

"So when are you coming back to school? Did it suck being here all day in bed?" Ariana sat down on the bed and laid back with Mayra.

"I should be back Monday. Might as well go ahead and take tomorrow off since it's Friday."

Ariana rolled her eyes but smiled.

"And yeah, it sucked. Someone's supposed to take care of you when you're sick, but my mom said she couldn't miss work." She pulled the covers up and stared at the television.

Ariana patted her hand. "Well, I'm here now. That reminds me." She pulled a folder out of her bag.

"I picked up all of your missing work for today. And tomorrow, in case. Good thing I did."

She handed it to Mayra, who opened it and groaned again, this time loud enough for the entire neighborhood to hear her.

"I don't want make up work." She threw it towards the end of the bed.

"At least you'll have something to do tomorrow," she said.

Another roll of the eyes, and she laid back down and put the covers over her head.

"So what else did I miss today that has nothing to do with actual work?" Her voice was muffled.

Ariana thought for a minute. "Two guys almost got into a fight in the cafeteria. But the teachers stopped it." Mayra popped her head out.

"What about Lucas?" She looked at her with a smile.

"What about him?"

"Did you talk to him?"

"Eh. Just about the project. And a little at lunch."

Mayra nodded. "Did you guys pick someone to do the project on at least?"

"Not yet. Tomorrow we will. I'll let you know."

"Are we still on for filling out our college applications together next weekend?" Mayra sat back up again, and Ariana put the folder of makeup work on her lap.

"You know it."

"Good. Because that application is long, and I know I'm gonna need your help. Plus I don't want to be here by myself all weekend."

For some reason, she felt that wasn't the reason for Mayra's slowly-forming smile.

"You need to get Lucas's number," Mayra blurted.

"What? Why?"

"Because. He's cute. You're cute. Two really good reasons you two should go out."

"What about you?" She stood up and grabbed her stuff. "I'm not going out with anyone until you do too." Ariana thought that should buy her some time.

"Okay." Mayra said coyingly. "You promised."

"What does that mean?" she asked.

"That if and when I decide to have a boyfriend,

you need to give Lucas a chance."

"How do we even know he wants a chance? I don't want to give him a chance. I barely know him." She was almost shouting for some reason.

"I can *see* the sparks going on between you two." Mayra said.

"You're worse than that matchmaker on TV," she said.

They both laughed.

"So what time is your mom getting home?" Ariana asked. She needed to head home herself and grab something to eat before starting on her pile of homework.

"Midnight, probably after." She was flipping through channels now.

"That sucks."

"Yep." Ariana got her stuff together and stood up. "I'd gladly keep you company, but you know my parents. Hey, you want to stay at my house? We can take care of you."

Mayra sighed. "No thanks."

"Why not?"

She shrugged. "I don't want everyone to see me like this."

"Okay, well, I'll swing by later then, check up on you. You want me to bring you some dinner?"

"Nah, not hungry. And thanks." Mayra gave her a small smile.

Ariana left, feeling uneasy about leaving her best friend home alone and sick.

###

Ariana watched Jimmy stare at Mayra with his mouth slightly open. It was obvious he was still in love with her. His childhood crush on her had morphed into outright love.

It was Friday night, and Jimmy, Ariana, and Mayra were at the mall grabbing something to eat.

Mayra was just staring at her almost empty bowl of Chinese fried rice and noodles. She was obviously feeling better.

They had eaten way too much.

"I have to go to the bathroom," Ariana said, standing up. She thought Mayra would tag along, but she didn't. "I'll be right back."

"'Kay," said Mayra. Jimmy looked up at her and nodded before going back to staring at Mayra with his arms crossed in front of him. His whole body was leaning into her from across the table.

Ariana tore her eyes away and walked off to the bathroom, which was at the opposite side of the food court.

A few minutes later, Ariana was headed back, and she couldn't believe what she was seeing. She walked slower and hoped Jimmy and Mayra didn't see her approaching.

Jimmy was holding Mayra's hand and talking to her. She nodded her head and said something back, but Ariana was too far away to hear what it was.

She walked up the table quickly, hoping to catch a hint of what they were saying, but Jimmy quickly let go of Mayra's hand as she approached.

Mayra turned and smiled at her. "Ready to go?"

"Yeah." She decided to not bring up anything here. Her mind flashed back to last year the hospital, when she had seen them…but she had forgotten about it. Until now.

They got up, threw their leftover food away, and headed back to the car.

"You guys want to go anywhere else?" They had already played some arcade games, walked around at the mall, and gotten something to eat.

"Watch a movie at your house, Mayra?" Jimmy asked. It was still early out.

"Sure," she said without meeting his eyes.

So Ariana headed home. They talked and laughed about the weird people they had seen at the mall as they drove home.

Jimmy texted their parents that they were at Mayra's as they pulled in. Mayra's mom wasn't home, as usual.

They walked in and sat down on the couches in the living room. She noticed Jimmy sat on the other side of Mayra instead of by himself in the recliner like he usually did.

"What do you guys want to watch?"

They settled on a horror movie.

Ariana couldn't concentrate on watching the movie, though. She kept glancing over at Jimmy and Mayra in case they were holding hands again. But they didn't. When the movie was over, Jimmy and Ariana headed home, leaving Mayra to get ready for bed.

"You sure you don't want to stay over at our house instead of staying here by yourself?" Jimmy asked her as they walked towards the door.

"I'm good. Thanks, though," she replied as she walked them to the door.

"Good night," Ariana said.

"Night."

Jimmy gave her a hug. Seemed friendly enough.

As they walked towards the car, she went ahead and asked. "What was that about?"

"What?"

"I know you saw me see you guys holding hands. Is she into you?"

"Nah. We're just friends."

"Friends?" They each closed their doors, and she turned on the car.

"Friends."

"Is that going to change in the near future?"

"I don't know the future, so I don't know."

"So there's a possibility?" she asked as she pulled out of the driveway and drove the short distance to their house.

He shrugged.

She didn't know what to say.

"Jimmy, just tell the truth."

"I did. You know I like her. I don't think she likes me like that, though." He looked away.

She parked, and Jimmy got out of the car and shut the door. He went inside without waiting for her.

chapter three

That Monday, Mayra was back in school. Ariana led her to their next class. They zigzagged around the crowded hall, clutching their things to their chests.

"Now you'll be able to help us out with that project. Not to mention I'll actually have someone to talk to."

"Yeah, yeah."

"Wish you were still at home?" Ariana glanced at her.

"Yeah, yeah." They walked into Spanish class. Lucas wasn't there.

"Where's your big man?" Mayra said as they sat down.

"Mayra! Someone's going to hear you!"

She shrugged.

They put their books on their desks, and Lucas walked in right as the bell rang. Mrs. Randolph closed the door. "Just in time, Lucas."

"Sorry," he replied in Spanish.

He sat down at his desk.

"Remember, today is the day you have to let me know who you're choosing for your project and paper. It's all due next week." She began handing out packets of stapled sheets as she continued in Spanish. "This contains the instructions and rubric for the assignment. The outline is due this week, and this blue paper lists the kinds of presentations you can choose from. The green is the rubric, including how much time you'll have to present."

Lucas passed a packet back to her, and she opened it and began looking through it.

"This is going to be ton of work," Mayra said.

"It's twenty percent of our grade," she replied.

Mayra sighed. She wasn't the only one.

"Let's head to the library then."

A few minutes later, Mayra and Ariana were sharing a computer, and Lucas was on his own right next to them.

"So what's the plan?" Mayra asked.

"We still need to choose someone since we didn't get to work on this on Friday, but I think we've narrowed it down."

She showed her three artists they liked. "I like that woman with the weird paintings," Mayra replied.

"You want to do her?" Ariana looked at Lucas.

"Not really. She has a mustache and a unibrow. But I don't mind choosing her for this project," he said.

Mayra laughed loudly.

"Not what I meant," Ariana said, turning back to the computer. She could feel her face turning red hot.

"I don't think we're going to get this all done by next week," Mayra said, calming down. Ariana was thankful for the change of subject. "I think we're going to have to meet at my house to work on it this weekend."

Ariana stared at Mayra, mouth open.

"Sounds like a plan. When?" Lucas was still typing. Now Ariana stared at him. He had sounded pretty eager.

"Saturday. We can pitch in and get something to eat." Mayra smiled at her.

"Sure. Where do you live?" He turned towards Mayra.

"Give Ariana your number, and she'll give you my address. I forgot my phone in my book bag back in the room." She went back to saving some stuff on the screen. "We live on the same street anyway."

More staring at Mayra. Plus a kick in the foot while Lucas reached for his phone in his pocket. Mayra smirked.

"Ready?" he asked Ariana.

She took out her phone. She had no choice. She nodded.

She saved his number as he recited it. She sent him a text with Mayra's address. "It's the blue house on the right."

"Okay. Thanks." He looked at the message he had just gotten. "I'll go tell Mrs. Randolph who we chose."

He left and walked to the opposite side of the library where Mrs. Randolph was helping some students.

"What the hell?" Ariana said as she turned towards Mayra.

"I just did you the biggest favor of your life." Mayra took her phone out of her pocket and checked it.

"No. You didn't," Ariana said. "What am I going

to do?"

"First of all, make sure you wear something cute on Saturday. Not those gym shorts you always wear." Mayra gave her a stern look before putting her phone away.

Her mouth fell open again. "Those are comfortable!"

"Yeah, well. If it's comfortable, it's probably not cute." Mayra went back to the computer.

"Who cares?" Ariana asked, trying to keep her voice down.

"Me. I care. You need to lighten up a bit. Lucas is a really good guy. I'm not saying go out with him. But he's a good friend to have at the very least."

"How can you know that? You haven't even been here."

"I can tell."

"You sure didn't tell with Carlos," she shot back in a whisper.

"Eh. I had a bad vibe sometimes, but it was too late when I finally realized why." She looked at her. "It's easy to tell Lucas is a nice guy. And ask anyone. I hear he's sweet."

"You've been back one day, and you've already been…snooping?"

Mayra laughed. Ariana looked to see if Lucas was coming, but he was just now talking to the teacher.

"I watch out for my best friend. You have nothing to worry about when it comes to Lucas. Trust me."

"You know what? I haven't said anything. Actually, I forgot. But I saw what was happening between you and Jimmy at the mall the other day—"

Mayra looked like her eyes were about to pop out.

"We're all set, guys." It was Lucas. He sat down. "We have ten minutes before lunch. Who wants to help me research what these paintings signify?" He did air quotes with his finger on the last word.

"Ariana does," Mayra said. "I'm working on the outline for the paper."

###

"What is your problem?" Ariana asked Mayra as they walked to lunch. She tried not to be overheard. Lucas was walking with a group of guys, and she and Mayra had fallen behind.

"What are you talking about?" Mayra kept looking ahead.

"I sense avoidance here." She pursed her lips as she thought. "You're in denial."

"The only one who seems to be in denial is you. About Lucas." Mayra stopped at the drink machines and put in her dollar.

"I. Barely. Know. The guy. He's cute. I'll admit it, but—"

"You really think I'm cute?" someone said.

She spun around.

Lucas.

"I was talking about another Lucas." She turned back around, trying not to hyperventilate.

"No, she wasn't," Mayra said as she pushed some buttons and waited for her drink.

"Okay. I'm leaving," Ariana said. She used her left hand to cup her right elbow so that her face was blocked from Lucas's view and walked off. No way was she sticking around for that conversation.

For maybe the second time in her life, including

the one time when they were nine and Mayra had made her drop her just-unwrapped popsicle in the dirt, she was mad at her best friend.

She entered the cafeteria and power walked past their usual table. She found an empty table at the back and sat down facing the window. She saw two tears hit the table, and she let her hair fall down around her face as she looked down and put her hands on her forehead. Her elbows were on the table, further blocking everyone off.

She was focusing on breathing when someone touched her shoulder.

She wanted to tell Mayra to go away, but she didn't want her to realize she was crying.

"What's wrong?"

Oh no. Now she really couldn't show her face.

It was Lucas. He took a seat next to her. She couldn't see his face through her wall of hair.

She sniffled, trying not to blubber all over the table.

"Napkin?" He handed her one. She took it and wiped her nose.

"Wanna talk?" His voice was so soft it was almost a whisper.

She shook her head.

They sat there like that for a few more minutes. Finally, he squeezed her shoulder lightly and left.

She shook her head and sighed. How embarrassing. She swept her hair out of her face and covered her face with her hands. She hadn't even gotten a drink. She licked her lips, wondering whether a cold lemonade was worth passing the table where Lucas, Mayra, and everyone else were sitting at, probably having a good time. She did not want to answer any questions about why she had been crying. The truth was, even she wasn't sure. She used the napkin to wipe her tears. She swallowed. It was going to be a long lunch.

Mayra sat down. "Hey."

She played with the napkin. "Hey."

"Sorry."

"You didn't do anything," she said quietly.

"Yes, I did. I've been acting like a jerk for no reason."

"Why?" She looked at Mayra, who looked out the window. It was raining.

"I guess I've been trying to get my mind off of certain things."

"Like what?"

"Like the fact that I like someone." She sighed. "I really like someone."

"Who?" Now Ariana was curious.

"It doesn't matter because it wouldn't work."

"How do you know?"

"I just do. But I need to get over it. Our friendship isn't worth sacrificing."

Then she knew.

"You're talking about Jimmy."

They finally looked at each other.

Mayra nodded. Her chin quivered like right before she cried.

"Since when do you like him?"

"I don't know." She looked around the lunchroom. "I've always loved him in a way. He's your brother. And then after everything last year, I don't know. I just started feeling something else entirely, and it's been driving me crazy. I mean, he's your little brother."

Mayra had tears in her eyes.

"First of all, he's not little. He's at least six inches taller than us. And yeah, he's my younger brother, but only by a year." She didn't know why she was defending Mayra's feelings for Jimmy instead of being weirded out by them. Because she was weirded out by them.

"You don't sound very surprised."

"I'm not. At the mall the other week, I saw you two holding hands. It was obvious there was something going on." She decided not to mention their kiss when Jimmy was at the hospital last year. It just felt wrong that she had witnessed something like that between them.

"I just don't want us to ever stop being best friends. I don't think this could ever be easy. This is high school. Relationships come and go. Fast. The odds are that we'll break up, and then what'll happen?"

Ariana shrugged. "We keep being friends."

Mayra sighed. "I don't know."

"We both know Jimmy's been in love with you since we were kids."

Mayra chuckled. "Isn't that crazy?"

"Are you thinking of giving him a chance?"

"I don't know. Sometimes yeah. Sometimes no. I'm just not sure, so for now, we'll just keep being friends."

Ariana nodded. "So no more being a jerk to me?"

"I can't promise I won't try to nudge—"

"Push."

"You and Lucas together because I see the chemistry, but I promise no more being a jerk."

They smiled.

"I think you and Jimmy might have chemistry."

Mayra turned towards the table and looked down. "Aren't you worried about what might happen? What could change?"

"Yeah, a little. But I also want you guys to be happy. You'll never know what could happen if you don't give it a try."

"True." She looked at her. "Sorry."

"It's okay. I don't know why I broke down like that." She wiped at her eyes again. She could feel the tears coming on again. "This is hard to say, but I think what happened with Carlos bothers me more than I thought. I can't stop thinking about it sometimes." A few tears ran down her cheeks. Mayra put her arm around her shoulders.

"He's not here anymore. He moved."

"I know. And sometimes I just hate myself so much for even loving someone like him. And being with him for so long."

"Don't beat yourself up over it. Everything's okay now," she said. "You are the strongest person I know. Besides my mom."

She smiled. "Thanks."

"Come on. Let's go get you a soda."

As they walked past their usual table, Lucas looked up at her and gave Ariana a small smile.

###

"So we still need to write the conclusion for the essay and finish the slides for the presentation on Monday." Ariana said as she stared at her laptop.

It was Saturday afternoon, and Mayra was laid out on her couch with her eyes closed and her laptop on the floor. "I need a break. Please. My brain is literally fried."

Lucas laughed and shook his head. He was at the kitchen table with Ariana. She was working on the paper with Mayra, and he was putting together the slideshow.

"Fine." Ariana closed her laptop and checked her phone. They had been at it for over an hour and a half.

"I'm going to the bathroom." Mayra got up from the couch, put her laptop on the table, and headed to her room on the other side of the house.

Count on Mayra to give her unwanted alone time with Lucas.

Lucas closed his laptop too and looked at her. He sighed, and they both looked away. He hadn't even mentioned her breakdown the other day, not even after lunch when they had gone back to the library to work.

"So about the other day…" he began. She looked at her notebook. "Are you feelin' better?"

"Yeah. Thanks."

He nodded, and she looked up at him. He gave her a small smile.

"So what are your plans for tonight?" she asked, trying to change the subject.

"First you tell me I'm cute, and now you're asking me out?" he asked.

"Oh my God," she said. Lucas laughed and kept his gaze on her. Ariana wondered why he was being a flirt if he was interested in Mayra.

"I was just messing with you." He still had a smile on his face. Ariana loved the way his eyes crinkled when he did.

"I was just making conversation."

"I know." He played with his pencil, looking down as he tapped it on the table. "Later, I have to take my mom grocery shopping. Then I have to go to work."

She nodded. "Sounds much more exciting than what I'll be doing. Which is nothing."

"Doubt it. My mom doesn't drive, so I take her everywhere. Her and my two little sisters."

"What about your dad?"

He looked out the window. "He's not in the picture." He looked back at her.

"Sorry."

"Not your fault."

"So where do you work?"

"At the mall. In that clothing store next to the food court."

"Gotcha. Must be nice. Bet you get a fat discount."

"One of the few benefits of working at the mall."

She laughed. "Well, I'll have to remember to swing by and do some shopping when you're there so you can give me that discount."

"Okay," he said with a smile. "If that means I get to see you later."

They stared at each other for a few seconds before Ariana looked away. She couldn't shake the feeling that Lucas gave her. He had a completely different vibe than Carlos. And she was starting to think maybe, just maybe, Lucas was into her and not

Mayra.

"Are you hungry?" she finally asked.

"Yeah. I could go for something. Are you thinking we should ditch Mayra?"

She looked towards Mayra's room. "It's been a while. I'm gonna go check on her." She walked towards Mayra's room, trying not to be self-conscious about how she walked.

She knocked a couple of times and walked in. She shut the door behind her. Mayra was on her bed, watching TV. "What are you doing? I thought you said you were just going to the bathroom."

She shrugged. "Tripped and fell on the bed. Then the TV magically came on."

Ariana rolled her eyes and joined her on the bed. "How convenient."

"You guys done making out already?"

Ariana rolled her eyes. "We were just talking. Are you hungry?"

"Eh. Kinda. I ate right before you guys came over. Did you see his car? Not bad, right?"

"Yeah. Well, we're hungry. Maybe we could go grab something real quick and bring you a dessert or something."

"Sure. Just text me. Hey, you think your parents are going to say anything?"

"Uh, they don't have to know," she said slowly, looking around the room.

Mayra winked at her. "Take your time then."

"Okay. We won't be long." She got up and closed the bedroom door behind her. Lucas was on his phone. He put it away as she came closer.

"So what's the plan? We going to eat?"

"Mayra's not that hungry. She said we could go and bring her back something later."

She stood in front of the couch and looked down at Lucas. He stood up and looked down at her. He was a few inches taller than her.

"My car, then?" His chest was less than six inches away, and she could smell his cologne. She felt goosebumps go down her spine.

"Sure."

Her parents wouldn't mind.

chapter four

Fifteen minutes later, Ariana and Lucas were eating at a local taco place, the one at the back of the Mexican mini mart in town. It really was pretty good. She was eating a torta de carne asada with extra salsa roja, and Lucas was eating four tacos with brisket and salsa verde. She had ended up texting her mom that she and Mayra had gone to get something to eat. She felt a tiny bit guilty for fibbing but decided it wasn't a big deal.

"Hm." She savored the soft fajita meat in her mouth, the cool sour cream, the fresh tomatoes, and the warm buttery bread.

"Good?" Lucas was chewing a bite of taco. He took a sip of his handmade lemonade.

She nodded. "Awesome. Thanks again for the food. You didn't have to do that."

"Wasn't about to let you pay for it. What would my mom say?" He smiled and took another bite.

Ariana smiled back. "It was my idea." She took a swig of her lemonade. "Man, Mayra doesn't know what she's missing out on."

Lucas nodded. "Got that right."

They were sitting across from each other in a

booth.

About ten minutes later, they were both done and wiping their mouths with their napkins. Lucas sat back and relaxed.

"So what are your plans after graduation?" he asked.

"Well, my dream would be to get into UGA. They have a good business program there, and that's what I want to major in."

"That's cool." He sat back up and played with his napkin.

"What about you?" She began putting all her trash on her plate.

"I think I'm gonna go to the community college. Sometimes I wish I could go to the Georgia State University or another college, but I don't think that's going to happen."

"How come?"

"My mom and my siblings. They need me. My sisters are only eleven and nine. It'll be a while before they can help out and drive my mom around."

"Are you going to be happy with going to college here, though?"

"The community college here isn't a bad college. And I'll still get a degree and be close to home. Plus the tuition is really cheap, and I can keep my job. Maybe move up the chain to manager or assistant manager in the mean time."

"That's true. It sounds like a good plan."

He nodded.

"What do you think you're going to major in?"

He looked around and back at her. "I'm not sure yet. You don't have to choose right away, right?"

She shook her head. Ariana felt like maybe he was getting uncomfortable. "So should we get going?"

"Sure." He checked his phone. "We can work on the project for another hour or so, and then I gotta go." They got up and gathered their trash.

"Okay. That works. Let me just go order something for Mayra."

On the way back, it was quiet in the car. She tried to think of something to talk about. She snuck a glance at Lucas. He had one hand on the steering wheel and the other on the cup holder. He was so relaxed.

She was gripping Mayra's bag of food, glad her hands had something to do.

"So, uh, what do you like to do in your free time?" Lucas asked.

"Well, I don't work like you, so I have tons of free time. I actually think it'd be neat to get a job. I think I'll get one over the summer, but for now, I just hang out with Mayra. I also like to read and listen to music, and I have like three AP classes this year, so I actually do a lot of homework too."

Lucas nodded.

"I realize I must sound pretty boring."

He smiled. "Not at all."

"Plus I'm in DECA competitions and stuff. It's fun, and it'll look good on my applications that I did it all four years."

"What do you do in there?" Lucas asked, eyes still on the road.

"We do projects, like business plans and speeches, and compete against other schools."

"Hm. Didn't know that. Did you compete last

year?"

She nodded. "First place in Business Speech."

"Nice." He laughed, but Ariana didn't feel embarrassed at all. In fact, it made her smile grow larger. She liked how comfortable she was starting to feel around Lucas. "Do you like sports?"

"Um, I play basketball with Jimmy sometimes or go for walks with Mayra, but I'm not good enough to play for the school. What about you?"

"I'm an assistant coach for my little sister's basketball team."

He worked, volunteered, and helped out at home?

"How do you find time to sleep?" she asked.

He smiled. "I don't sleep very much."

No wonder he didn't have a girlfriend, not that she had asked. But she could tell, and Mayra had done some more snooping, of course.

"What are you thinking about?"

She looked straight ahead. "Just that your life is pretty impressive compared to mine. I think you have a better chance of getting in to any college than I do, with your resumé."

"No way. You're way smarter than me. I can tell."

She rolled her eyes. "Whatever."

They looked at each other, a little too long.

She looked away, and he turned back to the road.

It was silent again. And awkward.

She was trying to think of something to say when he pulled into Mayra's driveway.

She had no idea what to think of Lucas. He was a great guy, obviously, but maybe that's all he was: a great guy. Someone who was just nice to her and didn't have time for a relationship anyway.

###

The next day, Mayra and Ariana were at Ariana's house. Her dad was making fajitas on the grill, and her mom was making rice and refried beans to go with it. Mayra and Ariana had helped make the salsa, and Ryan and Jimmy were shooting hoops, seeing who could make the most free throws without missing. Ariana and Mayra could see them through the window in the kitchen. They finished up and walked outside.

"So. How was it? Going out to eat with Lucas." Mayra emphasized the first syllable of his name. They sat on the front porch, enjoying the sun and breeze. The leaves on the trees were turning orange and red. Ariana loved the change of scenery that fall brought.

"It was good. The food was good. The conversation was good." She looked at Mayra and smiled.

"Do you see yourself going out with him? Be honest."

"I don't know. To be honest, I kinda thought he was into you at first."

"Oh wow. It's so obvious he likes you."

"You think so?" Ariana said.

"And anyway, he's clearly not my type." Mayra sat up, her elbows on her knees. "So if he were to ask you out right now, what would you say?"

She shrugged. "He's a nice guy. I don't know."

"You think so?" She couldn't help but smile. She remembered the feeling of being so close to him and smelling him. She felt something in her chest.

"You like him, huh?"

"He's a nice guy. A really nice guy."

"Do you think you're ready for another boyfriend, one who's not a jerk?"

Ariana gave a small smile. "Maybe with a little more time. I still want to get to know him more. Plus, he's pretty busy from what he told me."

"What about your parents?"

"What about them?" She squinted in the sun, looking down their street and the curve it took before it disappeared.

"Would you tell them? Do you think they'd let you?"

"Yes. I'd tell them. Remember last year? And I don't know. I think they would. But I don't want to even bring that up to them until I know for sure. No need for a fight or an argument or something."

"What about you? Have you thought anymore about Jimmy? Have you talked to him about it?"

"No." Mayra looked up at the sky and then at Jimmy.

"Does he know I know?"

"A little."

"You guys should talk and decide."

"We have." She paused. "Maybe I want to take things slow like you."

They looked at each other. "I wonder who'll cave first." Ariana said. They smiled, Mayra's beginning slowly at the corner of her mouth. She actually blushed a little.

Ariana's mom came down the side porch stairs with a big pot of rice. "Girls, please go get the pico de gallo and tortillas."

They walked back inside, and each of them came

out with something in their hands.

Mayra was carrying the pico de gallo. Jimmy ran over, all sweaty, and helped her, basketball forgotten in the grass. "Thanks," she said quietly.

Her dad had brought out a table from the garage so they could eat outside in the perfect weather. Everyone grabbed a plastic chair and a plate and began getting some food. Ryan gave everyone a soda.

"Hmm. This is so good." Jimmy was stuffing a taco into his mouth.

Ryan was displaying actual manners and taking small bites. "Gracias," he said, after wiping his mouth.

"De nada. Siempre eres bienvenido en nuestra casa," her mom said. Mayra winked at Ryan and smiled.

"Solo que ande con una de mis hijas. Entonces lo tendré que ir de 'tras de usted," her dad joked.

He had referred to Mayra as one of his daughters. Ariana looked at her. She was smiling at Ariana's parents, but her eyes looked wet.

They all laughed, except Ryan, who didn't know whether to laugh or just look respectful. "What did he say, man?" he whispered to Jimmy.

"My mom said you're always welcome here, and then my dad said unless you become Ariana or Mayra's boyfriend. Then he might have to hurt you."

Ryan laughed and began pointing at Ariana and Mayra, shaking his finger and acting like he was pushing them away. Her parents seemed to get the message and smiled.

"So what are your plans for college, Mayra?" her mom asked. She was using a spoon to pour salsa on her taco.

"I'm applying to the college here in town. I don't know what I'm going to study yet, though."

"Isn't that the one you want to go to, Ariana?" Her mom looked at her, putting her food down.

"No. I'm applying there too, but I want to go to the University of Georgia. It's about two hours away, but it has the best program in the state for business, which is probably what I'm going to study."

"What are you going to do two hours away by yourself?" her dad asked while he made his own taco.

"I'll figure it out. I'll get a dorm and some scholarships, graduate, then I'll be back in four years to look for a job. And I'll visit a lot."

She tried her best to sound optimistic, but her parents didn't look very happy.

"Why can't you go here, mija?" Her mom wasn't eating anymore.

"Because. I like that school. The counselor says it's a really good school. I want to go visit it in the spring. Maybe you can come with me so you can see what I'm talking about."

Her parents didn't say much after that.

###

After lunch, Ariana's parents stayed outside talking and resting while Mayra and Ariana got up to go inside. Jimmy and Ryan left to grab a bag to put all of their trash in.

"Where are you going?" her mom asked.

"We're going to go work on our college applications. They're due next week. And I'm looking for scholarships."

"Oh okay, then. I'll just get the boys to help me

clean the rest of this up."

Ariana gave Jimmy and Ryan a wink before heading inside.

They headed straight to Ariana's room. Mayra closed the door behind them. Mayra grabbed her laptop from Ariana's bed and opened it up.

Ariana opened her applications too, and they began working, asking each other for help every now and then.

"What do you think has been the life experience that made me into a better person?" Ariana looked up at Mayra.

Mayra stopped typing and looked at her. "I imagine you shouldn't talk about what happened with Carlos. I don't know. How about a difficult class you've taken? Or getting along with your parents?"

She thought about Mayra's suggestions but decided against them. It should be something academic. DECA, she realized. The business speech she gave and what it taught her. The admissions people would probably like that. She began typing.

A few minutes later, Mayra asked. "What are three values I stand for?"

Ariana laughed. "You should know that. I don't know. Think of stuff they want to hear. Hard work. Perseverance. Helping others. Stuff like that."

Mayra nodded and went back to typing.

Mayra finished before her since she was only applying to the community college. "Well, I just hit submit, paid the application fee, and got the confirmation email. I am done." She got up and stretched.

"I'm done with that one too, but I'm only halfway

through the one for UGA, and I still have to research scholarships."

"I'll do that later," Mayra said. "My brain has refried. Let's go outside for a while. It's almost dark."

"You had one essay!" Ariana said, laughing.

"I know! I poured my life's effort into that five hundred word thing. I'm ready for some fun."

"Aren't you gonna apply to any other colleges? What if you don't get in to that one?" She looked up at her.

Mayra pursed her lips. "If I can't get into this college, I'm not getting into any college." She walked out the door.

Ariana groaned and kept working.

About an hour later, she could hear everyone outside having a good time. Her parents were laughing, and Jimmy, Mayra, and Ryan were playing basketball. She wished she was out there, but she was almost done.

Her brain felt like it was about to explode.

She carefully hit submit on the UGA application. She had saved it for last. She closed her eyes, hoping she got in early. Otherwise, she'd be going to the community college in her hometown.

She read the confirmation page carefully. She'd find out in about two months if she had gotten in early. Either that, or she'd be deferred or denied admission. She tried not to think about that as she closed her laptop.

When she got outside, her parents were getting ready to come in. Her mom patted her shoulder on the way in. Ariana's dad was behind her. Jimmy, Mayra, and Ryan were still outside, sitting down in the grass, talking. It was getting dark, and they had already cleaned up.

"I'm done with college applications," she said as she sat down next to Mayra.

"Are you really going to UGA?" Ryan asked.

She nodded. "If I get enough scholarships."

Jimmy was looking up at the sky.

"Are you guys gonna miss me?" She couldn't resist.

"Nah," Jimmy said. They laughed. "Just kidding. You better come see us a lot. Maybe you can take me to see your dorm and stuff."

"Meet girls," Ryan added.

"Maybe."

"UGA's not bad at basketball, I think. Maybe I could there too when I graduate," Jimmy said.

Mayra was playing with some blades of grass in her hand.

"That would be cool." She imagined sharing an apartment off campus with him. "What about you, Ryan?" Ariana turned towards him.

"No idea. I don't even know if I want to go to college. High school sucks enough already." He looked down as he dribbled the basketball in his hands mindlessly.

"It'll be fun," she said. "You make your own schedule. You'll be so independent, even when it comes to class. Everyone treats you like an adult. Because you are one."

"I like that part. I'm just not sure I have the grades to go."

"I'm sure your grades are great. When it comes time, I'll help you apply. Believe me, this is not a regret you want to have for the rest of your life."

"Is that how you feel?" Mayra asked.

"Sort of. I mean, can't you feel it? It's like we'll be starting over with a blank slate. We can be who we want, do what we want. We'll meet so many new people, and at the end of those four years, you're ready to get a job, get paid good, get a house, start your life."

Jimmy laid back and put his arms underneath his head.

"I think you could also do that here. And still be close to your family and friends." Mayra said. Ariana shrugged.

"It'll suck not having you here," Mayra went on.

Ariana gave her a small smile. "We'll still be best friends. And you can still apply to UGA. Come with me."

Mayra looked down. "You know I can't go there." They had already talked about this. Mayra didn't have as good grades as Ariana, not even the three minimum AP credits. She'd have trouble paying the tuition, and her mom couldn't afford it.

Jimmy sighed. "Sometimes I want to grow up, and other times, I just wish we could stay in high school forever."

chapter five

Mayra, Lucas, and Ariana took off their fake mustaches, something the odd female artist Frida Khalo had been famous for, although hers had been real. The class had loved the fake mustaches they had handed out during their presentation, and Mrs. Randolph had put hers on right away.

Now, they were walking to lunch together.

"How do you think we did?" Lucas asked.

"Well, we went over the time limit by like two minutes, but other than that, I think we did really good. Nobody fell asleep like with the first group," Ariana said.

"So funny," Mayra said. A senior in the back row had begun drooling on his desk after falling asleep. Mrs. Randolph had gently woken him up and chided him before the class could get too many pictures on their phones.

Lucas shook his head and laughed. "Who does that?"

They stopped at the soda machines so Mayra and Ariana could buy something to drink.

"Want something?" Ariana asked Lucas as she put some money in. He hadn't made a move to get something.

"No, thanks." He smiled.

She held an orange juice in her hand. "Come on. My treat. It's the least I could do for you buying me lunch the other day."

Mayra was off to the side, waiting to see if Lucas would give in.

"If you don't choose, I'll get something for you."

"No, really. I'm good."

"Fine. I warned you."

She put in another dollar and a quarter and was about to press a random button.

"Fine, fine. I'll have some lemonade."

She looked back at him and smiled and turned back around to press the button.

A lemonade fell down, and she reached in for it.

She handed it to him. He took it, and they headed into the cafeteria.

They got in line. It was long today. "You gonna buy me lunch too?" he offered.

They smiled at each other. "No. I don't work, remember? You think I'm made of money or something?"

Lucas laughed and pushed his hip into her.

"You're funny," he said. Mayra winked at her. She tried not to smile so hard, but it was close to impossible. Lucas fell in behind her as they got their food and paid. They grabbed napkins and utensils and walked over to their table.

As she ate and everyone talked, Lucas's leg kept brushing hers. He never apologized for it or acknowledged it, but it kept happening. She didn't have a problem with it. Meanwhile, she tried to talk with Mayra, and they'd join the conversation with the others too. They were talking about their plans after school was over.

"Anyone at this table not going to college here?" a guy asked. He was the same one who had fallen asleep.

Lucas spoke up. "Ariana is going to UGA." Everyone stared at her, impressed.

"Nice," someone said.

She blushed and smiled. "If I get in." Ariana kept eating her lunch after someone else spoke up about moving to California.

She nudged Lucas with her body, and he nudged back, looking down at her and smiling.

After lunch, they headed back to class and sat through the rest of the presentations.

When the last one was over, Mayra leaned towards her, "Ours was probably the best one, right?" Ariana nodded. Some groups had obviously not put that much effort into it.

At the end of class, Mrs. Randolph handed out their rubrics with their grades. Theirs landed on Lucas's desk.

"Ninety-four!" he said, turning around and giving Ariana a high five. He gave the sheet to her, and she leaned towards Mayra so she could see it.

They had just gotten points off for going over the time limit, but the teacher had commented on their creativity, especially the fake mustaches.

"Am I a genius or what?" Lucas said. The fake mustaches had been his idea, and obviously, it had paid off. "This calls for a celebration."

"What are you suggesting?" she asked. She

crossed her arms and waited for him to talk.

"Let's go out to eat or watch a movie or something. Mayra, you in?"

Mayra looked up from the rubric. "Huh?"

"Lucas says we should celebrate by going to a movie or dinner or something."

"When?" She folded the paper and handed it back to Ariana.

Lucas shrugged. "This Friday?" He looked at each of them.

"Oh, I can't. I have to do this thing with my mom. I already told her like a month ago I would." Then she lit up. "But you two should go. Have fun for me."

"You sure?" Lucas asked. "We can go next week if you want."

"Nah. You guys go."

"Okay." He looked at Ariana. "I'll text you?"

What else could she say? "Uh, yeah. Text me."

The bell rang, and everyone filed out, including Lucas. He gave a wave before leaving.

Ariana and Mayra got up too but fell behind.

"What the hell was that?" she asked Mayra.

"That was me getting you a date with Lucas." She smiled as she said it, like it was brilliant. And she tapped Ariana's nose too.

"It was so obvious you were lying! Your mom works Friday nights. Besides, my parents make Jimmy tag along, remember?"

"Let me take care of that," she said with a wink as they walked to their next class.

###

"So according to your parents you, Jimmy, and I are

going to a movie. Come to my house like you always do, and we'll figure it out from there," Mayra explained.

"Ugh. It's like last year all over again," Ariana replied, frowning. She did not want a repeat.

"No, it's not. You're going to a movie with a really nice guy. He's not your boyfriend, although that could change by the end of the night."

Ariana smiled. Good thing they were on the phone so her friend couldn't see. She sighed. "I'll be at your house in an hour."

"Don't worry. I already talked to Jimmy. He knows what's going on."

"Okay." They hung up, and Ariana began getting ready, although she wondered if Jimmy would have a problem with her going out with Lucas without her parents knowing. They had already asked permission for all three of them to go out together, but that wasn't what was gonna happen, and it made Ariana nervous.

Twenty minutes later, she got a text from Lucas.

We still on for tonight? :)

She replied.

Yep :)

She had been texting Lucas for a couple of days. Before, their texts had always been about the project they were working on. Now they talked about other stuff. She liked talking to him. He was funny and kind. And kind of hot. She had made up her mind yesterday that if she had another boyfriend in high school, she wanted him to be like Lucas.

She finished getting her hair done and changed into something nicer than what she wore to school, but not too flashy either. She finally settled on blue skinny jeans with a black v-neck top and nice sandals. She straightened her hair and put a few pins in it and then put on some makeup, a bit more than usual. When she looked in the mirror, she felt like a million dollars.

There was a knock at her door, and Jimmy came in.

"You look nice."

"Thanks." She turned towards him.

"You ready?" He hung out by the door.

"Yep. So what did Mayra tell you?"

"That you're going out with a friend." He sat down on her bed. He was a bit dressed up himself. She wondered where he was going.

"And where are you going to be, and why aren't you complaining?" she wondered out loud.

"Because let's say I'll be on a date of my own." He winked.

"Who?" she pressed.

"You don't know her," Jimmy said as he lay back.

"Well, I want to know her if you've suddenly fallen out of love with Mayra and in love with this girl. Does Mayra know?"

He nodded. "Don't worry." He put his arm around her, and they went to living room, where her parents were watching TV after having had dinner together. She took her purse from Jimmy and slung it on her shoulder.

"We're leaving. We'll be back later." They gave each of their parents a hug and kiss.

"Call me when you get there," her mom said. "Remember to be back by eleven. Are you picking up

Ryan and Mayra?"

"Ryan couldn't come today, but we're getting Mayra right now." Jimmy answered, a little too quickly.

Ariana wondered what he and Mayra were up to.

They said bye one last time and shut the front door behind them. Less than a minute later, they were in Mayra's driveway.

"Mayra told me she wasn't coming today," she said, looking at Jimmy.

"She's not," he said.

"Then why are we here?"

"For my date." He unbuckled his seatbelt and got out of the car. She rolled down the window. "I'm not going either."

"What is this?" She stared at Jimmy.

"You remember last year when I got Mom and Dad to let us go to that party?"

She nodded.

"Remember what our deal was in exchange for that?

She tried to remember. Then it clicked. She gasped. "You? Mayra?"

He nodded with the biggest smile on his face she had ever seen.

"Have a good time, sis." He began to walk away.

"Jimmy!"

He came back and shrugged. "What?"

"Are you guys going to…"

"No. It's a date! And I'm a gentleman." He looked at her like she was crazy. "We're hanging out and watching a movie. Ordering in." He winked.

She couldn't believe what was happening. She

looked at her phone. It was too late to cancel with Lucas. She would look like a jerk. Besides, she didn't want to cancel on Lucas.

"Have fun, sis. But not too much." Jimmy walked up Mayra's porch and knocked on the door. She had no choice but to leave and drive to the movies.

But not before texting Mayra.

WHAT THE HELL???

###

By the time Ariana arrived at the movies, Mayra had answered her text.

:)

She couldn't believe that Mayra and Jimmy had tricked her. She sat in her car, wondering what they were up to. She shook her head to get rid of the image that had just invaded her mind. Surely they were just watching a movie, not even touching, much less kissing or who knows what?

Her phone buzzed again. It was Lucas. He was inside waiting for her. As she had gotten closer and closer to the mall, where the movies were, a knot in her stomach kept growing from the nerves.

She didn't think this was a date, but it kind of felt like it.

As she got out of her car and locked it, she wondered what the night would bring.

She checked herself in the car window. There was nothing obvious like something in her teeth, so she went inside to meet Lucas.

She saw him right when she opened the door to the mall. He was near the ticket booth with his hands in his pockets. He looked just as nervous as her.

She walked up to him, not knowing whether to

just say hi or give him a hug or shake hands…

"Hey," she said. She settled for keeping her arms at her sides.

"Hey." Lucas came towards her, and they had an awkward hug. She smelled his cologne and closed her eyes for the briefest of seconds before pulling back.

"You look nice," he said.

She tried not to blush. "Thanks. You too."

He really did. He looked like he had stepped out a fashion magazine, especially with his always-smiling eyes and perfectly white smile. Working at that clothing store obviously had its advantages.

"Are you hungry?" He looked down at her and indicated the concession stand.

"Not yet. I thought we were going to watch the movie first, so I had a snack."

"Oh. Yeah." They began walking towards the ticket booth. "What movie do you want to see?"

"Doesn't matter." They looked at the movie posters on the wall and the electronic sign above their heads with movie titles and start times.

"What do you like to watch?"

"Anything really? I like action, thriller, romantic comedies."

"Have you seen that new car racing movie?" He pointed at a movie poster with two racing cars on it.

She shook her head. "Mayra, Jimmy, and I were going to watch it last time, but we ended up watching something else. I hear it's good."

"Me too. Should we see that one?" They looked at each other.

"Sure." They got in line.

A few silent minutes later, it was their turn.

Ariana quickly got out some cash from her pocketbook, but Lucas handed over a twenty to the lady before she could even complain.

"Lucas!"

"What?"

"I was going to pay for my ticket." She grimaced at the fact that her comment came out kind of whiny, but she didn't want Lucas spending all his money on her.

"I got it."

The lady handed them their two tickets, and they began walking upstairs towards the movie theaters.

"But you help out your family and stuff. You don't have to buy me anything. We're just friends."

As soon as the words came out of her mouth, she wished she hadn't said them. They felt wrong. But it was too late. They stayed quiet for a minute after that. Once they got to the top of the stairs, they looked for their theater and headed that way.

"I think it's this way," he said. She followed him down a hallway to the left, and sure enough, a sign above the theater on the right indicated their movie. They went in and climbed the stairs to the top. It was dark and empty except for a couple of people towards the bottom. She almost tripped, and Lucas grabbed her hand.

"You okay?"

"Yeah." Except for her dignity.

He held her hand the rest of the way up. By the time they got to the top row, their hands were sweaty. They sat down, and their hands fell apart. Ariana caught herself wishing they hadn't and wondered if Lucas was thinking the same thing.

More people began coming in until the theater was almost full, and the previews began playing. She looked at Lucas, and he smiled at her. They laughed at some of the previews together. Lucas leaned over to say something in her ear.

"You sure you don't want something to eat or drink?"

She turned towards his face, and he didn't back away. His face was just a couple of inches away, and she tried not to look at his lips, but it was too late.

"I'm good," she whispered.

For a split second, she thought he was going to kiss her, but before that thought had even fully entered her mind, he was facing forward again and resting back in his seat. She turned back to the screen and tried to focus on the movie.

###

When the movie was over, Lucas held Ariana's hand again as they maneuvered through the crowd to leave the theater. People were buzzing and laughing about the movie. They stepped out into the hallway and began walking towards the exit. He let go of her hand again.

"What'd you think? Pretty good, right?" He glanced at her and kept walking

"Yeah, it was pretty awesome."

They walked out of the mall and into the parking lot.

"You hungry?" he asked. They stopped on the sidewalk.

"Yeah. You?" She adjusted her purse on her shoulder. The movie had been almost three hours. Way longer than she'd thought.

He smiled. "Starving. You want to go get something to eat? We can go in my car if you want."

"Sure." She nodded and followed him to his car.

"Right over here," he said, and they walked in between some cars. They got to his car, and he opened the door for her.

She couldn't meet his eyes. "Thanks." She got in, and he walked to the driver's side.

He got in and turned on the car.

"So where we going?" he asked.

She remembered the tacos and torta they had last time. "Let's go where we went last time."

"Yes. I kinda wanted that too." They smiled and headed towards the mini mart/restaurant.

A few minutes later, they were there.

They went inside, ordered, and sat down. This time, though, Lucas slid in beside her in the booth. It was cold in there. Ariana's arms were covered in little bumps from the cold, and she shivered. She rubbed her arms.

"Here," Lucas took off his jacket and put it over her shoulders. It was toasty inside from Lucas's body heat. She sighed and hugged it closer.

"Thanks. Aren't you cold, though?"

"Nah," Lucas replied. He began playing with a straw wrapper. Ariana took a sip of her drink.

"Do you work tomorrow?" she asked, looking at him.

"Yeah. The whole day."

"That stinks."

"Yeah. But it's better than being at home with nothing to do. And I get paid tomorrow."

"That's true. So what other classes are you

taking?"

"Statistics," he replied.

"I'm in statistics. Do you have Warner?" She looked at him.

He nodded. "First period."

"I have him last."

"I also have chemistry," he said.

"Taking that next semester," she said.

"And Spanish. And Art III."

"So you like to draw and stuff?" she asked.

"Yeah. Anything really. Painting. Clay. I've been taking art since eighth grade. I don't do it in my spare time anymore because I work all the time, but I do it in school."

"That's so cool."

They saw their food land on the counter a few feet away, and Lucas sprang up to go get it. Ariana got up too, to get salsa and lime slices. And some extra napkins.

They sat down again.

"Oh my God, this looks so good." Lucas grabbed a taco and took a huge bite.

Ariana laughed. She had her torta in her hand, and she took a big bite too. "Mm."

They finished chewing and drank from their drinks.

She caught Lucas glancing at her cheesy torta. "Want some?"

He shook his head but glanced at it again.

"Come on." She turned it around to the unbitten side and put it up to his mouth. He smiled and took a bite. She loved this. He grabbed one of his tacos and gave her a bite.

She put a thumbs up. They had been a few inches apart in the booth, but now, after trying each other's food, their bodies were touching. They stayed like that the rest of dinner.

After their last bites and swigs of soda, they threw away their trash and headed out.

"That was amazing," Ariana said as Lucas opened her door.

"Shhyeah." She couldn't stop looking at his smile. It was radiant.

He drove them back to her car at the movies. She pointed to where she had parked it, and he parked in the space right beside it. She couldn't believe the night was already over. She had forgotten all about Jimmy and Mayra. She didn't even care what they were up to anymore if she could just keep spending the night with Lucas. But it was already really late, and she had to be home soon.

Lucas came around to open her door. She got out, not knowing what to do. How would they say bye? It was like before the movie all over again, except they felt more comfortable with each other. Still friends, but maybe more.

Maybe.

Lucas shut the door and smiled at her. She smiled back.

"Did you have fun?" he asked. He leaned against his car, and she did the same.

"Lots," she said quietly. "Thanks for the movie. And the food. Seriously, I'm gonna pay next time."

"It was nothing." He moved so he was in front of her, and there was only a small space between them. She moved so she wasn't leaning on the car anymore.

He put his arms around her and took a step closer. Ariana stood on tip toes, and then she was completely enveloped by him. She inhaled and closed her eyes. The side of Lucas's face was touching hers. She felt his ear on hers. He had one arm around the small of her back and the other on her shoulders. He squeezed her a little, and she did the same. Just as she was sure it would never end, he pulled back, holding her hands for a few seconds.

"I had a great time with you."

She nodded and looked up at him. "Me too."

"I'll see you in school Monday?"

"Yeah." They turned towards her car, and she fumbled to unlock it.

"Drive safe."

She got in and he closed the door for her. He stepped back and leaned back on his car again.

Ariana tried to remember how to pull out of a parking space and simply drive. Her head was still buzzing from Lucas's hug, but she managed to get out of the parking lot without hitting anything.

Then her mind turned to Jimmy and Mayra.

chapter six

Ariana went into Mayra's house without knocking, without thinking. The lights were off except for the bathroom, and the door was halfway closed. The television was on, but the movie was long over because the main menu of the DVD was on the screen. They had been watching some chick flick, apparently.

She saw them on the couch, covered with a fuzzy blanket. She walked over and noticed they had clothes on. She exhaled in relief, her hand on her chest. Her keys jingled in her hand as she pushed her hair out of her face. Mayra was leaning on Jimmy's shoulder, and Jimmy's head was on top of Mayra's. They looked so peaceful she almost didn't want to wake them, but it was past time for her and Jimmy to get home.

She nudged them both. "Guys." She nudged a little harder. "Hello, I'm back."

Jimmy opened his eyes and looked around and down at Mayra, who was also waking up.

"I know you lovebirds must have had a nice time and all, but we were supposed to be home like twenty minutes ago, Jimmy."

He sat up and grabbed his phone from the coffee table. "Crap. It's almost eleven thirty?"

"Uh, yeah. I've only been gone like four hours."

"Shit." Jimmy said as he stretched his arms into the air and stood on his tip toes.

"What were you guys up to?" She stared at Mayra, who was in a tank top and some tiny shorts. She was rubbing her eyes.

"Just watched a movie and ordered in." The leftovers and trash were still on the coffee table.

"Is that all you guys did?" she asked as Jimmy began cleaning up.

Jimmy just winked and said, "We don't kiss and tell. Sorry." He messed up her hair with his free hand on his way to the kitchen. She barely reached his shoulders now, he had grown so tall.

"Bleh."

Mayra came over and gave her a hug.

"You guys good then?" Ariana asked.

"We're still technically friends. We want to take things slow," she said. "How was your date?"

Ariana rolled her eyes and sat down on the couch. "It was not a date. It was a…celebration."

"Okay. How'd your celebration go?" Mayra and Jimmy joined her on the couch.

"Yeah, who's the dude?" Jimmy asked.

"Funny how you actually care about that now that your date is over, huh?" She reached over and playfully punched him on the shoulder.

"His name is Lucas, and he's in our Spanish class. He's a senior. So where'd you guys go?" Mayra looked at her.

"We saw that new racing movie, and then we

went to eat tacos and tortas. Really good."

"The movie or the tortas?" Jimmy asked. She noticed how his hand was around Mayra's waist, but she looked away before he noticed she had noticed.

"Both. He's really nice."

"Nicer than Carlos?" Jimmy asked.

She flinched a little at the sound of his name. "He's nothing like him."

"Good." Jimmy squeezed her shoulder, and they all got up and said good night to Mayra. Ariana walked to the car first and turned it on. Jimmy followed a minute or two later.

He got into the car and closed the door.

"So you guys had a good time, huh?" Jimmy said.

"Yeah. We did. We're just friends, but I don't know. Could be something more eventually."

"Do you like him?" he asked as she pulled out of the driveway and onto the street.

"I don't know. But for now I'm okay just like this."

He nodded.

"What about you and Mayra?"

"Just friends too. For now. Maybe we'll take the next step later on."

"That's good. If I've learned anything in high school, it's that you can't rush things."

"Tell me about it."

"What do you know about relationships? I thought you'd never had a girlfriend?"

"Not really. Not real girlfriends. I've kissed girls and stuff—"

"And stuff?" She stared at him, trying not to laugh as she parked the car behind her dad's truck.

"But I've never had a real girlfriend. I've just always liked Mayra. And look how long it's taken for us to realize we might be right for each other. I'm sure not about to mess that up because I want to get laid or something."

They got out of the car.

"Ew," she said.

Jimmy put his arm around her shoulder, and they went inside.

###

Ariana wandered into the book section of the grocery store and picked up a book with pretty girl on the cover. She flipped it over and began reading the back.

"Boo," someone whispered in her ear. She jumped and turned around. She knew it wasn't Jimmy. It had been a different but familiar voice.

Lucas.

"What are you doing here?" Her heart was still racing, but she found herself smiling back at him. For a split second, she'd thought Carlos had somehow found her.

"Um, I have to buy groceries too, you know."

"Sorry. I meant hi." She put the book back on the shelf.

"You gonna get that?" He nodded at the book.

"Eh. Probably not." She looked back at him. He looked nice, as usual, with fitted jeans and a semi-tight shirt. She was in a t-shirt and sweats with a ponytail. Curse destiny making them bump into each other now. "So you're grocery shopping?"

"My mom is. I'm looking for my little sisters because we're about to go get in line to pay."

"Well, I think you're in the wrong section. If I were a kid, I'd probably be in the toy section."

They began walking down the aisle.

Lucas laughed. "I was just on my way there, actually, when I saw you."

The store was packed, and they moved out of the way of shopping carts pushed along by parents and grandparents.

"Didn't work today?" She glanced at him.

"I go in a bit later," he replied.

She nodded.

"I had fun the other night. We should do it again." He stammered a bit. "Mayra and your brother can come too." They looked at each other. "What I meant was that, you know…"

"I'd love to go." She blinked, not believing Lucas was pretty much asking her out at the grocery store while she was in sweats.

"Really?" His smile returned.

"Yeah. I had a great time. And I can't stop thinking about those tacos," she replied.

He smiled.

"One rule, though," Ariana said. They were at the toy section now.

"What is it?" His eyes were glued on hers.

She tried to contain her smile. She could just hear Lucas's thoughts of panic from the look on his face.

"I pay for my stuff this time." She nudged him and finally smiled.

"Oh, I don't know if I'll be able to follow that rule," he said, looking ahead.

"Well, if you want to go out with me again," she loved the way that sounded but stammered herself, "then you'll have to follow it."

"I'll think about it," he said.

They kept walking and looking down the aisles for Lucas's siblings. When they got to the end, they saw two girls playing with some bicycles.

"That's them. Amy, Jessica! Let's go." He motioned to them, but they just ran away. Lucas sighed and turned to her. "I have to go."

"See you later." She was about to walk away when Lucas pulled her into a hug. She hugged him back and smiled as they pulled back.

"Bye," he said.

"Bye." And she saw Lucas run off after some giggling voices around the corner.

Someone picked her up from behind, and she screamed.

"Jimmy!" He put her down.

"So that's Lucas, huh?" He put his arm around her, and they began walking back towards the grocery section of the store.

"Yes. Stalker."

"I just happened to be walking by…" he said, shrugging but smiling.

Lucas walked by a few aisles down, holding his sisters' hands in his. He turned and looked at Ariana one more time, smiling.

She smiled back, thinking he must be such a great big brother.

"He's cute," Jimmy said, and Ariana just stared.

"I mean, if I were a girl, I guess I'd think he was cute."

Ariana just laughed. "Okay…"

They walked back to the grocery section of the

store.

"He seems like a nice guy. When do I get to meet him?" Jimmy went on.

"Um, how about never? We're just friends," Ariana said.

"For now. I can tell he likes you, though."

"You didn't even talk to him." She laughed.

"I can tell with these things. He likes you. You like him." Jimmy's voice sounded like a xylophone.

Ariana just pursed her lips.

"I get a good vibe from him. And I've heard good things too. You have my permission to fall in love with this guy."

Of course Jimmy had been investigating along with Mayra.

"Thanks? Although like I said, we're just friends."

She thought about that. Were they just friends? She knew Lucas was a busy guy with a lot of responsibilities, but she couldn't stop thinking about him. And maybe he felt the same way.

###

The next week at school, Lucas, Ariana, and Mayra were headed to lunch from Spanish class when Mayra saw some people she knew and left to go talk to them.

"I'll be right back," she said as she walked off.

Lucas and Ariana kept walking towards the cafeteria. Ariana stopped for her usual drink from the machines. Then they got in line, got their food, and headed to their usual table. Mayra joined them a few minutes later.

Ariana noticed Lucas kept staring at her throughout lunch, and she couldn't figure out why.

They talked along with everyone else, and sometimes just the two of them, but he kept fidgeting and tapping his foot.

"You okay?" she asked as he tapped the end of his fork on his lunch tray.

"Yeah." He looked at her again and took a deep breath before putting down his fork.

Then the bell rang, and they exited the lunchroom. Ariana tried to get her mind off of Lucas and how different he was acting.

At the end of the day, she was walking to her car and enjoying the light breeze. It wasn't hot anymore, but just a tiny bit chilly.

Her phone buzzed, and she took it out of her bag.

It was Mayra.

Hey. Staying after to work on social studies group project. Due tom. Ugh. Riding home with Kayla later.

Jimmy wouldn't be riding home with her today either. He was staying for a basketball meeting, and she'd be back for him later. Her parents had agreed to let Ariana keep taking Jimmy like last year, but she couldn't wait for him at school like before. She had to come home in between and check in with them.

Ariana switched to thinking about her presentation next week for her Business Principles II class. The DECA members of the class were already preparing for the spring state competition. She wondering if she should do business speech again when Lucas fell in step beside her.

"Hey," he said.

"Hey. Don't you have work today?" She looked at him as they walked.

"Nope. Not today. I'm off."

She nodded. "What are you doing today?"

"Nothing. Just homework and relaxing at home."

They arrived at her car.

She had taken her time walking to her car from her last class across campus, so most of the parking lot was almost empty by now. Even the buses had left.

"What about you?" he asked.

"Same."

There was an awkward silence, and Lucas shoved his hands in his pockets and then took them out again.

She gave him a small smile, sensing he was nervous.

"Hey, I want to…ask you something." His eyes shifted from the ground right to her eyes.

Her mouth fell open a bit. She screamed inside, wondering if he was about to ask her what she thought he was. She held her books closer to her chest.

"Here." He took her books and put them on her car. Then he held both of her hands and looked right into her eyes.

"I know we haven't known each other that long, but I really like you. I think about you all the time, and you're just…awesome."

He looked down and then back at her. He used his thumbs to massage her hands.

"Will you be my girlfriend?" Lucas said.

For a few seconds—or maybe minutes, Ariana couldn't tell—nothing was said. She simply absorbed Lucas's words, focusing on them, on him, on the feel of her hands in his. Saving the moment in her memory.

She looked at him. She hadn't stopped looking at him. She nodded.

"Yes." She made herself stop nodding like a bobble head. "I want to be your girlfriend."

She couldn't believe she had just said that. But he had. Lucas smiled the most beautiful smile she had ever seen. Before she knew it, she was in his arms, being lifted up, and pressed into his chest. She found herself hugging him back with her arms around his neck.

He put her back down. Their foreheads were touching. She readied herself for a kiss, but it didn't come.

"You don't know how long I've been wanting to ask you that."

She smiled. "Really?"

"Couldn't you tell how crazy I was, am, over you?" Her hands were in his again. They were oblivious to the cars and people around them.

"I thought I was just imagining things," she said. She couldn't believe how much had happened with him in just a few weeks of knowing him.

Lucas laughed and took her face in his hands. No kiss, though. She couldn't help but close her eyes for a couple seconds. She looked back at him.

"I have to tell you something," she said.

###

Ariana was home. She put her stuff in her room and came back to the kitchen. Her mom was in there. She had just gotten home and was defrosting some meat for dinner.

"How was school?"

"Good." She tried not to smile too much from what had just happened at school, but it was hard. "Mom, I have to tell you something."

Her mom stopped unwrapping the meat package and looked at her.

Ariana didn't know how to begin. She took a deep breath.

"Oh, God. You're not pregnant, are you?" Her mom's eyes looked like they were about to pop.

"What? No!"

"Oh. Okay. Then what is it?" her mom asked, now more relaxed.

"This guy I know…" Her mom pursed her lips. "He's in one of my classes. And he's a really good guy. He asked me to be his girlfriend today." Ariana was fidgeting with her hair. She looked at her mom, who was looking down at the meat package.

"I don't want to do what I did last time. I want you guys to know what's going on. I'm going to be eighteen in less than two months. You can't tell me that by then I'm still not allowed to have a boyfriend. Or when I'm at college." She waited. "Mom?"

"Your dad will be here soon. We can talk to him about it when he gets home."

She nodded and went back to her room. She lay down and got out her phone.

She had a text from Lucas.

I miss you already. How did the talk with your parents go?

She replied.

Dad's not home yet so no answer yet. But I'm almost 18. What are they going to say?

Good luck, he replied.

Twenty minutes later, her dad was home. She knew better than to talk to him before he had something to eat, so she waited a bit longer in her room, trying to focus on a paper that was due in a couple of days.

Finally, she walked into the living room where he was sitting.

She sat down next to him, and her mom joined them in the living room.

"I told your dad what you wanted to talk about."

She turned to her dad, who was just staring straight ahead and grinding his teeth together.

"What do you think? Is it okay if I have a boyfriend? I'm almost eighteen, Dad."

He exhaled loudly. There were several seconds of silence, but Ariana willed herself to wait for her dad to say something first.

"There will be rules," he said finally. But she didn't hear the rest of what he said because she was hugging him.

Her mom continued while her dad grunted. "You can't go out with him by yourself. That would lead to all kinds of things. For example, sex, which can lead to pregnancy. And if you want to go to that college as much as you say you do, you don't need to be risking anything."

"I know. I'm not going to do anything dumb. He really is a great guy." She tried not to scream or jump in excitement.

"You can go out with him only if Jimmy goes too," her dad said.

She nodded. She could live with that. Or work

her way around it.

"And we want to meet him," her mom said.

That caught her off guard.

"Isn't it a bit early for that?" She stared at them.

"No. We want to know from the start who you're with," her dad said.

Now that would be mortifying. But she was sure Lucas would do it for her. Carlos, probably never. But Lucas. He would do it. She nodded. "When?"

"Today. Tomorrow. The sooner the better," her mom said.

"Okay. I'll ask him." She checked her phone. "I have to go get Jimmy from the school, but I'll be back in about thirty minutes."

"Don't go around making any detours," her dad said. She just smiled and shook her head.

###

Ariana called Lucas while she waited for Jimmy to come out of his basketball meeting. She was a couple of minutes early.

"Hey," he answered.

"Hi." She was sure Lucas could hear her smiling on the other end.

"What's up? What'd they say?"

"They're not in love with the idea of me having a boyfriend, but they said yes."

"That's great." Now she could hear him smiling. Ariana thought of how much she loved the sound of his voice. Just a tiny bit husky.

"I never thought they'd say yes after... Anyway, they said there will be rules, like Jimmy has to tag along when we go out."

"That doesn't matter to me. I'm more than cool

with that."

"Well, Mayra could come too, so it'd be a double date."

"That works. Like I said, all of that doesn't matter to me. I'm just glad you talked to them about it."

She smiled. "There's one more thing." She tapped the steering wheel and looked to see if Jimmy was out yet. He wasn't.

"What is it? It can't be that bad."

"They want to meet you." She exhaled.

"Seriously? When?"

"As soon as possible."

"Wow." She heard him breathe. "How about today?"

"Really?"

"I mean, it's not going to be easy. When is something like that ever easy? But if that's that they want, I'll do it. Besides, I have to work the rest of the week. I want to be able to see you this weekend."

She smiled and wished he was with her so she could give him a hug. "Can you be at my house in twenty minutes?"

"It's the one at the end of the street, right?"

"Yep."

"At least I'll get to see you."

Ariana saw Jimmy come towards the car with his bag in tow. "I can't wait. See ya later."

They hung up, and Jimmy got in the car.

"Who were you talking to?"

"Lucas." She turned on the car. He nodded.

She turned the car on and maneuvered out of her spot. "Mom and Dad are going to meet him in twenty minutes."

Jimmy did a double-take. "You mean…"

"He asked me to be his girlfriend, and I said yes." They left the parking lot. For once, she couldn't wait to get home.

"And Mom and Dad are cool with this?"

"Yep. I talked to them about it just now. Told them I'm almost eighteen, and they said there will be rules, but honestly, I don't care."

"Good for you." He had a huge smile on his face.

"Why are you all happy?"

"Because I get to meet him too." He laughed, and Ariana groaned.

chapter seven

As Ariana's car went around the street corner and their house came into view, she could see that Lucas was already at her house. She parked near the mailbox since they were short on space in the driveway. Lucas was just getting out of his car, and he smiled as Ariana got out of hers. Jimmy was right behind her.

"Hey," she said. She turned around and glanced at Jimmy. "This is my brother, Jimmy. Jimmy, this is Lucas."

They shook hands. Jimmy was taller than Lucas, of course, but Lucas had a bit more bulk on him.

"What's up, man?" Lucas asked.

Jimmy nodded. Ariana just stared at their male ritual. "Shall we go inside?"

She led the way. She opened the front door, and they all went inside.

"We're home," Jimmy announced, putting his book bag and gym bag in the hallway before heading to the couch. Her mom and dad were in the living room, waiting. She had called them on the way home saying Lucas would be coming over. Her dad looked as serious as ever, and her mom had some drinks ready.

"Mom, Dad," she said in Spanish. "This is Lucas." She looked behind her, and Lucas stepped forward with his right hand out.

"Nice to meet you," he said in Spanish to each of her parents. Her parents stood up, and he shook each of their hands. Her dad nodded, and her mom smiled.

Ariana didn't know what to do so she sat in the empty sofa next to her parents, where Jimmy was already sitting. Lucas joined her. They didn't hold hands or anything. Lucas glanced at her, and she smiled.

"Tell me who you are," her dad said. "Where are your parents from?"

Ariana saw Lucas take a deep breath. He began speaking in Spanish.

###

Over an hour later, her parents were finally done talking with, or rather interrogating, Lucas. They had asked about his family, his grades, his job, his goals for the future. Ariana was surprised they hadn't asked if he had a retirement account or something. Then they'd gone over all the rules of their relationship and what would happen if he didn't follow them. Lucas had looked terrified and even sweaty nervous at one point, but he had survived, and now she was walking him to his car. As they went out the front door, Jimmy followed them for a bit, and Ariana hugged him.

Lucas walked ahead of them. "I can tell he's a good person," Jimmy whispered.

"He is. He really is," she replied, letting go. Jimmy

closed the front door as he went back in while Ariana followed Lucas to his car. It was dark out already. They conveniently went around to the other side of his car, where it would be hard for someone inside her house to watch them.

"What'd you think?" Ariana said with a smile.

"A little scary, but I think they liked me. Right?"

"Not completely sure either. It's hard to tell with them, mostly my dad, but I think they did." She looked up at him. He pulled her close and wrapped his arms around her. She leaned her head on his chest and closed her eyes. Lucas breathed deep and began stroking her back. She shivered a little. She didn't know if it was from the chill outside or from Lucas's hands on her.

"Are you cold?" he asked.

"A little," she said. Any excuse to get closer to him. Instead, he took off his jacket and put it on her.

She looked at him while gripping the super soft edges of the sleeves. "Thanks."

Lucas put his arms back around her. "Do you want to go out with me this Friday?"

She nodded and whispered. "I'd love to."

"I should probably go now. Don't want to make your dad mad," he said. She squeezed him harder. "I'll text you when I get home, and we'll see each other in school tomorrow."

"What do you think everyone's going to say?" She looked up at him with a smile.

He smiled back. "That it's been a long time coming."

She laughed. "Really?"

"Yeah. My friends could tell I really liked you."

"You should have heard Mayra."

He laughed. "Yeah, she definitely helped me realize maybe you felt the same way about me."

Ariana shook her head. They pulled apart, and Ariana waited for a kiss from Lucas, but, again, it didn't come. He kissed her forehead instead and walked her back to the front door.

"I'll see you tomorrow, okay?"

"Yeah." She hugged herself from the chill.

He walked back down and got in his car and drove away. It was then that she realized his jacket was still on her.

Ariana watched his car go around the corner, and then she went inside. Her parents were in the dining room, about to have dinner.

"Come and eat," her mom said, eyeing Lucas's jacket on her.

"I'll go get Jimmy." She went the opposite way to his room and knocked before going in.

He had just gotten out of the shower and was putting on a shirt.

"Hey, you have a six pack," she said. It was weird seeing her little brother all muscular.

"Pssh. I've had a six pack," Jimmy said as he pulled his head through his shirt.

"Impressive."

"Does Lucas have one?" he said with a smile.

"I wouldn't know." She rubbed the sleeves of Lucas's jacket, wondering if he did.

"Sure."

"Anyway, Mom and Dad said it's time to eat."

He followed her to the dinner table, and they had dinner as a family. Ariana couldn't stop smiling. She couldn't believe how well everything had gone with Lucas and her parents. Then she wondered what it would take for Lucas to kiss her on the lips.

###

The next morning, Ariana and Jimmy pulled into Mayra's driveway to pick her up on their way to school. She realized she hadn't even told her the news about Lucas. She had been busy texting Lucas until midnight last night. She was kind of tired but way too excited to even yawn.

Mayra came out of her house and got into the front passenger seat. Jimmy was in the back.

"Guess who has a boyfriend?" Jimmy said before Mayra had even shut her door.

She stared at Ariana, and Ariana shook her head, smiling.

"You and Lucas?"

She nodded. "Yep. Last night. He came and talked to my parents and everything."

"Aw. Congratulations." She leaned over and gave her a hug as best as she could. "You two deserve each other."

"Thanks, Mayra."

"So your parents were cool with it and everything?"

Ariana nodded and smiled.

"Wow. They've really come a long way."

"Uh huh," said Jimmy from the back.

They began the drive to school. Fifteen minutes later, they were in the parking lot, getting out of the car and walking towards the cafeteria for breakfast.

Ariana wondered where Lucas was. She didn't normally see him in the morning, but maybe that would change now that they were going out.

They each grabbed a chicken biscuit and an orange juice and sat down. She looked at Jimmy and Mayra. They were sitting next to each other opposite from her, but she hadn't heard anything lately from Mayra about them. She supposed they really were taking things slow.

Her phone buzzed, and she looked around for teachers before taking it out. It was Lucas.

Good morning, princess.

"What are you smiling about?" Jimmy asked. He was on his third chicken biscuit.

"Nothing."

"You better tell me about nothing later," Mayra said with a wink.

Ariana laughed and replied to Lucas's text.

Good morning, handsome.

Her day was already getting off to a great start.

As she and Mayra walked to their first period class, she saw Lucas waiting for her at her locker. He had a different jacket on today since she still had his other one at home. She'd slept in it, breathing in his scent the entire night and waking up super cozy.

She walked up to Lucas, and they hugged.

"I missed you," he said. She opened her locker and took out some things.

"Me too." She looked up at him.

"Where's your first class?" Lucas watched as she put a notebook inside her bag.

"I have AP Lit with Harrison."

"That's on my way. Can I walk you?" She shut her locker and took his hand.

"Let's go."

They said bye to Mayra, and Jimmy had already gone off to his first class. They had a few minutes before classes started for the day, so they took their time walking to the English wing. She loved the feel of Lucas's hand in hers. She squeezed his hand, and he squeezed back, harder.

Then they were in front of Mr. Harrison's room. They turned to look at each other.

They stepped out of the way as a couple of girls walked into class. She noticed one of them glance at Lucas, but she ignored it.

"See you in Spanish?" he asked, taking her hands in his.

She nodded. There was hardly anyone left in the hallway now. "The bell's about to ring. You don't want to be late."

He gave her a quick kiss on the cheek and took off. So forehead and cheek but still not on the mouth. It had to a matter of time before they kissed for real.

She walked into class and took her seat. She opened her notebook to a fresh piece of paper to do the warm up on the board. She tried to focus as some girls talked behind her. She didn't really know them, but they were starting to become annoying with their laughter and whispering. She looked around for Mr. Harrison as the bell rang. He wasn't in the room. One last person came running, realized the teacher wasn't even there, and slowed to a walk as he reached his desk.

Then Ariana heard her name mentioned behind her.

She turned around. One of the girls had said it.

They tried to look away and stop laughing as she stared at them.

"I'm just sayin'. I wouldn't want to go out with the ex-girlfriend of someone who went all psycho. Not to mention if she was drunk and half naked and everyone got it on video." The girl who was talking had her back to her. Her friends were kicking her and shushing her. "What? I'm not afraid to say what I think." She turned around and stared back at Ariana with a smirk.

It was Wendy, a girl in her class who loved to talk smack.

Ariana stared back, not knowing if she should do something about what Wendy was saying. She was frozen in the moment, not believing what was happening, and then Mr. Harrison walked in and closed the door.

"Good morning, everyone. I apologize for my being late. I forgot your graded essays in my car. When I call out your name, please come up here and retrieve your paper."

"Wendy." He held out her paper and looked down at the rest of the essays. Wendy got out of her seat and strutted to the front of the room. Mr. Harrison continued as Ariana grinded her teeth, trying to calm her beating heart.

"Ariana."

She got up and walked towards the front of the room. Wendy stared at her as she walked back to her desk, as if daring her to do something.

As they passed each other, Wendy hit her shoulder, hard. The room was silent, as just about everyone realized what had happened. Ariana turned around, and so did Wendy. She didn't apologize.

Before she knew she was moving, Ariana had pushed her on the shoulders, knocking Wendy down onto a desk. Wendy managed to catch herself, but got up lightning fast to come at Ariana. Ariana moved out of the way.

Then Mr. Harrison was in between them. "Stop now! Both of you to the front office. I will not have this in my classroom." He pointed to the front door, everyone's essays on the floor.

Wendy seethed, staring at Ariana. Ariana stared right back, not realizing she was biting the inside of her mouth.

"Now." Mr. Harrison was louder this time. Everyone else had started talking and whispering. Ariana decided she wasn't going to give them any more reason to keep talking about her. She walked out and straight to the principal's office, leaving Wendy behind.

chapter eight

Ariana was sitting in the lobby of the front office. Wendy was across from her, still staring at her. And probably imagining herself getting Ariana back for knocking her down.

Ariana wondered how such a perfect morning had turned into this mess.

She'd never gotten in trouble in school in her life. Not even for chewing gum. That wasn't her. But she had gotten so angry so quickly. For a split second, she admitted to herself that her reaction scared her.

Was she turning into Carlos? Was this how he had turned into the person who had been responsible for what had happened last year?

Then she looked at the paintings on the wall, listened to the secretary talking on the phone, anything to get her mind off the thought that had just crossed her mind and the crazy nut who was in front of her.

A door to her left opened and the assistant principal, Mr. Sandhill, stepped out of his office. He signaled to the both of them with his finger, beckoning them. "In my office, please."

He didn't sound happy. Ariana got up first and

went right in. Wendy trudged behind her. They each took a seat, and so did Mr. Sandhill.

"Mr. Harrison has just informed me of what happened in his classroom this morning. One of you pushed the other?" He looked from Ariana to Wendy and back.

"Yeah. She pushed me," Wendy said, looking Ariana up and down like she was scum.

"Why don't you tell him why?" she said, glancing at Wendy.

"For no reason. I didn't do anything to you."

Ariana scoffed.

"You two young ladies need to tell me the truth," Mr. Sandhill said, looking from one girl to the other.

"She was talking about me with a bunch of other girls. They were laughing at me. I hardly even know her, so it beats me why she was even doing it."

Wendy just rolled her eyes.

"Then, when she was walking back to her desk and I was going up to get my essay from the teacher, she pushed me on purpose. So I pushed her back." She glared at Wendy. "I don't even talk to her." Ariana felt hot again.

"I did not touch you."

"Oh my God. At least have the…the decency to admit it."

Balls, she wanted to say, but not in front of Mr. Sandhill. She leaned back in her seat and crossed her arms. Then she began thinking about how all of this might affect her getting into college. What if she got suspended? What if they wouldn't accept her because of her behavior?

"Since we can't seem to settle this, I'll just have to

find out myself what happened." Mr. Sandhill told them.

"I just want to say that I am telling the truth. And you can check my record. I've never gotten in trouble before. Never. I have excellent grades. I wouldn't have done anything like this except for being provoked. Which I was. And even then, I regret my actions and want to apologize."

"Let's see what Mr. Harrison has to say first." He picked up his phone, looked at a laminated sheet taped to his desk, and dialed a number, putting the phone to his ear.

It was a few seconds before Mr. Harrison picked up. Mr. Sandhill spoke into the phone, nodding often. He went on like that for a couple of minutes.

Wendy sighed next to her.

Finally, Mr. Sandhill hung up and looked at Ariana with a stern glare.

Then he turned to Wendy.

"Ariana, please step out of my office."

She looked at Wendy and Mr. Sandhill, then slowly got up and left, closing the door behind her.

She took a seat right by the door, trying to listen to what was going on, but the secretary was on to her. She gave Ariana a stern stare and waited for her to sit back in her seat.

A few minutes later, Wendy came out of the office. She stormed into the hallway. Mr. Sandhill came out of his office and motioned for Ariana to come back in.

She took a seat, wondering what was about to happen.

Mr. Sandhill just stared at her with his chin on his

knuckles. "I hate to do this, Ariana, but you're the one who pushed Wendy down."

"Wh—" She almost fell out of her seat, but Mr. Sandhill put up his hand.

"Mr. Harrison said a couple of students told him what happened. I know Wendy was verbally bullying you and then ran into you on purpose. Thank you for being honest with me. However, I can't let this slide even though you do have no history of misbehavior."

Ariana's mouth was slightly open as she tried to process what Mr. Sandhill was saying.

"You'll have one day of in-school suspension. Wendy has the same for what she did. If you two can't get along, then I don't want you saying a word to each other. Because if this happens again, you can rest assured that both of you will be suspended outside of school."

It was quiet in Mr. Sandhill's office for a few seconds. Tears entered Ariana's eyes. "Is this going to affect my college applications?"

Mr. Sandhill sighed. "It depends. I'll remove this incident from your record if there's no more trouble from you two. An out-of-school suspension definitely will affect your applications, so I'd watch it if I were you."

Mr. Sandhill finished writing something on a pink slip of paper. Then he slid it towards Ariana. "I need you to sign this. You'll have ISS next week."

She signed her name on the bottom of the paper. She could hardly see the line where she was supposed to sign because her eyes were so full of tears. She willed them not to overflow. She slid the paper back to Mr. Sandhill.

He tore off her copy. "You may go back to class. We are in second period now."

Ariana got up and left without a word. The tears had silently splashed onto her face.

###

"My parents are going to kill me," Ariana told Mayra at lunch. She looked down at her tray. Today it was peanut butter and jelly sandwich with some soup. She made herself take a bite of the sandwich, knowing later she'd be starving otherwise. Meanwhile, Lucas was still getting his lunch. She hadn't told him yet.

"Wendy is such a bitch. So she got one day of ISS too?"

Ariana nodded and looked down at her tray. "They just gave me permission to go out with Lucas, now this."

"Well, I bet when you explain to your parents what happened, they'll understand."

"I don't know. I've never been in trouble before in school. This is bad. I basically started a physical fight. It would have gotten worse, but Mr. Harrison stepped in." She looked at Mayra. "Believe me, Wendy was getting ready to throw punches."

Mayra shook her head as she bit into her sandwich.

"I don't even talk to her."

"She's just one of those people who love to talk shit about other people. They thrive on it. She was in one of my classes last year. I let her know early on she wasn't about to do that around me. I think she just loves the attention."

Ariana rolled her eyes and stared off into space. This day was not supposed to have turned out like this.

Lucas sat down next to her with a tray of chicken pasta. He kissed her on the forehead and looked at her. They hadn't really had the chance to talk since Lucas been late to Spanish class and the teacher had put them in different groups for an activity.

"Hey," he said with a smile. He dug into his food.

She gave a small smile.

"What's wrong?"

She sighed and looked at him. "Haven't you heard?"

"Heard what?" he said as he lifted his drink to his mouth.

"I got a day of ISS."

He almost choked. "What for? I thought you never got in trouble."

"She doesn't," said Mayra.

"This girl named Wendy in my lit class was talking shit about me going out with you," she paused. "Then she pushed me as she was walking by. And I pushed her back."

Lucas's eyebrows furrowed. "Wendy? Our grade? Short hair?"

"Yeah…You know her?"

Lucas played with his food. "Yeah… She's my ex. I went out with her for a couple of months last year."

"Seriously?" Ariana just stared with her mouth open. She grossed herself out at the thought of them kissing. Or worse.

"Dude. You just lost some cool points," said Mayra. She had been trying to act like she wasn't listening, but obviously she had been.

"I have to agree with Mayra," Ariana said.

Lucas blushed and put down his fork. "Can we talk about this later?"

Then she blushed. She thought of her ex, Carlos. Wendy was nothing next to him. Carlos had done some really horrible things. Or rather Carlos's friends. Wendy was just all talk. Mostly.

"Sorry," she took his hand, which was on his leg.

He took a deep breath. "Don't worry about it." He went back to eating, although definitely less enthusiastically. "So what happened?"

"She was talking about me and you and why you'd even want to be with me after…"

He looked at her. She tried to focus on her words, just her words and getting them out. "After what happened last year. With my ex, Carlos. And the pictures from this stupid party."

"I don't care about any of that."

"So you know what happened?" She turned to him.

"Well, yeah. I didn't know you, but I saw you two together, and he was in one of my classes. I pretty much heard what happened."

What a horribly, awkwardly small world, she thought.

"Were you friends with him?"

He shook his head. "Never really liked him."

She nodded.

"You know he didn't even graduate?" he said as he began eating.

She hadn't even really thought about that until now. She felt like gagging for some reason. Why did everything feel like her fault?

"So when's ISS?" Lucas continued.

"Next week. I just hope this doesn't affect me getting into college." Tears threatened to invade her eyes again.

Lucas hugged her with his arm and squeezed her. "I'm sure everything's gonna be fine."

Ariana was just amazed at how sweet Lucas was after what she and Mayra had said. There was no comparison to Carlos.

###

Ariana and Jimmy got out of the car and headed inside their house. Their mom was already home, and Ariana was wondering whether she should tell her parents about the day of ISS she had gotten individually or together.

Or not at all.

Jimmy patted her shoulder as she went inside first. She had already told him what had happened, and he'd pretty much heard about it anyways. News traveled fast at school. From what he had heard, Wendy was not happy she hadn't gotten the chance to fight back.

"According to what I've heard, you're now officially a badass," Jimmy had said.

"Not the reputation I was hoping for," Ariana said. The attention she had gotten last year from the drama with Carlos had been more than enough to last her a lifetime.

Maybe she shouldn't tell her parents. That might just ruin things for her and Lucas.

She put her stuff in her room and followed Jimmy back to the kitchen to see what her mom was cooking. Her second favorite. Tostadas made with shredded pork, lettuce, chopped tomatoes, sour cream, and extra hot salsa.

"How was school?" her mom asked as she cut up the lettuce.

"Good," Jimmy said.

"Ariana, did you see your boyfriend?"

"Yeah. He walked me to class, and he's in my Spanish class so we had lunch with Mayra and some other people."

"Remember, it's not good to spend too much time alone with boys at your age. You're still new at this, so it's easy to get carried away, but what you do determines what kind of reputation you will have."

She almost wanted to say that this wasn't her first time having a boyfriend, but she didn't want to bring up the past. She settled for nodding and staring at the lettuce.

"I got a day of in-school suspension." There. She had said it. Quick, like ripping off a Band-Aid.

Her mom put down the knife and put her hands at her waist. "You've been suspended?" Ariana cut in before her mom got into the full swing of her angry mood.

"It's in-school suspension. Just one day."

"What did you do? Does it have to do with Lucas?"

"Some other girl was talking about me. Then she pushed me in front of everyone. So I pushed her back."

She looked at her mom.

"How did this happen? Why didn't you just tell the teacher? You should have let him resolve it. Then it would have just been that other girl in trouble."

"I know. I didn't think. Not that the teacher

would have been able to do much. The other girl, Wendy, would have lied. She lied to the assistant principal's face."

Her mom shook her head. "What has this generation come to?" She resumed cutting some lettuce and began on the tomatoes.

"So when do you have the day of in-school suspension?"

"Next week."

Jimmy was browsing around the kitchen, looking for something to eat. He opened the fridge.

"It's really not that bad," he said. "Most people would have gotten out-of-school suspension for being in a fight."

Ariana stared at him. He had said the word. It had not been a fight. Could have turned into one had the teacher not intervened. But it had not been a fight. No matter what everyone else said or thought.

"And I mean, she had to defend herself, you know?"

"There are other ways to defend yourself. Not just with your fists." Ariana's mom turned to her as she put the lettuce and tomatoes in separate bowls. "Is this going to affect you getting into that school?"

"Maybe. I don't know."

"Well, if you went to school here, that wouldn't be so bad. That would be one good thing that came out of it."

Ariana sighed. "Why can't you understand that I don't want to go to school here? The other school's bigger and better. I've researched it. They have really cool dorms, free tutoring, and everything."

"I guess, in the end, it's your choice," her mom

said, pinching her cheek. "You're almost eighteen. We can't tell you what to do anymore." She sighed.

chapter nine

Ariana went to her room to lay down until her dad got home so they could all have dinner together. Then, she would tell her dad what had happened. Maybe he would take it as well as her mom had. Maybe.

What her mom had said about her age was true. Her birthday was coming up in like a month. With everything that had happened, she had completely forgotten about it.

She was going to be freakin' eighteen. Her mom's words rang in her head.

We can't tell you what to do anymore.

How had she gone from being told what to do with every second of her life to this? To deciding what her life was going to be? If she got in early to UGA, she had to go there. It was part of the deal for applying early. Leaving her family behind would suck. Not having Mayra along for the ride would suck even more.

Then another thought entered her head.

Lucas.

How could she leave without Lucas? He was smart. Not incredibly smart, but he got As and Bs.

Had he even applied to UGA? What if he did but didn't get in?

They had just started their relationship, and this December when she found out if she got in to UGA might be the beginning of the end of it.

She grabbed her phone and texted Lucas.

Can you talk?

Within a minute, her phone was ringing from Lucas's call.

"Hey, are you okay?" He sounded rushed.

"Are you at work?"

"Yeah. But it's not too busy. I have a minute."

"I just wanted to ask you something."

"Okay."

She took a deep breath. "What are we going to do in the spring when we go to college? Did you apply to UGA?"

"Um, yeah, I was going to apply, I guess. I don't think I'll get in, though. And if I do, I'm not sure I can go anyways."

"Why not?"

Silence.

"I can't afford it. My mom and siblings need me here. She'd never be able to handle everything on her own. Remember?"

"Oh," was all she managed to say.

"I'll be right there!" Lucas said to someone else. "Hey, I gotta go, but let's talk about this later, okay?"

"Bye." She put her phone on her bed.

She realized her life had just gotten much harder. She almost wished she was still being told what to do.

###

The next day at school, Ariana and Lucas sat on their

own at lunch. Lucas was already there, picking at his taco salad.

"Hey," he said as she sat down.

"Hey." She put her plate down and opened her drink before touching her food.

"Sorry I never called you back last night or texted. I got home really late and fell asleep after taking a hot shower." He put his arm around her and pulled her in for a small hug.

"It's okay. You don't have to apologize." She said it without looking at him, just focused on her food.

"You're not mad?"

She looked at him and smiled. "Why would I be mad about that? You work. Of course you're going to be tired."

He smiled back. "Okay." He took a bite of his food and a sip of his drink. "So about what you said yesterday."

She sighed. They hadn't even been going out a week and already their relationship was in trouble.

"What are we going to do?" he asked.

"I have no idea. I really want to go to UGA. They have the best program for what I want to major in, which is business. And it'd finally be a chance to get away."

Now Lucas looked away.

"Not from you. Just this. This town. This school. These people. I need that. I need to be independent."

He nodded.

"I want you to come with me."

Lucas sat up straighter and stroked her hair. "You'd want to do that? Even though we haven't been together even a month? Even though we've known each other less than two?"

She nodded. "It feels right."

It was his turn to sigh. She knew what she was asking him. To leave his family behind, one he couldn't leave behind even if he wanted. How could she ask him to do that? Because she was selfish, she thought.

Lucas kissed her lightly on the head. "Let's see what happens first, okay? If I can even get in. Then we'll figure it out. I promise we'll figure it out." He kissed her forehead, and she closed her eyes, hoping they did figure their lives out.

###

That Friday, Ariana looked out her window. Still no Lucas. But he would be here any minute probably. She looked at herself in the mirror one more time. She had looked up some new hairstyles on Pinterest and chosen a cool-looking kind of bun that didn't look too hard. Mayra had given her some pointers on makeup and helped her pick out an outfit.

Lucas had called her parents the other day and asked if he could take Ariana out for a few hours. No one had been more surprised than Ariana when they said yes, as long as she was back before eleven. Perhaps they really had liked Lucas then. And they had taken the whole thing with Wendy pretty well.

Ariana saw headlights coming around the corner, and she went to the window to see if it was Lucas. She recognized his car and saw it pull into the driveway. She smiled, grabbed her purse, and walked to the living room, where her parents and Jimmy were watching TV. She'd offered to drop off Jimmy at the movies, but he had declined. Ryan would be coming over to watch a movie with him instead.

"Just don't get too crazy," he had said while winking.

As she sat down on the couch next to Jimmy, her father just stared. She looked down at her outfit. It wasn't too bad, was it? Her mom just smiled and pinched her cheek.

"Boyfriends, makeup, and skirts," her father mumbled while he shook his head. She went over and hugged him, trying not to laugh. She was actually wearing a dress.

There was a knock at the door, and Jimmy got up to go open it.

"Come in," she heard him say. She turned around and saw Lucas all dressed up and walking into her living room. He was kind of tall compared to the average Latino male, but he looked plain short next to Jimmy. Ariana tried not to stare at his perfect frame. Dress shirts looked really good on him. The sleeves were folded up, and he also wore dark blue jeans and brown dress shoes.

Ariana walked over and gave him a hug. He squeezed back briefly before walking over to her parents and shaking both their hands.

"Como estan?" he asked.

Her mom smiled. It was obvious she liked his manners, and Ariana couldn't help but think that was awesome.

"I'll bring her back before eleven." Lucas said in Spanish as he took Ariana's hand.

Her parents nodded. Her dad looked kind of serious, but that was probably more because of the fact that Lucas was a male about to escort his daughter out of the house than anything else.

"Have fun," Jimmy said, not noticing the half glare from their dad. Ariana waved and they walked to the door.

Once they were in his car, Ariana buckled in.

"So where we going?" she asked.

"You hungry?" he asked as he headed to town.

Twenty minutes later, they were in a nice Italian restaurant downtown.

"Have you ever been here before?" Lucas asked as the hostess walked them to their table.

She looked around the restaurant. It wasn't full, but a lot of people were starting to come in. "No, but it looks good," she said as she saw a waiter with some plates of pasta walk by.

"It's delicious," Lucas said as they sat down at a booth. The waitress handed them their menus and left.

Lucas looked at her with a smile. His eyes bore into hers.

She looked down and back at his eyes. "What?"

"Nothin'." But he wouldn't stop smiling.

She thought about their graduation, just a few months away, and what would happen to them. She tried not to think about it and instead wondered if Lucas was finally gonna kiss her tonight.

###

At half after ten, Lucas and Ariana were walking out of the movie theater.

"That movie," Lucas said, "was hilarious."

Ariana laughed, remembering the scene with Chuck Norris. "I cannot wait until that one comes out on DVD so we can watch it with Jimmy and

Mayra. They're gonna love it."

"Maybe we can come and see it again with them sometime," Lucas said.

"Pay to watch it again?" she said.

"Yeah. You've never done that?"

She shook her head.

"Oh my gosh. It's the best. Nothing like watching your favorite movies on the big screen. We'll have to do it in a week or two. It can be a double date, and maybe your parents will let us stay out longer."

"Maybe." They got to his car, and he opened the car door for her. She got in, and he came around to get in himself.

She rested her head back against the seat and closed her eyes for a minute.

"You tired?" Lucas asked, rubbing her shoulder.

"Yeah. I guess I just had a tough week." She turned to him and took his hand in hers.

"When do you have to do ISS?"

"Wednesday." She sighed. "Just want to get it over with."

"It's not as bad as it seems." She looked at him.

"You've had ISS?"

"Once." She rested her head on his shoulder.

"What for?" She checked her phone. They had a little time.

"Can't remember. Maybe talking during a test or something like that." Lucas stared at the ceiling as he talked.

"You did that?" She studied his face, trying to imagine him getting in trouble.

"I think I was laughing at something someone else said, and I got the blame."

Ariana laughed.

"It was freshman year, and everyone hated that teacher. And she hated us."

"I hardly remember freshman year," Ariana said.

"Yeah, I want to forget it."

They laughed, and their eyes met. Lucas reached down and brought his lips to hers, hardly brushing her lips at first. But she turned her body and put her arms around his neck, trying to get closer to him in the cramped space.

Lucas put his hands on her waist and kissed her harder. A groan escaped from Ariana's mouth, and she felt a little embarrassed, but Lucas began breathing real heavy, pulling her closer. She realized he had been holding back before. And she was glad he wasn't now.

He pulled back, but his nose was still almost touching hers. She realized she was out of breath herself. Ariana looked at him, wondering why he had stopped.

"Is this okay?" he asked, rubbing her hand.

She nodded, and they were kissing again. His hand went back to her waist, but this time, it slid slowly to her thigh. Her hand automatically covered it. Then she slid her hand all the way up his arm instead, then onto his chest.

Meanwhile, Lucas moved to her neck, and she closed her eyes. Not long after that, he pulled back and kissed her softly again on the lips.

"I should get you home," he said, looking at his phone and back at her. "We're cutting it close."

"Yeah," she replied, out of breath, even though she wanted to say no. Lucas had just blown away her expectations of their first kiss.

chapter ten

It was Wednesday, which meant ISS for Ariana. She was not looking forward to it.

She finished her breakfast at the school cafeteria. Even the food sucked today. Breakfast was sausage biscuit, and she didn't trust the sausage at all. She drank her orange juice and ate the biscuit with some grape jelly.

Mayra, Jimmy, and Lucas were making conversation, but she wasn't paying attention.

The bell rang. It was time for her day of torture to begin. She automatically got up and headed towards the cafeteria doors, her trash in hand and her backpack slung on her shoulder. She threw the trash away and headed out with a sigh.

"Hey, wait up, beautiful," Lucas said as he caught up and grabbed her hand. "Let me walk you."

"I guess," she said.

"It's really not that bad. Think of it as a mental vacation from everyone and everything," he said with a smile.

She stared at him. "Really? That's the best you got?"

He shrugged, and they kept walking.

"I told you that she has ISS today too, right? And I cannot get into any more trouble if this is going to stay off of my record."

"You'll be fine." It was obvious Lucas knew who she was talking about.

They were at the designated ISS room. Which she had never even been in. She tried to prepare herself, but it was no use.

"I'll see you later, okay? It's one day. It'll be over soon," Lucas said. He gave her a peck on the lips before leaving for his first period class. She watched him walk away, wishing they could skip school or something to get away today.

That made her think of senior skip day next semester. At least that made her smile, thinking of the possibilities with Lucas.

She walked into ISS, shutting the door behind her. There were a couple of other people there, students she didn't really know. There were several long tables, but they were all enclosed by three wooden walls to minimize any kind of social interaction.

She recognized the football coach at his desk in a corner. "Sign in. Take a seat," he said without so much as a glance.

Ariana looked to her right and saw a clipboard with today's date and a list of names. She found hers and printed her name and the time.

She looked around as she contemplated where to sit. She found a spot with a half decent view of the only window with the blinds open.

She put down her backpack and took a seat. Wendy wasn't here yet. She wondered what she was supposed to do. She tried to look around without being obvious. Everyone else seemed to be taking a nap.

The bell rang, and Wendy ran in. They made eye contact over the desk cubicles, and Wendy smirked as she took a seat at an adjacent table. Now they could see each other if Wendy turned her head a bit.

Ariana rolled her eyes, and positioned herself so the cubicle hid her face. The last thing she needed was any additional trouble.

The coach began calling out the roll, making a note of some guy who hadn't shown up.

"I'm noticing we have a couple of new people here today, so I'll review the rules very quickly," the coach said, looking directly at Wendy and Ariana. She wondered why he seemed so bitter. She guessed being the ISS teacher probably wasn't the most enjoyable teaching position.

"There is absolutely no talking, under any circumstances. And none of that "what if I'm bleeding to death or on fire" crap. There is to be absolutely no use of devices. In fact, get ready to give them to me."

He held up a clear plastic container.

"If you think you'd rather keep your phone in your pocket and pretend you don't have one, think again. If it even so much as thinks of vibrating, get ready to spend another day in here with me.

"Third rule. You are to absolutely always be working. When you come up here to give me your phone, I will give you your packet of work for the day. If it's not done by seventh period, guess what? You get to spend the next day with me. And on the off chance you do get done early, don't worry. We'll come up with something for you to do. At the end of the day, you will bring your packet of work to me. Don't ask to go to the bathroom or drink water."

He paused for a second to swallow before continuing. "There will be three breaks today and not during class change. You will also walk to the cafeteria with me to get your lunch and walk straight back here to eat. Then you'll walk back to drop off your tray. Any questions?" He paused to look around for about two seconds. He was still standing next to his desk. "I didn't think so."

Ariana looked around. There was one kid with his head still down, but it seemed that the coach's speech had woken everyone else up. She saw a couple of people check their phones one last time. She did the same. Nothing. She sighed.

"Silently walk up and drop off your phone. Make sure it is off."

One by one, everyone slowly got up and walked to the coach's desk where he had placed the plastic container. Ariana was at the end of the line. Wendy was right in front of her with her arms crossed, her phone in one hand. Ariana turned hers off.

She watched the coach hand packets to each student in line with hardly a glance.

It was finally her turn. There was just one packet left on the desk. The coach handed it to her as he sat back down without even calling out her name. She put her phone in the plastic bin and headed back to her seat. She used both arms to carry the packet back to her desk. It weighed at least three pounds.

###

By lunch, Ariana was sure she was losing it. She was making steady progress with her work. She had even begun eagerly, hoping to finish a bit early and lay her head down at least. But after three hours in, she was starting to get antsy, silently tapping her foot and looking around more and more, mostly behind her since she couldn't look in front of her without standing up a little and risk being seen by the coach. Meanwhile, the coach would grunt every now and then or shift in his seat. Other than that or the occasional cough, it was completely silent.

Except for when the bell rang and classes changed. That was the only way she was able to keep track of time. She pictured Lucas walking to his next class. I should be walking with him, Ariana thought. Her hand in his, a hug before he rushed off. Eating lunch together and talking about things. Instead, she was stuck in ISS. Ariana glanced at Wendy, who had her head in her hands.

"Time for lunch," the coach announced. "No talking. Grab your food and come straight back."

They all got up quickly and walked to the cafeteria. Ariana stretched her legs and arms as she walked behind everyone else. They entered the cafeteria. There wasn't anyone in there. It looked like everyone else had already had lunch. She sighed and got in one of the two lines. Wendy went to the other one.

She grabbed a drink from the vending machine before heading back to the ISS room. Ariana held her styrofoam plate in one hand as she got a dollar and some change out of her jean pocket and pushed them into the slots. As she bent down to retrieve her soda, someone bumped into her, hard. Her food went everywhere, and the styrofoam plate was the only thing left in her hands. Her hamburger patty was on the floor, the bun next to it, along with a pool of diced peaches and the syrup.

Before she was even done processing that her entire lunch was on the floor, she looked up to see Wendy smirk before walking off with her lunch tray.

She got up lightning fast, her drink still in the vending machine, and power walked to Wendy. Wendy turned around, chin held high.

"You bi—" she began.

"Something going on?" The coach appeared from around the corner. She saw him look behind her at the mess next to the machines before looking back at her. "Clean it up, grab another tray, and get back to class. You," he said to Wendy. She turned around and looked at him. "What are you waiting for?"

He and Wendy left but not before Wendy glanced back at her with a smirk.

Ariana's fists were shaking, and she was breathing like she had just run a 5K. What had just happened? Why was Wendy making her day a living hell? She stood there, thinking of the things she could do to her, before slowly walking back into the cafeteria for napkins.

A few minutes later, she had cleaned up most of the mess and informed the lunch ladies that she had dropped her tray.

"I got most of it," she told one of the lunch ladies as she looked down at her new tray of food. "Sorry."

"Don't worry about it. I'll clean it in just a sec."

She walked back to ISS without another word, grabbing her drink on the way.

As she walked past Wendy, she forced herself not to put her small tray of peaches down the back of her shirt.

###

Ariana had to think. Surely it was almost time to go home. The seventh period bell must have rung at least thirty minutes ago, maybe forty.

She looked at her last worksheet. All of her teachers had sent along several of them, and the coach had obviously put in a nice thick stack of mundane ones as well.

She closed her eyes for a few seconds and took a deep breath. Her brain felt like sludge. She couldn't think anymore. She desperately needed social interaction.

Ariana made herself open her eyes and slowly finish these last math problems. She didn't care if they were right. She just wanted out.

She stared at the last row of problems, and her eyes teared up. When is the bell gonna ring? she wondered.

Just as she began her last problem, the afternoon announcements came on.

She put her pencil down and put the stack of papers back in the manila folder. Then she put her backpack on around her shoulders and folded her left leg to sit on so she could glance at the coach. She eyed the plastic container of cell phones. The announcements were finally finished, and everyone else was moving around, just as anxious to leave. She resolved not to look in Wendy's direction.

"When I call your name, turn in your packets and pick up your device," the coach said.

Thankfully, Ariana was one of the first people called. She power walked up to his desk and handed him her packet with both hands before reaching in for her phone. She turned it on while she returned to her desk. By the time she was seated, everyone else was called up and the bell finally rang.

The sound rang loudly through her ears, and she smiled as she got up and left. As soon as she stepped out into the hallway, she checked to see if she had messages, but before she could check, she felt someone grab her from behind and hug her.

She turned around. It was Lucas.

"Hey," he said quietly, his eyes gleaming.

She closed her eyes and kissed him, not caring who saw. Her arms went around his neck, and he hugged her waist. After a couple of seconds, they parted, and Ariana noticed someone staring at them. It was Wendy. Just as she met her eyes, Wendy turned quickly and began walking away in the opposite direction. Ariana tried to put a word to the look she had seen on her face. She looked like she had just been slapped.

###

"Did you see that?" Ariana asked Lucas, still staring after Wendy.

"What?" Lucas asked.

"Wendy," Ariana said. "The look she gave me. Us."

They began walking towards his locker. "To be honest, I don't pay attention to her. What happened with her is in the past."

Ariana wanted to ask what had happened between them but figured it wasn't the right time to ask. And she didn't know if she wanted to know anyway. It still bothered her that such a good guy like Lucas had fallen for someone as evil as Wendy.

She sighed, and they walked to his locker around the corner and down the hallway.

"It was so boring in there. I seriously thought it would never end," she said as she watched Lucas grab stuff from his locker.

"Yeah, it pretty much sucks. I wish I could take you out to distract you from it, but A, I don't think your parents would love the idea of me taking you out on a school night, and B, I have to work," he said as he shut his locker. They took each other's hands and walked out of the school.

It sucked that Lucas had to work so much. She had looked forward to talking to him after school to get her mind off things, and really just to hear his voice. But they wouldn't be able to chat until ten o'clock tonight when he got home, and even then, he would be tired, have to shower, do homework, and get to bed. They mostly texted, especially during the week.

She needed something else to do, besides college stuff.

She made a mental note to start preparing for this year's DECA competitions. Either that or find a hobby or do a sport. She thought of Mayra, but she didn't want to take too much of her time now that she also hung out with Jimmy. She wondered if either of their parents knew about those two. Probably not.

"What are you thinking about?" Lucas asked.

"Nothing." She tried to smile. "Just that I miss you."

Lucas laughed a little and put his thumb and finger on her chin. "I'm right here, babe."

She hugged him and pressed her face into his neck. Her arms were around his neck, and she didn't care who saw.

They walked up to their cars. They were parked next to each other. Ariana had beat Mayra there. She'd be back for Jimmy later.

"I'll see you later, okay?" Lucas said softly as he kissed her on the cheek.

But she grabbed him around the waist before he could turn around and leave. She put her hands on his face and pulled him towards her. She took his mouth in hers, pulling on his lips and feeling his skin against her nose. Lucas squeezed her until their bodies were meshed together. She heard a car honk, maybe at them, but she didn't open her eyes or pull back to see. She felt a hot pang in her chest as Lucas groaned inside her mouth.

A few seconds later, Lucas stared at her, mouth still open. "What was that?"

I love you.

She caught the words before they came out of her mouth. She just stared at his eyes, wondering if he was thinking the same thing.

Lucas closed his eyes as he came in for one more kiss, although shorter. "I'll call you later."

Another kiss before he finally left, and she got into her car. She thought about her birthday coming up, and she realized Lucas was the best thing that had ever happened to her. The best gift. She couldn't stand to lose him now.

chapter eleven

"Hey, just two and a half weeks left until your birthday," Mayra said as they drove home, interrupting Ariana's thoughts on last year. "Did you know that?"

They were driving home from school. Jimmy was at practice.

"It snuck up on me this year. I forgot all about it," Ariana said. She focused on the road and tried not to think about last year's birthday. It made her want to gag at everything that had happened.

"It's your eighteenth birthday. How could you forget it?" Mayra teased.

She shrugged.

"So are you doing anything?"

"I don't know. I guess just a family dinner like last year. I don't know if I feel like doing much."

"We can go to my house again if you want. Rent some movies." Mayra said while she looked at her phone.

Ariana wanted to pretend she hadn't heard. It reminded her too much of Carlos.

Mayra glanced at her. "Or, hey. Let's go out. Double date. Dinner and a movie."

Ariana nodded and smiled at Mayra. "That sounds fun. We can still do the family dinner, just on a different day."

"Yeah." They turned into their subdivision. "So I wonder what Lucas is gonna get you for your birthday." She drew out the first syllable.

She sighed. "I actually haven't told him yet."

"He doesn't know your birthday is coming up? Didn't he ask you when your birthday was?" Mayra asked.

"Don't get all…" Ariana searched for the right word. "You sound like my mom when I don't sort the laundry right."

They laughed.

"Still. How does he not know? Don't make me do something about this." Mayra was dead serious now.

"I guess it just never came up. I'm gonna tell him."

"When?" They were in her driveway now. Ariana put the car in park.

"I don't know. Soon."

Mayra stared, squinting her eyes a little.

"I will." She put her hands on the steering wheel, trying not to look away.

"Oh, hey. You know what?" Mayra said out of nowhere.

Ariana couldn't help it. She smiled. "What?"

"My mom said she might get me a car soon. She got a raise, and she's been saving up. Wouldn't that be awesome? Then I can finally get a job, and I'm gonna need a car for college anyway."

"That's great," Ariana said. She didn't mind at all giving Mayra rides, but she knew she'd much rather have her own car. She still remembered the feeling of not having the freedom to do anything or go anywhere on her own.

Mayra made to get out of the car, hooking her bag on her shoulder.

"Hey," she said as a thought popped into her mind. "How's it going with you and Jimmy? Have you guys decided on anything yet?"

Mayra looked out the window, leaving her arm on the bag handle. "Still just friends." She was out of the car now, about to shut the door.

"Is that what you want, though?" She didn't want to pry, but she also wanted to be there for them. The both of them.

"I have no idea. I really like him. It's not that. I just don't want to mess anything up."

"You know I'll always be your friend. No matter what," she said. "Him too."

"I know. I just," she paused. "I don't want to ever lose him. In any way."

"Well, you'll never what could happen if you don't try."

"That's what sucks about the whole thing."

"So the friend thing. Whose idea was that?" Ariana said.

Mayra sat back down. "Both of us. Mostly mine. He kinda wants to give it a shot. I'm still not a hundred percent sure, though."

"Are you worried at all what people would say? You guys are almost two years apart."

"Not really. It's not that. There are a few couples like that at school, and come on. We're about to go into real world. Age doesn't really matter anymore."

"True. And he's sixteen now. Since last spring. Almost seventeen," she said.

"Yep," Mayra said. "We'll see, I guess."

Finally, Mayra went into her house.

###

"So Ariana's birthday is next week," Mayra told Lucas. They were in Spanish again. Ariana gawked, looking up from her Spanish verbs worksheet.

Lucas looked at her. He didn't look like he was having fun. "Your birthday is next week?"

Now Mayra looked at her, wincing. "You haven't told him?"

Now they were both staring at her. She put her pencil down. "Can you guys stop looking at me like that? It's like I'm being cornered." She glanced around. Maybe she'd said that a little too loud, especially since everyone was really quiet today. She saw a couple of people stare from the corner of her eye.

"Why didn't you tell me?" Lucas asked, reaching for her hand. But she grabbed her pencil and began working again.

"It never came up. I was going to tell you this afternoon. Until Mayra opened her mouth," she whispered. She stared at Mayra.

"It's in less than a week," Mayra said, not whispering. "Of course I'm going to say something."

Ariana just shook her head. "We need to finish this study guide. The test is tomorrow, remember?"

She heard Mayra sigh and get up. Less than a minute later, she had the bathroom pass and was headed out the door. She heard it click quietly. The other groups were talking lightly as they thumbed through the Spanish textbook looking for the answers. Mrs. R had clearly said that the test would not be a "walk in the park." Ariana had an A in the class, but she wasn't about to start slacking off now.

Lucas kept writing in silence along her. She snuck a glance at him, and he caught her eye. He didn't look mad. Just serious.

"Why didn't you say anything?" he asked. It took her a few seconds to gather what he had just said, he had been so quiet.

She shrugged. "It's not a big deal."

"Not a big deal?" Now he was looking at her again, disbelieving.

She said what was on her mind before she chickened out. "It just brings back bad memories anyway." She wrote down an answer for question eighteen, looking back from the book and to her paper.

"Of course it's a big deal, Ariana. It's your eighteenth birthday. And I wanted to know about it. I want to spend it with you." There was a pause. "If that's what you want."

She breathed out. "Of course I want to spend it with you. I just don't want it to be a big deal. Mayra said we could go out on a double date. Dinner and a movie." She touched his hand. "Do you want to go with me?"

"Duh," he said. They smiled.

"My mom will probably cook something that weekend too, so you're invited." She squeezed his hand.

"You're gonna have birthdays the rest of your life, you know," he said with a smile. "You can't let one person ruin them all."

She smiled as she looked at him.

They began working, but Lucas said something else. "So what do you want for your birthday?"

Ariana finished copying a definition then looked up. "I don't want to sound cheesy or anything, but all I want for my birthday is you."

"Okay, that was so cheesy," Lucas laughed. "Seriously, though. I want to get you something."

"Really. I don't want anything. I just…want to be with you."

Lucas squeezed her hand. "That's a given. But just so you know, you're begging for a crazy gift."

###

"Happy birthday, sis," Jimmy gave her a big squeeze and lifted her effortlessly into the air. Their dad, who was watching an action movie on the couch, just laughed and shook his head. Ryan had just arrived, and he smiled but didn't move. He had already given her an awkward hug.

She struggled to breathe. When Jimmy finally put her down, she hugged him back.

"Thanks," she smiled. She fixed her purple floral dress and matching purple cardigan. Her parents had taken her shopping last weekend for her birthday, and she couldn't wait for Lucas to see her in her new outfit.

She wandered into the kitchen, where her mom was making her favorite meal: enchiladas potosinas. She salivated just thinking of a huge plate of the tiny orange tacos right in front of her with a side of fajitas. Her mom was finishing up chopping lettuce and blending her homemade salsa. Any minute now, she'd start frying the tortillas for the enchiladas.

"Tienes hambre?" her mom asked.

"Starving," she replied in Spanish. She leaned on the kitchen counter and observed her mom move about. She made a mental note to learn how to make enchiladas before she moved out. Or got married.

"What time is Lucas getting here?" her mom asked as she carried stuff to the dining table.

"A few minutes, probably," she replied. They had gotten out of school for the weekend a couple of hours ago, but he had gone home to take a quick nap.

She walked back into the living room and sat down next to her dad. He put his arm around her neck and brought her close. She let herself lean on his shoulder. Jimmy and Ryan were on the other sofa.

"So how's basketball going?" she asked.

"Good. Tryouts are next week. Ryan's trying out again this year. I finally convinced him." He put his feet up on the coffee table and put them back down again when their dad shot him a look.

"You'll probably make it, right? Ryan too, I bet. " she said.

"Hope so," Ryan said. "I didn't get to play much last year."

"You will," she said.

Ryan had gotten taller too, and now he was almost six feet. What are Jimmy and Ryan eating? she wondered. Oh yeah. Everything.

"That's the plan."

"You guys better come to all our games. First one's next month," Jimmy said.

"We'll be there."

"You too, Dad?" he asked.

"I'll go to as many as I can," he said. "But you'd better win. Or there's no point in me going." They laughed.

There was a knock at the door. Ariana jumped up to get it, hoping she didn't trip in her new pair of high heels.

She opened the door. It was Mayra.

"Oh, hey."

Mayra came in for a hug, shifting a present she carried to her side. "Happy birthday, best friend. How does it feel?"

"Honestly? Like any other day." She put her hands at her side.

"Except now you can legally do whatever you want," Mayra whispered with a grin on her face.

Ariana laughed. "There is that." She glanced behind her, but her dad was distracted by the TV.

"This time next year, we're going to be in college. Can you believe that?"

Ariana shook her head.

"Deciding our schedules. If we go to class or not. What time to go to bed. Whether to eat our vegetables."

"Don't get too crazy there, Mayra," Ariana said.

"Oh, that's just the PG stuff," she replied with a wink. "Anyway, happy birthday, and here's your present."

Ariana took it and looked at it. "Should I open it now or wait?"

Mayra shrugged. "Up to you."

"I'll wait. Savor the surprise."

Ariana stepped out of the way so Mayra could come inside. "It's not much, but I hope you like it,"

Mayra said, nodding at the present.

"I know I'll love it." She shut the front door but not before giving one last peek outside. No Lucas.

Mayra was wearing jeans, boots, and a nice top with a navy blue cardigan. She went over to the couch and shook Ariana's dad's hand then said hi to Jimmy and Ryan before heading into the kitchen to see what Ariana's mom was up to. She saw Ryan elbow Jimmy in the ribs.

She followed Mayra, and the three of them chatted a bit before the doorbell rang just a few minutes later.

"Lucas," Mayra said with a grin as Ariana went to go get the door.

"Hey," he said after she opened the door. She went in for a quick kiss on the lips before inviting him in. He had a wrapped present in his hands. "This is for you. Happy birthday." He gave her a long hug and only let go of her when Jimmy whistled from the living room. Ariana didn't want to see the look on her dad's face, so she kept her back to him and took the present.

"Thanks. I'll open it later. I wonder what it is." She looked at him for a clue, but he only winked and took her hand as they walked inside. This time, Lucas shook her dad's hand.

"Hola. Como esta?" he greeted.

"Bien, bien," her dad replied with hardly a glance.

Lucas gave Jimmy and Ryan some kind of secret bro handshake, and she maneuvered him into the kitchen to say hi to her mom and Mayra. Lucas shook her mom's hand as her mom smiled.

"Como estas, Lucas?" she asked.

"Bien. Gracias," he said.

He nodded at Mayra. "Hey." Mayra just smiled and went back into the living room.

Ariana took Mayra's present from the kitchen table and headed to her room. She dropped off Lucas with Jimmy.

"This is a great movie," she heard him say as she walked down the hallway to her room.

She put the presents down on her bed. There was a tiny bag from Jimmy, a small rectangular-shaped box from Ryan, and her parents had given her a hundred dollars in cash (gas for the rest of the year, they joked), which she had hidden in her purse. She put the presents together and smiled at them. Lucas's was the biggest. She couldn't wait to open them later on her own.

She went back into the living room and sat down next to Lucas and Jimmy. Mayra was also sitting on the couch. Not long after, her mom called them into the dining room. Mayra helped set the table, Jimmy and Ryan gave everyone a soda, except for her dad, who had a beer, and Ariana carried plates of food to each person.

She looked at Lucas. His mouth was slightly open as he looked at his huge plate of enchiladas. "I cannot wait to eat this," he said. "Your mom needs to come over to my house."

Ariana laughed and sat down next to him.

"Your mom doesn't make these?" She pulled her plate closer and opened her soda.

"Nope. Not where we're from."

Her mom finally came into the kitchen to join them.

"Buen provecho," her dad said as he dug in. Jimmy opened his soda and took a swig before grabbing a taco in each hand and eating.

Ariana waited for Lucas to taste the enchilada. She saw him chewing and close his eyes briefly before turning to Ariana. "This is like my new favorite food. No joke."

She smiled and began eating. She hadn't been able to stop thinking about her birthday last year and all the horrible things that had happened after. When she had been with Carlos. Now, all of that lay forgotten as she had birthday dinner with the people she loved the most.

chapter twelve

Lucas and Ariana were standing at Lucas's car. They watched Jimmy, Mayra, and Ryan walk down the street from Mayra's driveway. They were walking Ryan home. It was late. The movie they had watched at Mayra's house had just ended and her parents had called for them to head home. Her birthday had turned out pretty good.

She grabbed Lucas's hands and put them around her waist. Then she put her arms around his neck and kissed him. When they finally pulled away, he smiled. "Did you have a good birthday?"

"The best," she answered. "I can't wait to see what you got me, by the way."

He looked down and smiled, taking her hands in his. He brought them to his mouth and kissed them slowly. His eyes were closed. Ariana remembered to close her mouth before he opened his eyes and looked at her.

"I just can't believe I found someone like you. You're the best thing that could have happened to me," Lucas said, looking in her eyes.

She shrugged, not finding an adequate response to that. She settled for kissing him on the cheek and trying not to blush.

"Any guy would die to have a girl like you. You don't do drama like so many other girls. You actually try in school and don't think you're the best thing that happened to the world. One day, when my mom meets you, I know she's gonna love you."

"Uh. Way to bring on the pressure there, Lucas."

He laughed. "Don't worry. We can wait a little longer, although it would only be fair considering what I went through."

She shook her head and laughed. "But it was worth it, right?"

"Eh…" he said.

"Lucas!"

"I'm kidding. Of course you're worth it." He kissed her again. A few minutes later, she rested her head on his chest and heard his heartbeat. She closed her eyes. She never wanted this night to end.

"Hey," he said after a while.

"Hm," she said, eyes still closed. It was chilly outside, but she was warm in Lucas's arms.

"Did Wendy ever bother you again?"

She looked up at him.

"I never asked you, and you never mentioned anything else. That's all."

She shook her head. "She makes faces at me in class, but I ignore her."

He nodded and hugged her again.

"Jimmy and Mayra sure have taken a while," she said.

"What's up with those two?" Lucas said. "They have a thing for each other?" They turned to the street, but saw no one. It was dark out, and if they didn't get back soon, she'd have to go looking for them. Her parents would probably call any minute, wondering where they were.

"Yeah," she said. "They're not sure if they want to give each other a chance or just stay friends, though."

Lucas nodded. "I have a feeling those two are gonna get together real soon."

She smiled. "Me too."

They finally saw figures approaching. Mayra and Jimmy.

"Look at 'em. It's so obvious they were making out," Lucas said.

Ariana laughed and shoved him playfully.

"What are you two laughing about?" Jimmy said as he got closer.

###

Ariana sat on her bed, the small pile of presents in front of her. She picked up the one from Mayra first.

Instead of giving her one thing, she had given her a bunch of smaller things: lip gloss, eye shadow sets, earrings, and bracelets. There was also a little metallic, tree-like stand for all of her jewelry.

She began organizing everything right away and stared at it in admiration on her desk.

Ryan's present was next. She tore the wrapping paper carefully and set it aside. It was obvious he had wrapped it himself. She smiled as she looked down at a daily and weekly planner. She loved the pastel colored flowers all over the outside and the fancy curly font on the inside. Perfect for college.

She was touched. Ryan's family wasn't that well off, but he had probably saved up to get her this. She made herself a mental note to get him something really nice for his birthday next year.

She grabbed Jimmy's present and opened the tiny bag. There was a $15 ebook gift card for the eReader she wanted to buy with the money her parents had given her. She smiled. Jimmy had paid attention to her birthday wish hints. Mayra was gonna be a lucky girl to have such a sweet guy. She put the card away in her wallet, and proceeded to the present she had saved for last.

Lucas's present.

It was a tiny rectangular box, all velvety on the outside. Before she could wonder what it was, she opened it.

And gasped.

A bracelet. A delicately thin gold bracelet. No one had ever given her jewelry.

She wished she had opened it when he was there so he could put it on her. Asking Jimmy or her parents to help her put it on would be so awkward. She stared at it and held it for a few more minutes before putting it away in her backpack.

She began texting Lucas and then stopped and deleted the message.

She would ask Lucas to put the bracelet on tomorrow before their double date.

###

The next day was Saturday, and the day of their double date.

"You ready?" Jimmy asked as he walked into her room and sat down on her bed. She was putting on some eye shadow as she watched a demonstration video on her phone. She sighed in frustration. The girl in the video made it look so easy. She turned around and showed Jimmy.

"Does this look good?"

"Uh..." Jimmy said. He looked like he was answering a life or death question. "Yes?"

She looked in the mirror again. "It'll have to do. I don't have time to do it again. Or the patience."

She put away her makeup, tossed her hair over her shoulder, and then pulled some hair back to the front on each shoulder. She had curled her normally straight hair into soft waves.

"Okay. I just need to put on my dress—" She began as she looked in the mirror on her dresser.

"I'm leaving." Jimmy walked out and shut the door behind him. She smiled and grabbed the dress from her closet.

She hadn't been able to decide on this dress or another at the store, but looking at the dress now, she knew she had made the right choice. It had an empire waist, was free flowing, and light bubble gum pink. It matched her eye shadow. She hoped Lucas would like it. He had liked her dress from last night, so surely, he'd love this one. He hadn't been able to keep his hands off of her during the movie at Mayra's.

She grabbed the velvet box from her desk and put it in her purse.

###

Lucas finally pulled into her driveway a few minutes later.

She had been sitting on the sofa with her dad. "Be good, and don't do anything you'll regret later. That way, I won't have to do something I'll regret later," he said, his arms crossed, staring at the TV.

She smiled and gave him a hug as she got up to go.

"You can only give that part of yourself one time. Make sure it's with the right person and later on in your future when you're ready to get married and have kids."

Oh gosh. Were they really having this conversation right now?

She looked towards Jimmy's room. He was still in there doing his hair. And her mom was doing laundry in another part of the house.

She just nodded and tried to leave. "Okay, Dad."

"Jimmy and Mayra are going with you, and I'm trusting that all of you are going to be responsible, stick together, and get home early. Is that understood?" He hadn't raised his voice at all, but Ariana nodded silently.

"Ariana."

"Yes." But she looked away. She didn't know if it was from embarrassment or what.

"Manejen con cuidado." Lucas wasn't a crazy driver, so no worries there.

She finally walked out the front door and sighed with relief once the door closed behind her. She saw Lucas's car pull around the corner. She walked down the driveway towards their mailbox and met him there.

Lucas stepped out of his car and smiled at her. She went up to him and gave him a hug, putting her bag on top of his car.

"Did you look at your present yet?" he whispered in her ear as he held her at the waist.

"I might have snuck a peek," she whispered back.

She felt his nose and lips roam her neck, and she leaned her head to the opposite side to give him room. She tried not to think about whether her dad was looking out the window or not.

"Do you like it?" he asked as he pulled back.

She smiled. "I love it. Thank you." She got the box out of her purse. "Can you put it on?"

He gathered the bracelet in his hands, and she outstretched her own. She watched his face as he clicked the clasp shut.

"It looks beautiful on you, although it can't compare really," he said.

She brought her face to his, and their noses touched. She tried not to stare at his lips, but she couldn't help herself. Apparently, neither could he because he closed his eyes and brushed his slightly wet lips against hers just for a second.

"I love you," he said.

It took her a few seconds to grasp what he had just said.

"I love you." The words were out of her mouth before she could even wonder if she should say them out loud.

Lucas squeezed her and kissed her.

"I wish we were alone right now," he said as he kissed her under her chin.

She chuckled.

"I didn't meant that," he said with a laugh. "I just wish I didn't have to worry about your dad, mom, or brother watching me kiss you."

"Or me," someone from behind them said.

They turned around. Mayra.

She smiled and gave them each a hug. "You guys

were taking forever, so I just decided to come on over here."

"We're waiting on Jimmy," she said.

Just then, he came out of the house in a dress shirt, dark jeans, and fancy-looking brown shoes.

She looked over at Mayra as Jimmy came down the driveway.

"Sorry guys. My shirt was in the dryer. And then, you know, my mom insisted on ironing it real quick." He came and gave Mayra a hug. Her mouth was still slightly open. Jimmy looked hot.

"So where we going?" Jimmy asked, his arm still around Mayra's shoulders.

###

It had just gotten dark, but they had already had dinner and watched a movie.

"That movie sucked," Mayra said, sipping on her soda as they headed to a local ice cream shop.

"I thought it was good," Ariana said.

"It was so unrealistic," Mayra continued. "How can one guy, no matter how buff he is, land on the windshield of a car at like fifty miles an hour and walk around like nothing happened?" She rolled her eyes and put her soda in the cup holder beside Ariana.

Lucas chuckled and kept driving. "It was okay. The fight scenes were good."

"Heck yeah," Jimmy said from the back. "Especially the one between the two girls. That was epic."

They laughed.

Lucas parked, and they got out. The ice cream shop was in a small shopping center. Each of them ordered and walked out.

Ariana walked with Lucas towards one end of the shopping center. She looked back and saw Jimmy and Mayra walking in the other direction. She checked her phone and stifled a groan.

"What? Your parents call you?"

She shook her head. "No. I can't believe it's already nine-thirty."

"Yeah. That movie was long."

She kept licking her ice cream cone and leaned her head against Lucas as she walked. He put his arm around her. A few minutes later, they had finished their ice cream cones and thrown away the trash. Hardly anyone was shopping this late, and stores were closing.

They stopped at the far end of the stores and walked up a small hill. They sat in the grass.

She looked at Lucas and smiled.

"What?" he asked, returning her smile.

"You make me happy," she said, taking his hand. He leaned over and began kissing her, running his hand through her hair. She put her hand on his arm, feeling the tight muscle underneath his sleeve. They kissed harder, and before they knew it, she had leaned back in the grass, and half his body was pressed against hers.

His hand went to her waist and began to slide up. Right when she was about to get goosebumps, it slid back down. And further down to her hip. His thumb swept near an area that did make her shiver. Then it was on her thigh.

She pulled back.

"Are you okay?" he asked.

"Yeah," she said, catching her breath.

"Did I go too far?" He pulled his hand back and sat up straight again.

"No," she said, taking his hand. "It's just...I don't want us to get carried away...here."

They smiled at each other.

"Let's head back," he said.

They got up and went looking for Jimmy and Mayra.

As they walked closer to the ice cream shop, they noticed two figures leaning against Lucas's car. Jimmy was pressed up against Mayra, and her arms were around his neck.

She looked at Lucas.

"Should have walked slower maybe," he said with a wink.

"Look at those two," she said as they inched closer. "Supposedly they're just friends."

She coughed loudly. Anybody else may or may not have thought she had tuberculosis.

She saw Mayra push Jimmy away and pull her fingers though her hair.

They walked up to the car, and Jimmy wiped his mouth with his hand,. Mayra looked away and headed to the other side of the car to get in.

"We should probably get home, huh?" Jimmy said as he shoved his hands in his pockets.

Lucas laughed. "Probably."

chapter thirteen

Happy three month anniversary. I miss you.

Ariana sent the text to Lucas. Then regretted it. Maybe she should have waited and seen if he had remembered. She shrugged and kept walking to her car.

Jimmy's first basketball game of the season was tonight, and she, Lucas, Mayra, and her parents were going to be there to watch him and Ryan play. Jimmy and Ryan had just found out a couple weeks ago that they had both made varsity.

She was excited, although she had to admit it was also because she would get to see Lucas. He'd been working a lot lately.

As she put her bag in the backseat of the car and climbed in, her phone buzzed.

I promise I didn't forget. I overslept ;) See you soon.

She smiled. Poor Lucas. He'd probably gotten home past ten, had to have a late dinner and shower, and to top it off, do homework before having to get up again at six.

She turned on the heater in the car. She liked winter, but it was really cold this morning. She waited for Jimmy to finish getting ready. A few minutes later,

Ariana was starting to worry about being late to school when he finally came out the front door with his backpack and gym bag slung over one shoulder, a huge burrito in his hand, and an even bigger smile on his face.

He got in and threw his bag in the back along with his gym bag. He took a bite that almost encompassed half the burrito.

"Um, please don't get that on my seat," Ariana said as a random lump of refried pinto beans slopped onto the seat. Jimmy swiped it up with his pointer finger and put it in his mouth. "No need to worry about that."

"So mom made you breakfast?"

"Yep. You should have stuck around."

"No thank you," she said looking at the overflowing burrito and turning on the car. She backed out, looking through her rearview mirror.

"Completely understandable. Eating beans in the morning gives me gas all day too."

She stared. "Ew. I promise you. If I catch one whiff—"

"Relax. I'll open the window. Besides, I'm a gentleman," Jimmy said, taking another bite. "I would never do such a thing with Mayra in the car."

"Lucky Mayra," Ariana said to herself as they pulled into her driveway. They noticed a strange car near Mayra's house. It was burgundy and not too new but not completely crappy either. She noticed the front bumper was missing, and it was just parked in the grass.

Mayra came out of her house. She ran up to the car and got in the back. "Morning, guys. Guess what?"

"What?" Jimmy said with a mouth full of burrito.

"You know you're not supposed to have beans in the morning right? You know what they do to you," Mayra said.

Ariana choked back a laugh as Jimmy turned to her, no longer chewing his food.

"I might have already mentioned what happens to you when your body digests beans in the morning," Ariana said, looking out the window at the car again.

"I am going to kill you when we get home," he said under his breath, putting extra emphasis on "kill."

"Anyways," Mayra continued. "That's my new car. Well, not new. But you know, new to me. It's gonna take a couple of months to fix it, but as soon as it's ready, I won't be riding to school with you two anymore. Unless you two want to ride with me."

"Oh, I want to," Jimmy said, also looking at the car.

"That's awesome, Mayra. What all does it need?" Ariana said, getting on the road.

"Um, I forgot all the part names. But hopefully, it won't be too expensive."

"Maybe our dad can take a look at it. He knows some stuff about cars, and maybe he can help."

"Okay," Mayra said with a smile. "I'll tell my mom."

"And I can help dad," Jimmy said, winking at Ariana as he took another bite of his burrito.

###

Friday dragged on, but finally, it was time for the annual basketball pep rally at the end of the day.

They all got to skip their last class. Even though they were supposed to sit with their class, Mayra and Ariana sat together on the bleachers. They saw Ryan, Jimmy, and the rest of the varsity and JV basketball teams sitting across the gym and the cheerleaders doing flips and waving pompoms everywhere. The band was playing music, and everyone was chatting. Even some of the really strict teachers seemed to be in a really good mood today.

"Remember they got second place in state last year, but they're hoping for first place this year," Ariana said.

"With Jimmy, they definitely stand a good chance of that. Really, the whole team is pretty good," Mayra said, clapping as the school mascot, a bull, ran down the gym with a basketball, jumped on a mini trampoline, and dunked the ball.

Everyone shouted, clapped, and stood on their seats. Several people had their phones out, but the teachers weren't saying anything.

"You're staying for the game, right?" Ariana asked as they sat back down.

"Psheah," she said. "It's not like I'd have a ride home anyways."

They smiled.

They noticed the basketball team wasn't in their seats anymore. Suddenly, they ran out into the gym, some members of the team screaming and cheering. Others were just jogging with a smile on their faces. Jimmy was last, and he had a ball in his hand. He turned towards them, and Ariana waved. They caught his eye. He winked at Mayra—there was no confusing it—and then he ran and did a slam dunk, hanging onto the rim for a few seconds.

Some people had turned in their direction, but they ignored it, clapping for Jimmy. Ariana had never seen Mayra blush before. She pretended not to notice as she bit the inside of her cheek to keep from smiling too hard.

###

It was six o'clock that evening, and Ariana, Mayra, and her family were back in the school gym.

It was the last quarter of the game, and Jimmy's team was losing by five points. Ryan had played a short while but had just been benched.

"They shouldn't have been so cocky in the first half of the game," her dad said, mostly to himself. She nodded. The team had come back, but it still wasn't a sure thing that they would win. Just a few minutes were left, and each team kept making a basket. She realized she was chewing her nails, and she stopped. Lucas was beside her. He took her hand and smiled, kissing her on the cheek. Mayra was on his other side.

"I think they're gonna win," she said. "They have to. This isn't even a tough school."

"They're really not," Lucas said.

They watched Jimmy's teammate dribble the ball down the court, putting his hand up to indicate a play.

Jimmy was on the far side, moving around. Suddenly, he feinted to one side and then sprinted the other way, behind the hoop and to the other corner, which was practically empty. A split second after he got there, the ball flew through the air, straight at him. He caught it, faced the hoop, and shot the ball, even though a player from the other team was coming straight at him. That player jumped, high, trying to block the ball, but it was no use.

"It's a three," she heard Lucas say. But would it go in?

It did. The crowd erupted in applause. People stomped their feet on the bleachers and screamed so hard it was impossible to hear anything else. Arianna laughed and cheered.

"Just two more points," her dad said.

Her mom was busy taking pictures. "Si se puede!" she screamed.

"There's less than a minute left," Lucas said, looking at the clock and back at the game.

Thirty seconds later, they were just a single point behind. Jimmy's team had made another three pointer while the opposing team had scored two more points.

Seven seconds were left.

Ariana was tapping her right foot like mad, Lucas's hand forgotten at her side.

One of Jimmy's teammates went for the shot. It didn't go in.

The whistle blew.

"Oh my God!" Lucas said, standing up and sitting back down.

Two seconds left.

"What?" Mayra and Ariana shouted. "What does it mean?

"Foul. The other guy hit his hand. He gets two shots. He needs to make them or they'll lose or tie."

They turned back to the game.

Jimmy's teammate went up to the free throw line.

The gym fell mostly silent. The referee blew his whistle again, signaling for him to shoot.

He looked down. Sweat dripped down his nose, but he wiped it away. He bounced the ball a few times. Ariana could see him taking a deep breath. The gym was silent except for that one baby that could always be heard crying at public events. He looked at the basket, put the ball in his hands, and threw the ball.

In.

Everyone cheered.

The ref threw the ball back to him, and again, the gym was quiet. A baby was still crying. Ariana hoped the guy down there wouldn't be distracted because of it. He did the same thing. Bounced the ball. Took a deep breath. And the ball left his hands to make a long arc towards the hoop.

The ball danced on the rim for two seconds before going in.

Ariana, Mayra, Lucas, and her family stood up, clapping along with everyone else. The other team got the ball and began dribbling down the court again. They had two seconds to make a comeback. Not likely but not impossible. The guy flung the ball across the gym with one second left. It hit the backboard, gasps could be heard all around, but the ball bounced away.

Nothing. They had won. Jimmy ran and lifted the coach into the air. Meanwhile, Ariana and Mayra screamed and clapped along with their entire half of the stands.

###

Ariana wondered how to ask Mayra her question

without completely embarrassing herself.

They were at Mayra's house. They had just a few days until winter break. Ariana shifted on the bed. Mayra was at her desk, finishing up some homework. Ariana had finished a few minutes ago, and her stuff was already in her bag.

She watched Mayra's pencil scratch the worksheet in front of her. Mayra sighed, flipped the pencil over, and began erasing entire lines of writing.

"Mayra?"

"Yes? Kinda busy here if you didn't notice." She began writing again.

"I'll help you if you want. But I wanted to ask you something first." She leaned on her elbow and made herself not chew her lip.

"What is it?" Mayra asked, swiveling her chair around.

"So," she began, wondering just how to word her thoughts. "Lucas and I—"

"You're not a virgin anymore!" Mayra exclaimed, dropping her pencil on the floor.

"Oh my gosh," she said, sitting up. "I am a virgin. I swear."

"You want to not be a virgin anymore," Mayra said, hopping onto the bed. Her homework lay forgotten on the floor.

Ariana studied the bedspread. Mayra gasped. "Have you and Lucas talked about it?"

"No. Not yet. It's just… I want to be prepared."

Mayra nodded.

"I feel like I might be ready, but I'm not sure. But just in case we decide to…I want to get birth control."

"That's a smart thing to do," Mayra said. She got up from the bed and went over to her night stand. She opened a drawer and began rummaging through it. She got out a circular plastic container and some small square packages. Condoms.

"Here," she said, throwing them on the bed. "Take some of these." She scooted a few condoms towards her. Ariana picked one up.

"Don't these expire?"

"You've been researching," Mayra said with a smile.

Ariana stuttered. "I like to be informed."

Mayra laughed. "These are still good. It's always good to be double protected. I use condoms, not that I've had occasion to use them in a while since I just haven't gone out with anyone anymore. But I always carry some with me in case of a fling."

Now it was Ariana's turn to laugh.

"Not that I've ever had one. But you just never know when you'll run into a Channing Tatum look alike or something. Oh, and if a guy ever says he doesn't want to use a condom, no matter what excuse he gives you, grab your panties and run the other way."

Ariana laughed as she pictured Mayra running away in such a situation.

She picked up the round plastic container and opened it up. There were a bunch of tiny pills around a wheel. She noticed different colors. Mayra must have already taken some of them because there were some missing.

"Those are birth control pills. I still take them in case because they take a few weeks to start being effective. I got a bunch of these at a free clinic. I can take you if you want. I could just give these to you but you should go and get checked."

"What do you mean?"

"Basically, you get a check-up down there."

She blinked and asked. "Really? Doesn't my mom need to take me, though?"

"Uh uh. You can go by yourself or even with Lucas. They won't say anything."

Ariana nodded. "Let's go tomorrow." She also made a mental note to someday very soon have the talk with Lucas. She still wasn't sure about discussing it with her mom. She didn't want to risk getting in trouble. Everything was finally going okay, and she didn't want to mess that up. But she did want to be ready in case she and Lucas became ready to take the next step.

chapter fourteen

Ariana held the wheel of pills in her hand. Then she felt the bracelet on her wrist, remembering the moment Lucas had put it on her. She was in her room, standing in front of her dresser.

The lady at the clinic had been really nice and explained just how the pills worked. She admitted to herself that she had no idea when she would have sex with Lucas. They'd never talked about it. And they still hadn't taken things too far. They kissed. A lot. Hands went to other places, but for the most part, they hadn't gotten crazy. She smiled, realizing she liked that about Lucas.

Things with Carlos had gotten serious pretty quickly. She shuddered at the thought of having stayed with him. She hadn't even considered taking birth control then.

Now, though, things were different. She and Lucas were savoring their relationship, taking things slow. Partly because they didn't get to see each other that much, but she kind of liked that. She had time to focus on her classes and get the grades she wanted, and Lucas had to work and keep up with school. Not to mention helping out at home.

She had no idea what that moment would be like. When Lucas would see her naked. When she'd see him naked for the first time. But now she knew, that whenever it happened, it could be special. And they'd be able to completely enjoy it.

She swallowed the month's first pill and hid the bag of birth control pills deep in a drawer.

The lady had given her enough for six months.

She still contemplated whether she should have told her mom about it, but she shoved that thought aside, deciding she'd tell her some other time, when it felt right and she and Lucas were getting closer to taking things that far.

###

Ariana shivered in the cold. She and Lucas were outside her house.

He had swung by after work to see her for a bit. It was wet and cold outside, Ariana's least favorite weather combination. Her parents were inside watching TV. They had just had dinner.

She wrapped her arms around herself, but Lucas snuggled her, wrapping his arms around her from behind. They leaned against his car.

That was her parents' rule. They weren't allowed to be in his car alone while he came over, but it was still better than sitting awkwardly in the living room.

She wondered what it would be like to be in college together. Do whatever they wanted whenever they wanted. She couldn't wait.

"So how was work?" she asked before other kinds of thoughts began invading her mind.

"Boring. As usual," he said, resting his head on top of hers. "It was so slow. Weekdays always are."

"Hm," she said, closing her eyes.

"But at least I got to work on homework when the manager was in her office. So when I get home all I have to do is shower and eat. And go to sleep."

"You haven't eaten?" she asked, turning around. "You should have said something. Duh. I should have offered."

Lucas turned her around and wrapped his arms around her once again.

"Nah. This is better."

She smiled and put her hands on his arms. They had on jackets so she couldn't feel his warm skin. She turned around, and without letting go of each other, she kissed him on the lips. She needed to feel him. Because soon he would be gone.

A few minutes later, they pulled apart.

"So have you started applying to colleges yet? You're going to apply to UGA, right?"

He looked down before looking at her.

"I guess I'll apply, but I don't think I can go anywhere other than the community college here," he said.

"Why not?" It didn't even come out as a question. She knew the answer.

"One, I can't afford it. I'd have to find a new job, and even then, it won't be enough, even with financial aid. And you know I can't leave. I help my mom with the rent and bills. I can't do that if I have to pay my own rent and bills."

She fought the tears at her eyes. "I know. What are we going to do?"

She couldn't bring herself to say out loud the rest of what she was thinking. What were they going to do if they couldn't be together? Would they have to break up?

"I know I can't ask this of you," he looked down as he said it, "but have you considered going to school here? With me? We'd be able to be close to each other, stay together."

She sighed. "I don't know. I really want to go to UGA. I mean, I guess, if I don't get in, then yeah. I'll stay here. I just wish there was a way for both of us to get what we want."

She thought for a moment. "What if you applied for scholarships?"

It was his turn to sigh. "I only have okay grades. And that still wouldn't help my mom."

Now the tears were at her eyes. She bit her lip, forcing the frog in her throat to leave.

Lucas grabbed her chin and lifted it so she was looking at him.

"We'll figure it out," he said, hugging her. "I promise. I can't lose you."

"And I promise that if we can't," she said, hoping he heard her from being buried in his chest, "I'll stay here with you."

"It's okay." He hugged her back. "There's no point worrying about all this right now anyway."

She thought about that. It was already early December. She'd find out in a matter of days if she got in early to UGA or not.

###

Ariana blinked her eyes awake and immediately froze. She was staring at the ceiling but not really looking at it. There were a gazillion things flashing in her mind.

It was December fifteenth.

She was supposed to find out by today at 4 o'clock if she had gotten in to the University of Georgia early or not.

Her stomach felt queasy as she decided whether to check the status of her application before she went to school or not. She slowly sat up and gripped the edge of the bed. The carpet felt fuzzy and soft under her feet.

Ariana knew that if she didn't check now, she wouldn't be able to focus on anything else besides wondering if she got in. On UGA's decision about her, if she was worthy enough, basically, to go there.

She sighed and went over to the computer on her desk. She typed in her username and password.

Wrong. She sighed as she racked her brain for the right ones, and her fingers clicked at the keyboard again.

She was in.

Ariana paused the cursor over the See My Status button. There was zero indication of whether she'd actually find out. Maybe it'd just say it was still processing.

Yeah. That's probably what it would say.

She clicked and waited a several seconds for the page to load, tapping her fingers restlessly.

Then it appeared.

And her heart stopped, and her mouth fell open all the way.

Status: Deferred.

###

"Hey, what's wrong?" Lucas asked later that day. They were at her locker. They had a minute or two.

Ariana couldn't decide if getting deferred was as

bad as just getting plain denied. That's how it felt right now.

"Hello?" he said.

She looked at him and then away. How was she supposed to say it out loud?

This sucks so bad, she thought.

She sighed. "I found out about UGA today." She still didn't look at him.

"And?" Lucas pressed. He actually sounded excited for her.

She felt his realization as the seconds passed and she didn't say anything else.

"Hey, it's okay. You can apply somew—"

"I didn't get denied," she interrupted.

"So you got—"

"I got deferred," she said, finally looking at him.

He opened his mouth then closed it. Then tried again. "That's—what does that mean?"

"It means 'we're not sure, send us more info, and we'll think about it and let you know in April.'"

"Oh. Well, that's not so bad at all," Lucas said, putting his arm around her. They began walking to Spanish. "I bet you a hundred dollars you're gonna get in. In fact, they're gonna beg you to go there."

She smiled. He had a point. This wasn't so bad after all. She was just gonna have to wait.

Maybe this was even a blessing in disguise because she had more time to figure things out with Lucas and she wouldn't be locked into attending UGA.

###

I miss you.

Ariana smiled and texted Lucas back. It was

Christmas morning, and her family was getting ready to open presents. Just a week ago, they'd been gathered here celebrating her dad's birthday. She loved the holidays. So many good things.

Later, Lucas would be over for dinner, but they'd decided to spend the morning with each of their own families. Tomorrow, though, she'd be meeting his family for the first time. He had finally convinced her to come over, and she decided it was time to meet his mom.

Jimmy ran into the living room in just boxers and a t-shirt and jumped onto the couch where their dad was sitting. Ariana, thankfully, was on the floor next to the Christmas tree.

"So who's ready to open presents?" he said in English. Her mom came into the living room from the kitchen. Unlike everyone else, she was nicely dressed compared to the rest of them in pajamas.

Some of their extended family would be over later, but for now it was just them. Just how Ariana liked.

Ariana looked at the presents gathered around the tree. There were a few big presents, but most of them looked like clothes.

"Let's start opening presents," her mom said, sitting down next to her dad.

Jimmy began passing out presents until everyone had their small pile.

"Ariana, you want to go first?" Jimmy asked.

"Nah. You go. I want to see what's in that big box in your lap."

He smiled. "Well, if you insist." He wasn't even done with his sentence before he started ripping the wrapping paper off of that very box.

"Oh my G—" Jimmy managed before he literally fell over and clutched at his chest. Then he was back up and feeling every inch of the box. It was the latest version of his video game system. "This just came out. It's like four hundred dollars."

Ariana smiled, wondering what she had gotten. She looked at her parents, who had their arms around each other and were smiling.

"Open it," her dad said.

Jimmy ran for some scissors and was back in a flash, pulling the controllers out. Next, he unwrapped a couple of games. "So that's why you wanted Ryan to come shopping with us a few weeks ago. And then sent me to go get you like a dozen things at the store."

Their mom smiled, and Ariana laughed.

"Ryan is so coming over later."

He unwrapped some clothes, which he set aside.

"You're next, Ariana." The video game system was still in his lap. He had his arms around it, as if he was afraid it might disappear.

She started with the small presents. Clothes, a couple of gift cards to stores at the mall, and a new hair straightener. She'd had hers for ages.

"Thanks, Mom and Dad," she said. She looked at her big present. She wondered what it was. It wasn't as big as Jimmy's, but hopefully it was something just as good.

She'd splurged on an eReader a few weeks after her birthday, so she doubted it was that. Besides, the box was bigger.

She tore at the wrapping paper carefully at the

places her mom had folded and taped it together. When it was unwrapped, she set aside the paper and bow. She tried not to squeal because she realized what this was.

"A laptop?" she asked. She covered her mouth with her hand and looked up at her parents.

"For school, when you go to college. You'll have your own. Later, we can buy you the printer to go with it," her mom said with a sparkle in her eye.

Ariana got up and hugged her parents.

"How did you guys afford all of this?" She indicated the pile of stuff on the floor. Expensive stuff. They'd never had a Christmas this good.

Her mom looked at her dad before answering. "I got a promotion at work. That's why I've been putting in more hours. Part of it is that I'll be getting a Christmas bonus from now on."

"Sweet," Jimmy said, his mouth slightly open. "Does that mean you make more money than dad now?"

Her mom laughed. "Maybe."

"In this day and age, that is perfectly normal," their dad began. "Aqui no es como en Mexico." Nope, it wasn't like in Mexico at all. Ariana's mom kissed him on the cheek.

"Next thing you know, Dad'll be the one cooking around here and doing the laundry," Jimmy said as he took his huge pile of stuff to his room.

###

It was later. It was time to meet Lucas's family for the first time. His mom and two sisters.

She wondered what she should say after greeting them, and if his mom would like her.

"What are you thinking about?" Lucas asked her as he squeezed her hand. They were almost at his house. Her parents had trusted them to go alone.

She glanced out the window before turning back to him. "I just…want to make a good impression." She smiled as butterflies danced in her stomach.

"You will," Lucas assured. "You're smart, nice, everything my mom could want."

They pulled into his driveway and got out of the car. "This is it."

They walked towards the front door. It was smaller than her house but homey. Her heart warmed at the handful of toy cars out on the front lawn, the kind she, Jimmy, and Mayra would ride down hills when they were in elementary school. "Those used to be so much fun," she told Lucas.

"Still are," he replied as they walked in.

There were even more toys in the living room, and she saw his sisters dressed up but watching Christmas movies. His mom walked in from the kitchen. Ariana smiled when she saw his mom smile. She held out her hand as she came closer.

"Mucho gusto. Yo soy Ariana," she said. She remembered to not have fishy hands.

"Es un placer. Yo soy Marcela. Lucas se la pasa hablando de ti pero no me dijo lo bonita que eres."

Ariana blushed and looked at Lucas, who shook his head. Aw, he talked about her to his mom.

"Come in," she said and closed the front door.

She ushered them into the kitchen, and they took a seat. Lucas stood back up. "Want something to drink?"

"Water, soda, juice?" his mom finished in

Spanish. She already had the fridge open.

"Um, water please," Arianna said, looking back and forth between them.

Lucas's mom closed the door and went to the dishwasher for a glass. The house was silent except for the sound of the TV and the occasional laughs of his sisters. His mom set the glass of water down in front of her, and she said thank you before taking a few sips.

"Lucas says you're graduating this year too," she said, leaning on the counter.

She nodded. "I'm really excited."

"Any idea what you're gonna do after?"

"College. I'll be the first in my family," she said with a smile.

"That's so good. I wish I'd had that opportunity when I was your age. Lucas will be the first too." She sat down across from them. "Tell me about your family. Are your parents still together?"

She glanced at Lucas, who was looking down at the table but caught her eye for a brief second. "Yes. They're very supportive. My brother too."

"That's so good. I've been a single mom most of Lucas's life, but he's really stepped up and helped out." She smiled at him. "I can't wait to see him in college and have a career."

"Me too." She also smiled at him, especially when she saw him smiling too.

"Lucas says you're really smart. He's so lucky to have met such a nice girl. I can tell you're a good person, good for him."

She didn't know what to say to that. "There aren't many like her," Lucas said with a laugh.

"Lucas works so hard to make a little money and do well in school, but I'm glad he has someone else there for him too."

"He's a really good guy," she said.

Lucas's mom smiled one more time before getting back up to stir something on the stove. "Are you hungry? I was just making some flautas. I'm just about finished."

"Sure. Need some help?" She got up and began walking towards her.

"No, no, no. Please sit down." His mom waved her off. Ariana smiled and walked back to her seat. She liked it here.

Lucas stood up instead. "I'll grab the plates and stuff."

One of Lucas's sisters wandered into the kitchen. "Mami, I'm hungry." Ariana loved her long, brown hair and green eyes. They caught each other's eyes and the little girl, around eight years old, smiled before running and hiding under the table.

"The food's almost done, mija," his mom replied.

"Do you have to work today?" she said from under the table. "I don't want you to work today."

"I'm just going to work for a little bit. I promise. Then I'll be back to help you color, okay?"

She heard her sigh. "Okay."

Ariana peeked under the table. "Hi. I'm Ariana."

"Are you Lucas's girlfriend?" she asked, not tearing her eyes away from her.

"Um, yeah." She had read somewhere it wasn't good to lie to kids. "Hey, do you want me to color with you?"

"Yeah! Can you play with me?" Before Ariana

could even answer her, she ran out of the table and back into the living room. She was back about five seconds later with her slightly older sister in tow and a huge box of crayons and markers and several coloring books. The little girls opened the box and they each grabbed a crayon and began coloring.

"Sleeping Beauty is my favorite princess," the younger sister said.

"I like Tangled," the other replied, glancing at Ariana.

Lucas squeezed her shoulder as he set the table around them, and his mom smiled at them while she rolled flautas and placed them in the frying pan.

chapter fifteen

"That was so good," Ariana told Lucas as they sat down on the couch together.

"Explains the roll I've been getting lately around my waist," Lucas said.

"Oh yeah, that nonexistent roll," Ariana said as she rolled her eyes. She sighed. "I am so full. I don't want to move."

"Then don't," Lucas said with smile as he put his arm around her. "We can hang out here for a little bit longer."

She nodded and leaned her head on his shoulder.

His mom was in her room getting ready for work, and his sisters were coloring again, this time in the living room.

His mom came out a few minutes later. She looked completely different. She was in a fast food uniform, and her hair was up in a bun. She also had a little bit of makeup on.

"I'll be back later, around ten," she said as she gathered her purse, phone, and keys. "You two behave," she said as she walked around with her things and grabbed a coat.

"We will," one sister said.

"I wasn't talking to them," she mumbled as she passed Ariana and Lucas and winked.

Ariana blushed hard and cringed into the sofa.

"Stay as long as you want," his mom said as she bent down to kiss each of her daughters. Ariana and Lucas stood up as she came towards them. "It was so nice meeting you. Please come back and visit again soon. Mi casa es tu casa."

"Gracias," Ariana said as she gave her and Lucas a hug.

"I'll call you on my break," she told Lucas as she headed out.

They sat back down. "Got the house to ourselves," he said.

"Not exactly," she said with a laugh. "But that's okay."

Lucas turned on the TV and began flipping through channels.

"So does your mom work a lot?"

"Yeah. She works during the day Monday through Friday and afternoons on the weekend. Opposite of my schedule so only one of us is here usually to watch the girls."

She nodded. Something occurred to her. "Well, if you guys ever need a babysitter, especially your mom, I'm available. She looks like she could use a break."

He kissed her forehead. "I'll let her know, babe. Thanks."

She got her phone out and texted her mom.

I'll be home later. Still at Lucas's house with his sisters.

###

"So you were alone at his house?" Mayra asked. Ariana could practically see her eyes pop out slightly.

"No," she repeated. "His sisters were there, remember?"

"Oh yeah. But still, I bet you guys snuck off a couple times."

"No comment," she said as she closed her eyes.

Mayra laughed.

"His whole family was really nice," she said.

"That's good. Bummer his mom works so much. Sounds like my mom. What about his dad?"

"I know he's not in the picture. I've just never asked why."

"Oh. Maybe they're separated or divorced. That's what happened with my parents, except we all know my dad pretends we don't exist anymore."

"I'm not sure," Ariana said.

"Why don't you ask? Or is it something he doesn't like to talk about?"

"I'm not sure." Ariana felt kind of dumb. "Honestly, I just feel like it's none of my business."

"He hasn't brought it up, but maybe one of these days you could just ask. I mean, you guys should be able to tell each other anything."

Ariana thought about that. "I guess you're right. I'll wait for the right time."

"So did you spend the whole afternoon over at his place?"

"Yep. Just got back like thirty minutes ago."

"Wow. Your parents have come such a long way from last year."

"I know. It's like they're different people. But I think it's awesome how they trust me with Lucas. I think they honestly see how good a person he is and that we're honest, mostly."

"Still haven't done it?" She was referring to sex, of course.

"Nope," she said right away.

"Do you want to?" Mayra asked a beat later.

She hesitated. "I don't know. Maybe. We'll see. I've been taking the birth control, so I'll be ready in that sense, but I just don't know about being completely ready yet."

"There's no rush. Take your time because it only happens once."

She thought about that a second before another question popped into her head. "So what about you and Jimmy? Any action happening there?" she asked with a smile on her face.

"Um, no comment," Mayra said with a wink.

###

Ariana walked into her room, ready to crash on her bed. But she froze when she saw her mom holding her birth control.

Her mom looked at her, and all she could see was that big wrinkle of her forehead that she got whenever she was upset and the questioning in her eyes. She shook her head and stared at Ariana.

"What is this?"

As if the situation wasn't enough, the first thing that popped into her head was, "Birth control, duh," but she decided leaving her mouth to hang open was a smarter option.

"Why do you have this? How long have you had these pills, and why didn't you tell me?" Her mom had taken two steps towards her.

Ariana tried to remember if she had put her pills back this morning after taking her daily dose. She always put the plastic container back in her underwear drawer. Then she noticed the pile of folded laundry on her bed. Her mom must have noticed it when putting away her clothes.

Damn. She should have stuck it in the way back.

"Explain yourself, Ariana. Are you having sex?" She whispered that last word.

"No," she shook her head frantically. "I promise. I just wanted to be ready. I promise, mom."

"You're only eighteen. Why didn't you tell me?"

"I was going to. I just—I wanted to wait and be sure."

Both of them were still just standing there. "Where did you even get these?"

"There's a free clinic," she said quietly. "I went with Mayra."

Her mom sighed and took a seat on the bed. "Sit."

Ariana's heart was beating about a million miles an hour, and she hoped her dad didn't find out about this. She had wanted to tell her mom eventually, but having her dad know would just be so awkward.

"I know you're getting older, and you've shown me how responsible you can be, but this is too much for me. I need to know this stuff. You're still my daughter, and I need to know what's going on."

Ariana looked down and nodded.

"Whatever you do with Lucas is your choice. I personally think it's too soon to be thinking about this right now, but you're almost an adult. All I can do is give you advice from someone who's been there."

"I just wanted to be ready in case."

"Is Lucas pressuring you to do this?" her mom asked.

"No," she replied immediately. "Never. We're taking things slow, but I just didn't want to risk anything after…"

"Carlos?"

She nodded again. "We never did anything, but I —I just want to be prepared." She felt silly saying the same thing over and over again, and her voice was shaking, but she just wanted her to understand.

"I wanted to tell you. I was just waiting for the right time."

Her mom sighed again, and there was a second of silence. "You about gave me heart attack."

Finally, Ariana laughed a little and glanced at her mom. She was smiling a bit.

"I'm glad you're being careful. But like I said, it's only been a few months. Please wait."

She nodded, and her mom got up and left.

"Mom?"

Her mom turned around and looked at her in the doorway.

"Are you gonna tell Dad?"

She shook her head. "This can stay between us girls."

###

It was the first day back at school after the holiday break, and Ariana and Jimmy were actually relieved.

Even Jimmy had gotten sick of playing video games all day, and Ariana's eyes kinda burned from browsing Pinterest, Twitter, and Instagram so much. And the occasional educational website, like checking up on her UGA application status, even though it said processing every single time. She had already submitted the additional essay UGA had asked for. She just hoped it was good enough.

She would know in a few more months if she got in after all. She still wasn't sure how'd she deal with leaving Lucas, Mayra, and her family behind if she got into UGA, but she decided to cross that bridge when she got to it. If she got to it. There wasn't any guarantee she would get in, and she was doubting herself more than ever.

Ariana was about to grab some Pop Tarts from the kitchen cabinet, but remembered she was looking a little pudgier these days, probably from being such a couch potato over the winter break. Jimmy, of course, looked as ripped as ever. She went to the fridge instead and grabbed some Greek yogurt and proceeded to make some peanut butter toast. That or her thighs were threatening to not fit into her skinny jeans anymore.

She thought about the freshman fifteen that college freshman supposedly gained their first year of college. Oh gosh. UGA better have a great gym, she thought. She made a mental note to check it out whenever she visited. She wanted to visit soon and see the campus for herself.

"Ready to go?" Jimmy asked as he walked into the kitchen. He went straight for the cabinet where the Pop Tarts were and grabbed two packages and some orange juice.

Ariana tried not to stare as he gobbled it all down while she nibbled at her toast. She drank some of his juice to wash it all down (Jimmy didn't complain; he was a morning person), and got up.

"Let's go." She grabbed her backpack from the living room as well as her jacket, keys, and phone.

Jimmy was behind her.

She heard him yawn and turned around to see him stretching. "Winter break was way too short."

Ariana laughed. "Yeah, I think I changed my mind. I'd rather stay here and burn my eyes all day from the TV and computer. No more learning."

They headed out the door. Her dad had already left for work, and her mom was about to leave as well. She was coming in from going to start up the car. "It's cold," she said. "Make sure you got your jacket."

Jimmy held his up.

"I meant put it on," she said as she closed the door behind them.

"Oh," he said. They were already at her car.

A minute later, they were at Mayra's, and Ariana was still trying to unglue her eyelids.

Mayra, unfortunately, was also a morning person, so the whole ride to school involved trying to participate in their conversation despite wanting to focus on the road while keeping her eyes open and her mouth from yawning.

"What time did you get to bed?" Mayra asked.

"Like at two," she replied. "I couldn't sleep. My good sleeping habits were pretty much ruined over the break."

"I hate class but love school. Finally, I can interact with other people my age," Mayra said.

Ariana smiled. "And I'm happy to be seeing Lucas again on a pretty much daily basis. Monday through Friday, anyway. He had to work extra over the break, so it sucked not seeing him that much."

She glanced at Jimmy and Mayra. Jimmy was in the back as usual, but he looked at Mayra every so often. She wondered when they'd finally give each other a chance.

###

Ariana parked at her assigned space at school and spotted Lucas getting out of his car a couple of lanes down at his spot. She turned off her car, grabbed her backpack, and headed towards him, leaving Mayra and Jimmy behind to pretend they didn't have a thing going on. Even though it had been apparent over the break from when they had hung out how much they still liked each other.

Lucas's face broke into a smile as she approached, and she couldn't help but do the same. He still gave her butterflies, just like the first day he walked into Spanish class last semester. The suckiest part of this semester was that they didn't share any classes at all. They were going to resort to seeing each other before and after school only during the week, and she hated to ask him to get up extra early or stay extra at the end of the day and then have to rush off to work.

Her smile faltered a little. They would make it work.

Somehow.

He pulled her into his arms. His face was in her hair, and she was sure his eyes were closed just like hers. He squeezed her. They hadn't seen each other in a few days.

"How are you?" he asked quietly. They began walking towards school, hands held.

"Good," she said. "How about you? Did you get some sleep?"

She glanced at him.

"Some."

"Lucas," she sighed.

"What?"

"What am I going to do with you?"

She sensed what he was going to say before he said it. He looked at her straight in the eyes. "Whatever you want."

He came in for a kiss, and Ariana hoped no one was watching because she kissed Lucas like there was no tomorrow, no longer feeling the cold.

A few seconds later, they pulled away and kept walking, but now there was a bit of an awkward silence between them. He had never implied anything like that, not even playing around. And that's what he had been doing just then. Just playing. But there had also been a hint of something else.

Oh, God, she thought. Was he ready to…have sex?

They'd made out. A lot. But hadn't really gone beyond that.

Would he bring that up soon? Maybe she should bring it up.

How did you even start a conversation like that? Wait until they were about to…? No. Who knew what would happen with their hormones all riled up?

They stepped inside the school building, and Ariana tried to focus on other things, like what breakfast would be today. That peanut butter toast and yogurt had not filled her up for long.

They went into the lunchroom, and she saw

French toast sticks (not bad) and apple juice. Eh.

At least she had Lucas for a few more minutes before the bell rang.

They grabbed some food and looked around for a table. The cafeteria was packed since the bell was about to ring. Just about all the buses had arrived.

She was about to groan but stopped herself at the last minute when she saw the only table with enough room for the four of them (Mayra and Jimmy were behind them) also had Wendy and her pack of friends.

Perfect beginning to the new year and the new semester.

chapter sixteen

Ariana tried to quickly decide where it was best to sit, but apparently, Jimmy and Mayra were not paying attention because they went and plopped themselves across from each other so that the only two seats left were next to Wendy and her friends.

Mayra glanced at her and saw where Ariana and Lucas were trying not to stare instead of sitting down. Her mouth fell open slightly before mouthing "oops."

They saw Wendy look at them and roll her eyes. Then she smiled like she knew something no one else did.

Mayra looked at her like she might move to the seat next to Wendy, but Ariana strutted over and sat down before she could question herself any further. Lucas went around and sat across from her.

No one said anything. Jimmy was just looking between them like he no idea what was going on. Of course. He began eating, and Ariana remembered the breakfast in front of her. She opened her juice carton without looking anywhere but her tray.

She heard Lucas give a small cough, and she glanced at him. He looked at her before looking back down at his food.

Ariana decided she wasn't going to let Wendy have this.

She brought her head up and tried to act normal. So what if Lucas's ex was right here? She was not going to be the jealous girlfriend. She was not going to let Wendy get to her because of what happened last semester. She was not going to let her ruin anything else for her.

She focused on eating and following Jimmy and Mayra's conversation, laughing when something was funny instead of worrying about who was right next to her. Lucas did the same and relaxed.

Soon the bell rang, and she got up with Lucas to put away their trays and head to their first class.

First, though, she headed to her locker to grab a couple things.

Before she turned the corner to get there, Lucas stopped her.

He looked her in the eyes. "I love you."

She saw his chest rise from taking a deep breath before he kissed her on the lips.

"Okay, break it up," she heard. They took a step back and saw a teacher walking down the hall.

She turned back to Lucas. "What was that for?" Although she had an idea.

"Thank you," he said. "For knowing that I love you."

She gave him a smile. "I love you too."

"I'll see you later, okay?" He gave her one last kiss before walking in the opposite direction.

Ariana went to her locker, grabbed some stuff, and continued heading towards her first period class.

It was an advanced computer class she thought might come in handy when she tried to find a job or something.

She froze for a second when she walked in. Wendy was in this class. She made herself not look at her as she strode to the opposite end of the classroom, but she could see her smirk out of the corner of her eye. She already had English with her. Senior year was threatening to be hell.

###

The next morning, Ariana sat straight up in bed and looked at her phone. All in one swift moment.

"Shit!" she half whispered, half shouted.

She was gonna be late for school. Again. She couldn't get another tardy or her mom would get a phone call about it. And it was only March.

She and Lucas could not afford that. But that's what she got for staying up way too late last night texting him. She ran to the window and glanced out, phone still in hand. Her mom's car was still in the driveway, but she'd surely be leaving any minute now.

She ran into the bathroom before her mom saw that she was not ready. Just as she quietly closed the door, she heard her mom's bedroom door open.

There was a knock on the bathroom door.

"Ariana?" It was her mom. "You almost done?"

"Uh, yeah. Just about," she said, remembering to keep her voice calm and not too hurried, like her heartbeat right now. She began brushing her teeth while turning on her straightener.

"Okay. I'm leaving. I'll see you later. Drive safe."

She saw her hair in the mirror. Shit! Of course her hair had to look like a troll's today.

"Okay. Bye!"

She looked at her phone again. She had seven minutes to leave if she wanted to make it to school on time. She rinsed her mouth out while dialing Lucas. After a couple rings, he picked up.

"Hey, you okay?" he asked. She didn't usually call him this early. She wiped off her face.

"Yeah," she said, brushing through the tangles in her hair. "Just wanted to make sure you didn't oversleep like I did today."

"Nope. But it was not fun waking up this morning."

"I bet," she said quickly. "Okay, well, I gotta run. I'll talk to you later."

"Alright. Bye."

The call ended, and she peed faster than she had in her life. She put on a little makeup and checked her phone again.

Four minutes.

Arana brushed her hair and worked the straightener through just the wildest parts of her hair before turning off the straightener and unplugging it.

She ran back into her room and opened her closet. She grabbed a t-shirt and a pair of jeans. She pulled them on along with some socks and sneakers. At least her backpack was ready to go.

"Jimmy! You ready?" she called out. He'd better be, she thought as she ran into the bathroom for her phone

"Yep. Fifteen minutes ago," she heard. "Watching TV."

"You have got to be kidding me," she said to herself as she slung her backpack over her shoulder and headed out.

Two minutes later, they were at Mayra's driveway, but Mayra was putting her stuff in her car. Ariana didn't bother pulling in to the driveway.

Her mouth fell open, and she forgot they were running late. She rolled down her window, and she and Jimmy stared at Mayra.

"Surprise!" She held up her driver's license. "Finally traded my permit in for this baby this weekend, and my car is finally up and running. I'll see you two later."

Mayra winked and got into her car.

Ariana smiled and waved along with Jimmy as they continued to school.

"Well, thanks for the rides and everything, but I don't think I'll be needing your services anymore," Jimmy said.

"Whatever," Ariana said, laughing.

"Man, I can't wait to get my permit. My birthday is almost here, and I've been reading that driver's ed book. Watch me get it on my first try."

"Oh gosh. Can't even imagine you *and* Mayra on the road. What has the world come to?"

"Speak for yourself," Jimmy muttered. "I can't wait to have my own car and drive around like you do."

###

"So what are you up to?" Lucas asked over the phone.

"I just got done applying to some online scholarships. I've literally applied to like twelve scholarships. One of them is this huge forty thousand dollar scholarship, which I highly doubt I'll get, but oh well. I'll take what I can get. It just sucks because the application is basically my life story."

"Um, yeah, I have like no time for that, and they'd probably start snoring as soon as they opened my B average application."

"Actually, there are all kind of scholarships on here. You should really look. Watch me apply for you because there are ones for being Latino, being artistic, whatever. Not just grades."

"Oh," Lucas said, although he still didn't sound very interested.

"Now I'm filling out all the financial aid stuff for UGA. The priority deadline or whatever is coming up in like a week," she said without tearing her eyes away from her laptop. Her phone was on speaker next her on her desk.

"Yeah, I think the deadlines for the college here is way more relaxed. I got plenty of time," Lucas said.

Ariana laughed. "Still, don't wait until the last minute. So you never did apply for UGA, did you?"

"Nope."

Silence.

"It's okay. I don't even know if I'm going to get in," she said, finally looking away from her screen. She glanced at all the paperwork in front her, taxes and stuff like that from her parents.

"I think we all know that's BS," said Lucas. "Of course you're getting in. I saw your report card last week. Honors list again."

She could tell he was smiling. She sighed loudly. "I sure hope so."

Ariana thought about that. "I don't know. Maybe I'll just stay here and go to school with you and

Mayra."

"Listen. Go where you want to go. Don't sacrifice the next four years of your life for us. We don't deserve that."

Silence again.

She had a hard time knowing what to say. "Yes, you do. It's just hard. Making a choice." She shook her head and looked at her screen again. "Let's worry about all that later. No sense worrying about it now. Let's just be happy for now."

"Got that right." Lucas was sounding sleepier by the minute.

He had just gotten off of work. She got an idea.

"Hey, why don't you just send me all your stuff later, and I can help you out with all the financial aid stuff. I have nothing to do all week anyway."

"You are awesome," Lucas said.

"You know it," she said, typing again. She didn't know where they'd each be next year, heck in six months, but she knew she wouldn't be without Lucas.

"So when do you find out?" Lucas said kind of groggily. "You know, about UGA."

"Um, soon. The website says the letters get mailed out next week, but I can log on and find out immediately like last time."

"Wow. That sneaked up real fast."

She thought about that. "Yeah, it really did." She tried not to think about the butterflies in her stomach right now.

"My application's not even due yet, I think."

"Oh wow," she said. "Better get that done on time."

"Yeah, yeah."

"Better not be one of those bums who doesn't go to college either," she said with a laugh.

"Haha," Lucas said. "No worries there. I do not want to get paid eight fifty an hour my whole life."

"Can you imagine what next year is gonna be like?" she asked him as an image popped into her head of them cuddled together on an apartment couch watching a movie, with no worries about curfews.

"I don't know. I just know I want to be with you," Lucas said.

Ariana hated the feeling that popped into her stomach right then, like being with Lucas wasn't in her control.

###

Today was the day. April 15.

Like that cheesy saying. Today would start the rest of her life or something like that. Or her life might be over, and she wasn't sure which was which.

She was going to find out if she had gotten into UGA. Again.

"So you're getting the letter today?" her mom asked. Ariana was surprised she remembered. She had made it a point not to make it a big deal when she told them back in December.

"They get mailed out today, so I probably won't get it for another few days," she replied.

"Hm." They were folding some laundry in the living room, but Ariana had been folding the same shirt for a few minutes. She couldn't think of anything else besides whether she had gotten in or not. Her whole day had been like that, but she'd managed to distract herself.

A few days ago, she had decided she would wait for the letter to come in the mail. She didn't want to go through the same thing as last time. Just click and her dreams were almost shattered. She wanted to open an actual letter. The bad thing was she'd probably know right away anyway. A thin envelope did not hold good news most of the time when it came to acceptance letters.

But now, she wasn't so sure. She just wanted to know.

"I could check on the computer," she thought out loud.

"Well, then, go check," her mom said, not folding clothes anymore.

Her mom looked at her when she didn't get up. "Are you nervous?" she asked.

"Kind of," Ariana said with a small smile.

"If it's meant to happen, it will happen," her mom said. "Even though I don't really want you to leave."

Jimmy came in from playing basketball outside. "Ryan had to go home," he said. "What's up?"

"I find out today if I got in to UGA. Or I can wait for the letter in the mail."

"Dang. Well, are you gonna check or not?" he asked as he sat down next to her. He held up a pair of huge underwear.

"Who's is that?" he said as he flung it back inside the container.

Ariana laughed. "Not mine."

Her mom snatched it away and tucked it behind a pile of clothes. "It's to keep everything in place."

Jimmy tried not to gag. "Now I can't take that

image out of my head."

"Just you watch. You'll grow old soon enough and need them too."

Ariana tried not to think about that. She got up. "Yeah, I'm gonna check my application status now."

Jimmy jumped up from the sofa and followed her to her room.

"Tell me what it says!" her mom shouted after them. Ariana got her phone out and dialed Mayra.

It was Saturday, so Lucas was at work, but she wanted to surprise him anyway. And have time to think about things once she found out the decision.

"Hello?" Mayra finally answered.

Ariana sat down at her desk, and Jimmy stood behind her as she logged on to the UGA website.

"What's up?"

"I'm checking my application status for UGA," she said.

"I thought you were waiting for the letter," Mayra said.

"I changed my mind."

"Hey, Mayra," Jimmy popped in.

"Hey," she replied.

"You two finally going out or what?" Ariana said, mostly to stall. The page was loading. From there, she'd be able to click and find out.

"Maybe. Maybe not," Jimmy said.

"Seriously, though, why all the mystery?"

Jimmy shrugged. Now that she had them both together, maybe she could find out what was going on between them. They were always together anyway.

The page was ready.

"Hold that thought," she said, her voice a little

shaky. "You guys ready?"

"Let's do it," Mayra finally spoke up.

"Okay, I'm clicking on the 'show my application status' button," she said as she clicked.

A few seconds later, there it was.

Her heart jumped.

"No way," Jimmy said quietly.

"What? What?" Mayra said. "Don't make me go over there."

"I got accepted," Ariana said. "I GOT ACCEPTED."

She jumped up and down and hugged Jimmy. He picked her up and threw her on her bed, and she screamed, but from pure joy. She felt the mattress beneath her, and she spread out like she was making a snow angel. Her smile was so big it was hurting her cheeks. She stared at the ceiling.

Her heart was pounding, and she was breathing like she had just run a marathon.

She heard shuffling and other noises from Mayra's end of the conversation. "Be right there!" Mayra hung up.

Jimmy jumped and landed sideways on top of her.

Ariana struggled to get up.

Her mom appeared in the doorway and came in for a long hug. "I'm calling everyone right now. And as soon as your father gets home, we're taking you out to eat," she said with a smile, leaving the room again.

She looked at the words on the screen again.

Accepted.

chapter seventeen

Mayra stared at the screen as she sat in Ariana's desk chair.

The news had sunk in, and Ariana was sitting on her bed with her back against the wall, and her knees to her chest.

She had to tell Lucas.

"So when do you start packing?" Mayra smiled as she turned to look at her. "You better invite me to some of those parties in Athens. I hear they're freakin' amazing."

Ariana slowly looked at her. It had just hit her that in a matter of months she wouldn't be living here anymore. She'd be in an entirely new place. Alone. No Lucas. No Mayra. No Jimmy. No Mom and Dad.

She took a deep breath and tried not to let that thought paralyze her.

Mayra sat next to her. "You don't look so excited. What's wrong?"

"Yeah, what's up? You look like you're going to a funeral or something," Jimmy said as he went to sit in the desk chair.

"I don't know if I can do this," she whispered.

She looked down. Maybe that way Jimmy and Mayra wouldn't see the tears that had pooled in her eyes.

She took another deep breath and willed the tears to go back inside her.

"Of course you can do this." Mayra put her arm around her. Jimmy just looked on, kinda sad. It reminded her of last year when Mayra had been the one crying. Except she had shut herself in the bathroom and was on the floor crying when she and Jimmy found her.

"It's gonna suck if I go," she said a minute later.

"When you go. Not if," Mayra said. "And it's not gonna suck. There's this thing called Skype that we can use to communicate. You and Lucas are gonna be fine. Won't be easy, but you'll get through it."

"Seriously, though," she asked, mostly because she didn't want to talk about Lucas right now. She could feel the tears coming on at the thought of not being close to Lucas anymore. "You two give yourselves a chance already. You're gonna be here next year, Mayra. You already decided that. What's holding you back?"

Mayra took her arm off of her shoulder and glanced at Jimmy. There were several seconds of silence.

Jimmy got up before she was even done talking. They all squeezed onto her bed, and Jimmy put his long arm around Mayra and kissed her on top of her head.

"We're not in a rush," he said. "We have the rest of our lives to be together."

Ariana looked at Mayra, who was staring straight

ahead. "You don't know that," Mayra responded.

"I'll be right back. Just gonna go to the bathroom," Ariana said, getting off the bed and standing up.

She went in to the hall bathroom and shut the door quietly behind her. She could hear her mom talking on the phone in the kitchen.

She could tell Mayra and Jimmy were having a moment. If anything good came out of all of this, at least it should be that. If she and Lucas didn't end up together next year, somehow she'd find a way to deal with it, even if it felt like she being eaten alive from the inside out. But seeing Jimmy and Mayra together, happy, that would be amazing.

She stared in the mirror at herself. Her eyes were slightly red, but she couldn't bring herself to look herself in the eye.

She grabbed some toilet paper to wipe her nose. Her phone was in her pocket, so she took it out and texted Lucas. He was still at work and wouldn't be able to go out to eat with them.

She texted him.

I miss you.

Already, she missed him so bad. Her heart tugged at her inside her chest. She closed her eyes and pictured his smile and the feel of his warm skin against hers, the slight stubble on his face.

She hugged herself instead.

###

Ariana walked back into her room. As she did, she saw Jimmy and Mayra pull apart. Their faces had been really close. She smiled a small smile and sat in her chair.

There was a link for the next steps she had to take to go to UGA. She hovered over it but decided to look at it later.

"So you're coming with us to eat, right? My dad should be here soon," she said to Mayra.

Mayra looked up. "Yeah. Let me just go ask my mom. Want to walk with me?"

"Yeah," she said. They both stood up.

"I'm gonna go shower," Jimmy said, also getting up. She saw the way his hand was on Mayra's back.

They walked out of the house and headed down the driveway.

"You okay?" she asked Mayra.

"Yeah," she said. They walked slowly to her house and looked up at the sky. It was a fiery orange red, and there were some clouds scattered around. It was slightly chilly, but it felt good. Ariana made sure she didn't forget this view, this feeling.

"How about you?" Mayra said.

"I'm good. We'll figure it out," she said. "If Lucas and I are meant to be, then we'll be okay." She looked at Mayra. "How about you two? Sorry if I was being intrusive. I just—"

"It's okay. We all know it's obvious. Except for our parents."

They gave a small laugh.

"It's just hard," Mayra said.

"Can you imagine?" Ariana asked. "You think they'll be cool about it?"

"I hope so. I know my mom probably won't care, as long as I do good in school. I'm just not sure I want to tell anyone right away."

"I think my parents would love it. They love you

already." She looked at Mayra again, who looked back and tried to smile. "What's going on?"

"You know," she said. "I don't want to ruin the good thing we have. All of this. Our friendship. Mine and Jimmy's friendship. The relationship I have with your entire family. I don't deserve someone as good as you guys."

And before Mayra had even finished her sentence, they were at Mayra's driveway, and she had collapsed onto it, crying. With her knees pulled up and her head down and covered by her arms.

Ariana pushed back the tears in her own eyes and sat down next to her. She put her arm around her.

"What? Is that what you really think?" She looked around and behind them. They were alone. "Mayra, you are the coolest, nicest person I know. How could you think that? We're all one family. You're my sister."

Mayra pulled her head up and hugged her, and Ariana hugged back, squeezing her best friend. Mayra gasped for air from how hard she was crying.

"Please don't cry," she whispered. "You deserve to be happy."

Mayra kept crying but tried to talk. "My family is so messed up. I'm messed up," she said in between sobs. "How can Jimmy love me?"

Ariana didn't say anything. She had a feeling Mayra just needed to say some things out loud.

Mayra continued, her head on Ariana's shoulder. "Jimmy is such a good guy, and I've slept with more guys than I can count on one hand. He's never been with anyone. How can I—" She broke down crying again, and a few tears escaped from Ariana's eyes.

"If being with Jimmy is what your heart wants

and it feels right, then do it. Don't worry about that other crap. It's just not true." Ariana didn't know where the words came from, but she knew they needed to be said.

Mayra kept sniffling. Ariana squeezed her again.

"Come on. Let's go get you all dressed up. Cuz my best friend is not going to be sad today. No one is."

She pulled Mayra up, and they hugged before going inside.

###

About twenty minutes later, Mayra and Ariana were headed back to her house. Mayra's mom had been more than okay with her daughter going out to dinner with them. And she had congratulated and hugged Ariana on her acceptance.

"I knew it," Mayra's mom said as she got ready to leave for work. "You're going to do great things." She looked at Mayra. "Both of you. Have a good time. I can't wait until it's Mayra too." She hugged them again before they left and handed Mayra a twenty.

Now they were walking back up Ariana's driveway. She noticed her dad's work truck. Jimmy came out of the house. He was already dressed, his hair styled perfectly in place. She could smell the aftershave from here. When had he started using that?

Jimmy glanced at their dad's truck before saying, "Dad's almost out of the shower, and Mom's changing. Then we're leaving." He walked towards them. "Ariana, what are you in the mood for? Pizza? Burgers? Italian? All you-can-eat, five-dollar Chinese buffet maybe?"

"No idea yet." She was about to say she was gonna head inside to change really quick when she saw Mayra go straight up to Jimmy, put her arms around his neck, stand on her tiptoes, and kiss him hard on the mouth.

Jimmy's eyes stayed open for a split second while his arms hung at his side, paralyzed. Ariana's mouth hung open, and she saw her brother realize what was happening as he closed his eyes, kissed Mayra back, and put his arms around her waist. Then somewhere below her waist.

"Uh, I'm gonna go change now," Ariana said laughing. She walked off.

Mayra and Jimmy didn't even look her way.

"I'm gonna be brave like your sister," she heard Mayra say as she was about to close the front door behind her. "And go after what I want in my life."

###

Ariana watched Jimmy and Mayra hold hands under the table at the restaurant and gaze at each other like no one else existed.

Her stomach fluttered from how happy she felt for them. Even her parents noticed something was different, and she caught them glancing at them and then each other once or twice.

Sooner or later, they'd find out. If they hadn't already guessed.

She fidgeted with the gold bracelet on her wrist.

It was hard not to think about Lucas right now. She was supposed to be happy. And she was, but there was also a huge downside. The time had come to decide what she was going to do with the next four years of her life. What if she made the wrong choice? How was she supposed to know what the wrong choice was?

"So what do you do now that you've been accepted?" her dad asked as he cut up his steak.

She stammered as she processed his question. "Um, there's a list of stuff I have to do. Confirm I'm going. Set up a student account. I have to go to orientation in Athens. A bunch of stuff."

"And when do you have to confirm by?" her mom asked. She took a sip of her soda and studied Ariana's face.

Ariana squinted as she tried to remember. "I think in like a month they have to have it. And I think there's a deposit."

"You're set on going then?" her mom continued.

Mayra and Jimmy looked up from their silent conversation.

Ariana looked at all of them. "Yeah, pretty sure I'm going."

Her dad nodded. "You're an adult now. You get to decide. But we think it's a good choice for your life. You can choose to be anything you want to be, and that school will help you do it."

"Have you talked to Lucas about it? What does he say about all of this?" her mom asked.

Mayra gave her a small smile. Ariana put her hands in her lap and focused on the texture of the black cloth napkin.

"He's supportive about it," she said, not as loud as before. "He wants me to go." She sighed and tried to look at her food.

"That's good," her dad said. "I had a feeling he would understand. He's a smart guy."

She nodded. "He's a good person."

She had no idea how she was going to tell him, but she knew sooner was better than later.

Everyone finished eating not long after and got ready to head home.

"No dessert?" her mom asked.

Ariana shook her head and got up from the table.

Once she got home, Ariana picked up her phone and dialed Lucas. While she heard it ring, she sat at her desk with the phone laying in front of her and her arms holding her head with her elbows on the table.

"Hey," he replied. "What's up?"

He sounded like Lucas. Always in a good mood. Always with a smile on his face. She hated being the reason that smile wouldn't be there anymore, even if she wasn't there to see it. It was just as bad.

Maybe she should wait to do this in person. She had to be there to hold him, so they could hold each other. Because she had no idea what was in store.

"You there?" Lucas asked.

"Yeah, sorry," she replied, taking a deep breath.

"What's wrong?"

"Nothing. I just… How was work?"

"Work was work. Same old, same old. How was your day?"

It was like he was in front of her, and she could see his eyebrows wrinkle from trying to figure out what was going on.

"My day was good."

"Have you found out about UGA yet?"

"Mayra and Jimmy finally officially started going out I think," she interrupted.

"Seriously? Good for them."

"So have you showered yet?"

"Why?" He was back to smiling again.

And she couldn't help but laugh. "Get those thoughts out of your head. Anyway, want to meet up tomorrow before school? A little early again?"

"Usual time? 7:40?"

"Yeah. Just want to hang out a little and then we can head to breakfast."

Tomorrow she would tell Lucas about UGA, and hopefully, they would figure things out together. They had to.

chapter eighteen

Ariana saw that Lucas hadn't gotten to school yet. It was already 7:42am. She was sure he'd be here by now. She parked and turned off her car. Mayra would be here later.

Jimmy got out of the car and grabbed his book bag. Ariana was still in the car. She hadn't even taken the keys out of the ignition yet.

"You comin'? Jimmy asked.

"Um, later." She looked at Jimmy and tried to smile. "Gonna hang out with Lucas a little. We'll catch up to you."

"Telling him about UGA, huh?" he asked.

"Yep," she said, taking a deep breath and looking straight ahead.

There was a small pause, then Jimmy said, "See you later, then. Gonna go look for my girlfriend now."

She couldn't help but smile. "You guys are awesome together, by the way."

"Yeah, we kinda are, aren't we?"

She thought for sure he'd have something to say, some kind of opinion to share on the subject of her and Lucas, but he didn't.

She nodded, and he closed the car door and left. She could see him heading towards the school from her rearview mirror. She watched him and the crowd of people going into the school like that for another few minutes. She saw several cars pulling into the lot, but no Lucas.

She checked her phone again.

7:53am.

They weren't gonna have much time to talk. They had to have breakfast too, and that ended at a quarter past eight.

She sighed again and put her head down on the steering wheel and closed her eyes.

She was tired. Her head hurt from not getting much sleep last night. She was still high from the news of her acceptance into her dream college but that was mixed in with the ickiness she felt inside her at figuring everything out with Lucas and the sheer joy for Mayra and Jimmy finally being together.

She jumped at a knock on the passenger window. The door opened, and she looked up.

Lucas.

He got in and went in straight for a kiss. A long kiss. She only had time to close her eyes.

His hands were on each side of her face, and his lips pulled on hers, his tongue slipping in as well.

Something lit inside her chest, and she wrapped her arms around his neck.

One of his hands went to her waist and the other to her thigh.

Whoa.

A minute later, he pulled back, but her eyes remained closed, wanting to savor the intense moment they'd just had.

Slowly, she opened her eyes to stare at Lucas. His face was inches away from hers.

"Good morning," he said. His voice was in between a whisper and normal talk, and he was out of breath.

She realized she was too.

"I missed you," he went on. She couldn't decide whether to look at his mouth or eyes.

"I missed you too," she said. This time, she went in for the kiss. Not as long, though. "I want to hug you."

They weren't going to be able to in the car. Not like she wanted. She got out of the car, and he did the same. It had been a bit chilly before, but now the air around them felt perfect. Fresh.

They met in the middle at the hood and Lucas immediately put his arms around Ariana's neck and back while she hugged back and pressed her head against his chest.

She could hear his heartbeat. It was beating pretty fast at the moment. Lucas kissed the top of her head.

"What time is it?" She had left her phone in the car. He got his out of his pocket.

"8:03," he said, looking at the screen. "Why?"

"I don't want you to miss breakfast," she said.

"Any other reason?" They hadn't been looking at each other, but with that, she pulled back and his gaze was already waiting for her when she turned in his direction.

She had to do this.

"I got in," she said, hardly above a whisper. "To UGA. I found out last night."

"That is...awesome," Lucas said. He was smiling, but his eyes weren't locked on hers. "I really am happy for you. I know what we said before, but you —you have to go. There's no question about it."

He squeezed her, and her face was against his chest again.

"We're gonna figure it out," she said. "I promise. I don't care if we have to take turns driving to each other's school every weekend."

She wanted to say the words, but she was too focused on not crying.

I love you. I don't want to lose you.

She realized then that Lucas really did love her. Because he was willing to let her go.

###

That afternoon, Ariana trudged back up the parking lot to her car. She couldn't get her mind off of the next few months. It killed her inside not knowing what was going to happen, whether her relationship with Lucas would survive the changes coming ahead in their lives.

Her whole life was changing. It'd be completely different in less than six months. Maybe she'd change as a person. Maybe Lucas would. Maybe he'd meet someone while she was at UGA.

She didn't think she could handle that.

She shook her head and decided to look up at the sky instead of at the ground like she had been doing recently.

Ariana got to her car, and she opened the back door to put her stuff in the seat.

She was about to close the door. That's when she felt someone's arms around her waist. She didn't have to turn around to know it was Lucas. She knew his hands, his smell. She was smiling before she turned around.

"Hey," she said, looking into his eyes. "How was your day?"

"Okay," he replied. "I wish we had more classes together. We don't even have lunch together anymore. That used to be the best part of my day, even before we started going out."

Ariana laughed. "Really?" She remembered last semester how they'd started liking each other and how awkward it was to be around him at first, especially because of Mayra. But she was so happy things turned out the way they had, even if things might eventually end.

"How was your day?" Lucas asked. He was leaning on her car, and she was leaning into him.

"Okay. Lots of homework."

"Me too. Got senioritis yet?"

"Heck yeah."

"Me too." He laughed.

"Oh gosh," she said with a smile.

"I can't wait until graduation," he said.

She felt a pang in her heart.

Lucas whispered, "Actually, I can."

"I'm visiting UGA in like a week," she said, looking over at him for a second.

They stood there in silence for a minute, listening and watching the other cars leave the parking lot, then the buses drive away. The constant buzz was dying. She closed her eyes and felt the breeze on her arms while soaking in the bit of sun there was today. It was chilly, but Lucas was warm.

"Realistically, what do you think is going to happen?" she asked. Nothing from Lucas. "Do you think we should…" She couldn't bring herself to say it.

"Break up?" Lucas asked. He sighed. "The day one of us stops loving the other, definitely. But until then, we're going to fight to stay together, even if we're apart. We'll make this work."

He looked down at her, and she up at him.

He went on. "I promise you. You're it for me."

###

This is it, Ariana thought. She pulled out the driveway. It was a school morning, but instead of Jimmy in the passenger seat, it was her mom.

Jimmy was going to ride to school with Mayra today because Ariana was finally visiting UGA.

She'd get to see the campus in person and confirm this was where she wanted to go.

She glanced at her mom, who smiled at her while she sipped some coffee. She smiled back but found herself gripping the steering wheel a little extra. It was gonna be a bit of a drive, so they had to leave early. It was only 6:00 a.m., and they were already hitting the road.

"Is there anybody else from your school going?" her mom asked.

"Um, a handful of people, actually," she said. "Other Hispanic kids who are applying for the scholarship program."

So awesome but nerve-wracking. She had no idea what to expect come fall or even today. How should she act? What if she did something like ask an obviously dumb question?

At least everyone there was in her same boat, and the lady in charge of the program seemed really nice and funny. She had visited her school last week and gathered a small group of students who were going to be going to UGA.

"You know where you're going?" her mom asked, bringing her out of her thoughts.

"Yeah, I have my phone's GPS on."

Her mom nodded. "Good thing we're a little early then. We can stop for some chicken biscuits if you want."

"That's okay," Ariana said as she pulled onto the freeway. She pressed down on the gas and joined the lane to her left. There wasn't too much traffic yet. "Remember, they're giving us breakfast there."

"Oh, that's right." She took another sip of her coffee and glanced behind them as Ariana switched to the fast lane to get ahead of a slow mini-van in front of them. "So what exactly will we be doing today?"

"I'm going to shadow a student a little bit, so I'll be following them around to their classes. We'll get a tour of the campus, some free lunch at the dining commons, and just some information about a scholarship they're offering."

"That's good. Free food. Free money maybe. I like this school already."

Ariana laughed, at ease a bit. If there was something about her mom, it was that she loved free food. She just hoped UGA would be a good fit for her too.

###

"This is officially freakin' awesome," Ariana said as

she walked inside UGA's three-level gym. There were college students working out everywhere, most with earbuds in their ears and facing forward while breaking a mean sweat.

She walked over to an elliptical.

"And they have TVs with cable? Why does the freshman fifteen even exist?" She looked at the girl she'd been paired with. Her name was Nayelli. She was taller than Ariana and easygoing.

"I know, right? But you'd be surprised. No one tells you when to eat and when not to eat. You stay up studying and you get hungry? You can buy yourself something somewhere or go to Snelling, which is open 24/7."

She patted her stomach, which was almost flat. "I had to learn the hard way last year. I gained some serious weight but began eating healthier and coming in here a few times a week. So basically, don't stuff your face every day."

"Wow. I'll definitely keep that in mind." Ariana laughed.

Nayelli glanced at her phone. "I have a calculus class coming up in about twenty minutes. We should start heading that way, and you can see what that's like. There's only about twenty-five people in that class, though, which isn't as cool as the three-hundred people biology class I had last year."

"Three hundred people in one class? How do they all fit?" Maybe that was one of those dumb questions she shouldn't have asked, but Nayelli didn't seem to think so.

"There are these huge classrooms that are kind of like a mini stadium. The professor's at the bottom and there's this huge screen and the class kind of goes up and around a bit."

"Oh," Ariana said, trying to envision it as they walked back out of the gym.

"I'll show you a class like that later. I personally liked those classes better, but it's just a preference."

Ariana nodded as they arrived at the bus stop.

"Okay. We need to get on the East/West bus. Do you see one?"

Ariana glanced around. There was one bus leaving and one about to get where they were, but it said something else.

"Um, nope."

"It'll probably be a few minutes. In the evenings, though, the schedule changes and the buses come through a lot less frequently, which sucks if you don't have a car and find somewhere to park for free. Sometimes I get stuck waiting for like fifteen, twenty minutes, but now I just ride with one of my friends."

Pay to park? Ariana thought. She assumed she'd be bringing her car next year, but no one ever had to pay to park in her hometown. How much would it be just to park? She started thinking about all the expenses the program lady had mentioned earlier, like the meal plan, tuition, books, clothes, and everything else.

She knew her parents had a little money saved up since they had been doing financially better in the last couple of years, but not anywhere close to pay for all of her college.

Her stomach sank a little at the thought of not being able to come here because she couldn't afford it. There was that one scholarship and a few others she had heard of and applied to, but would they be enough? There was also HOPE, which covered her tuition if she got As and Bs, but she had to live here the first year in the dorms and she knew that had to be expensive.

"Do you have scholarships?" she asked Nayelli.

"A couple. I still work part-time, though. At this fast food place down the street from my dorm. So I can afford all the fees, books, and the meal plan. I mean, there's bus fees, technology fees, green fees. Plus like supplies and clothes and stuff. My parents weren't really able to help me out at all with my expenses, so I cover them myself."

Ariana thought about that. Fees on top of everything else?

"Oh, look. There's the bus we need to get on."

Ariana tried to focus on her steps as she got on the bus and took a seat next to Nayelli instead of wondering if she'd actually be coming here next year.

chapter nineteen

Ariana took her plate of food over to where her mom was sitting in a corner of the dining hall, which looked nothing like the ugly cafeteria back at her school.

She hadn't seen her mom most of the morning. All the parents had been in their own informational meetings about what to expect once their kids were in college.

The extensive variety of food at the dining hall had distracted Ariana from her earlier worries, especially because all the walking around had left her starving. She had piled plate after plate of food onto her tray, not to mention a tasty-looking fruit smoothie she was dying to try after being out in the heat.

Now that she saw her mom, though, she needed to ask about how they were going to figure out things financially.

"So are you liking the school?" her mom asked with a smile.

"I love it," Ariana said. Which would make it that much more devastating if she couldn't come here after all. She took a bite of her Philly steak sandwich.

"Hmm, this is so good." She took a sip of her smoothie. "Oh my gosh, this is better. And it's healthy. Why can't I eat like this every day?"

She glanced at her mom, who was giving her the look.

She decided it was time to change the topic. Her mom looked back down at her spaghetti and continued eating.

"So, Mom. Did they tell you about how much it costs to come here and everything?" She took another bite of her sandwich, enjoying the cheesiness.

"Oh yeah. Almost twenty thousand a year."

Ariana's mouth fell open, and she had to cover her mouth quickly with her hand so her food wouldn't show.

"You can't be serious." She kept chewing. She guessed it made sense with the dorm, meal plan, books, fees, and tuition.

Her mom nodded. "They're giving you scholarships, right?"

"I mean, I applied for some yeah, and I should have HOPE because of my grades, but I haven't really calculated how much I might need after that. It just depends how many scholarships I get."

Her voice got smaller and smaller with each word she said. It became hard to swallow, and she couldn't help but sigh and put down her sandwich.

"If you really want to come here, we'll figure it out. Don't worry," her mom said. She looked up at her, but looking at her mom's eyes, Ariana knew she was saying what a mom should say right now. She just wasn't sure if her mom truly believed that.

Her mom looked down. "We'll take out a loan every year if we have to."

"No," Ariana replied immediately. "It's way too much, even with your raise. I don't want to come here if it means you and dad getting into a whole bunch of debt. It's not worth it."

"We disagree," her mom said.

The one up side to not coming to UGA? At least she wouldn't have to choose between UGA and Lucas.

But she knew she'd always wonder.

###

"What's wrong, babe?" Lucas said. He put his hand on hers as they headed to his house. It was his day off. Her parents had finally said it would be okay to go over there as long his mom was there, and she would be. For a few minutes at least, before she left for work.

She'd left that part out, though. She needed some alone time with Lucas. Or at least as alone as they could get with his two sisters around.

She sighed but didn't really want to talk about it.

"You never really told me about what UGA was like. Did you love it or what?" He had a smile on his face. He truly wanted her to be happy. She could tell from the way he always asked for updates.

"It was awesome," she replied.

"Then what's up?" he asked. "Is it about…you leaving?"

"A little. It's just that I don't even know if I'll be able to go. It's kind of expensive, and it just depends on the scholarships I get, if any, because I'm not sure if my parents are gonna be able to afford to help me with much."

Lucas stared at the steering wheel in front of him after he pulled in to his driveway and turned off the car.

It was quiet for a few seconds before he asked, "Have you asked your parents about it?"

"Yeah. They can help me with a couple thousand maybe, but it wouldn't be enough. HOPE will cover my tuition, but then there's the dorm since I have to live there the first year, the meal plan, the fees, gas, and other stuff and I just don't want them to have to take out a loan or get into serious credit card debt or something."

More silence from Lucas.

"This is one of those times I wish I was a millionaire, so the people I love didn't have to worry about something as dumb as money."

Ariana smiled, despite her thoughts going a million miles an hour. She squeezed his hand. "This isn't your fault."

"I know. I just wish I could help. I don't really have much saved up. You know if I did—"

Ariana kissed him. Hard.

She finally pulled back a minute later. "I could never let you do that. What you do for your family, for your mom and sisters, is amazing."

She had tears in her eyes now, and if she kept talking, they'd flow down her cheeks. "Like we keep on saying, if it's meant to happen, it will happen." She looked at him. "Right?"

He smiled softly. "Right."

###

"Happy birthday to you," everyone sang around the

table. Jimmy looked around with a goofy smile on his face. "Happy birthday, dear Jimmy, happy birthday to you."

Ariana's phone buzzed. It was Lucas.

I miss you. Wish I could be there with you.

He had to work all day. He hardly had any days off and worked even more hours than before. Someone had quit, and they were short on people at the clothing store where he worked.

"It's actually a good thing, I guess," he had said as they talked about it while having lunch a couple weeks before. "I need to save up some money anyway. My mom kinda wanted to take my sisters to the beach this summer, so I can help pitch in. We've never been on vacation."

"When you said you needed to save money, I thought you meant for college in the fall," Ariana said, putting her fork down.

Lucas sighed. "That too."

Now Ariana's dad went over to the stereo in the living room and pushed play.

Estas son las mananitas…

The equivalent of the birthday song in Mexico began playing. It was one of Ariana's favorite songs to listen to, but it was really long, and she didn't know all the words.

Her mom squeezed Jimmy's shoulder and kissed him on the cheek. Ariana playfully bumped into Mayra, who gave her a smile. Ryan looked on politely from the opposite end of the table. It was a given he'd be invited to Jimmy's birthday every year.

When the song was over, they all clapped and cheered.

"Que le muerda," Ariana said, still clapping. Everyone joined her, except for Ryan, who watched and realized what was happening.

Ariana went over behind Jimmy.

"Take a bite," Mayra shouted.

"Yeah, right," Jimmy replied, staring behind him at Ariana, who was ready to shove his head into the cake as soon as he let his guard down for the briefest of moments.

"I'm protecting you from everyone else," Ariana said.

Jimmy laughed, and Ariana took advantage of his glance towards everyone else.

She shoved his face down hard, except his head was turned slightly to the side.

It worked, though. Jimmy came back up with over half his face covered in blue and white frosting.

"It's up my nose," he said, his voice funny. "And my eyebrows."

Everyone laughed and their mom led him from his seat to the kitchen sink. She heard the faucet come on as she headed back to where Mayra was.

They high-fived and looked at the cake. They had only messed up a small part of it.

Ariana's mom came back to the slice the cake and pass pieces around. Ariana went to help her.

"This looks so good," Mayra said, holding her plate. "I love pastel de tres leches. And it has strawberries." She grabbed a fork and took a seat to dig in.

"Ryan, can you put some water bottles on the table for me?" her mom asked as she continued cutting.

"Yes, ma'am," he said, walking into the kitchen to grab some from the pack. Ariana handed her dad a small piece. He wasn't big on sweets.

He came back in a second later with a handful of water bottles, and Ariana handed him his piece of cake.

"Thanks," he said, looking at it and walking back to his seat.

"I think that's everyone," Ariana told her mom. "Just us left."

Her mom set Jimmy's piece, the one that had been practically flattened, aside for him.

As they all sat down to eat and talk, Jimmy walked back in.

"You still have some on your chin," Mayra said with a smile.

Jimmy groaned and grabbed a napkin before sitting down. He reached for his plate. "Yes," he whispered. "My favorite."

A few minutes later, they were finishing eating. Their mom went to the kitchen to begin cleaning while their dad went outside to have a beer.

Jimmy looked in Mayra's direction and winked. She rolled her eyes but smiled.

"This time next year, I'll have a car and my license. I can't wait," he said.

"Good thing I won't be around then because the roads around here are gonna be a dangerous place to be," Ariana said.

It was meant to be a joke, but she couldn't bring herself to even smile. Instead, she swallowed hard to keep the knot in her throat from forming.

Not only was she going to give up her current

relationship with Lucas for a long distance one, going to UGA meant missing out on Jimmy's last two years of high school.

###

Ariana stared at the screen in front of her. She had senioritis bad. She had a huge project due the next day for Language Arts, and she still wasn't done. Not even halfway done. And she still had to work on her DECA project for this year's competition. She wasn't even halfway done with that either.

She was supposed to have finished the Language Arts project at least by now, but she kept putting it off. She thought for a minute. This was basically Mayra's life. Procrastinating even at the very last minute. What had she gotten herself into?

Each person was supposed to pick a book off the teacher's list (definitely not Hunger Games) and create this huge presentation about it. She had finally finished reading the book yesterday. Why she had picked the longest book on that darned list, she didn't know.

Now it was time to do the presentation, which was basically the hardest part, the actual work, and she couldn't bring herself to do more than opening PowerPoint.

"Gahhh," she said out loud, mostly to herself. Jimmy was taking a nap in his room, and her mom had let her off the hook from helping with dinner since she had this project. And her dad would be home soon.

She stared out her window towards Mayra's house.

Mayra was actually closer to being finished than

she was. If there existed the opposite of senioritis, she had it. She had picked a pretty short book, of course, but had read it pretty quickly. Had actually gotten into it. And was already halfway done with the presentation component. Ariana glanced at the time at the corner of her screen.

7:17 p.m.

She was probably already done by now.

She sighed.

She moved her finger on the trackpad and navigated to the Internet.

A few minutes on Twitter, Instagram, and her email turned into twenty minutes.

"Shoot," she said. And she knew her mom would be done with dinner soon. She was hungry, but then she'd have less time after sitting down to eat.

Just as she was about to exit out for good and get at least the first slide done, she saw an email from a scholarship she'd applied to. The big scholarship.

Her mouth fell open as she read the subject line.

Congratulations.

"Holy shit," she said as she clicked. Her heart was already beating about a thousand miles per hour as she tried to make sense of the words in front of her.

She had won the scholarship.

Just a few days ago, she'd heard from the HSF people who had organized her tour at UGA. She had been awarded a small scholarship from them. One thousand dollars, and she'd have to reapply each year to get it renewed. It had been exciting, but she knew it wouldn't be nearly enough to get her through college.

This was ten thousand dollars each year for four

years.

Her counselor had recommended her for it, and she'd spent a lot of time filling out the lengthy application, which had to include pictures, recommendations, essays, her family's financials, and her goals.

I guess they liked me, she thought. She smiled as she read the next steps over and over. She couldn't wait to tell everyone.

She took a screenshot and finally exited out. Then she just sat there for a few minutes.

This was really happening. She was going to UGA.

She got to work.

chapter twenty

Fifteen minutes later, Ariana still felt numb. But also hungry as she walked into the kitchen to wash her hands. Her dad walked in the front door and went into the kitchen. He gave her mom a kiss on the cheek and left to change, patting Ariana on the shoulder as he passed. She opened her mouth to talk but couldn't.

His clothes were dirty, and he looked tired. "I'm gonna go shower really quick. I'll be back."

Her mother nodded. "Ariana, go wake up your brother. Tell him it's time to eat," her mom said.

She nodded and left, trailing after her dad towards the other end of the house.

She knocked on Jimmy's door and walked in. Only his lamp was on, and he was all bundled up in his comforter. He was snoring a little bit. Ariana sat down on his bed and shook him some.

"Mom said come and eat."

"Hm," was all he managed.

She tore off the sheets, a smile beginning to make its way onto her face. "Let's go."

She got up and left, and Jimmy finally rubbed the sleep from his eyes and stood up. He looked like a zombie as he put on a shirt and headed to the bathroom. Ariana shook her head and headed back to the kitchen.

Ten minutes later, they were all seated with their food, except for their dad.

Her mom had made sopes, one of her favorite meals. Really just about anything her mom whipped up was considered a favorite meal.

She realized how much she'd miss her cooking next year as she looked down at her plate.

"How was school? What'd you guys learn today?" her mom asked as they all dug in. Her dad finally showed up and took a seat in front of a huge plate of sopes.

"Eh," Jimmy said in between bites. "Same old, same old."

"Ariana?" her mom asked as she looked at her.

Ariana looked at her but froze as she wondered just how to word what she was about to say.

Now her dad was looking at her too.

"Um, I actually just found out like thirty minutes ago that I'm getting a scholarship. You won't have to worry about having to pay for my school anymore." She slowly smiled as she waited for them to say something.

They looked at each other. "Is this the scholarship you were talking about a few days ago?" her mom asked.

"No, actually. This one is ten thousand dollars a year for four years."

Her dad put down the sope he had in his hand, and her mom took a swig of her drink.

"Are you freakin' serious?" Jimmy asked, his

mouth half full of food. “Forty thousand dollars?”

“Jimmy, swallow,” she said, trying not to laugh.

He resumed chewing and finally swallowed. He also drank some water.

“And you’re sure this isn’t a scam?” her father asked.

“Yep. My counselor helped me apply. They chose one person out of the state for it, and I won.”

“Congratulations.” Her mom got up, walked around the table, and hugged her. “We’re so proud.”

Her dad did the same and walked into the kitchen. He walked back out with some tequila and two small glasses.

“This calls for some real celebration.” He poured some tequila into each glass and handed the other glass to her mom. For a second there, Ariana thought maybe one of those was for her.

“When you’re twenty-one, you can have one too,” her dad said as he threw his shot back.

Her mom was much slower but drank the whole thing. Ariana noticed her take a napkin and wipe at her eyes several times.

“Don’t worry, Ariana,” Jimmy said as he walked over and put his arm around her. “We’ll have ours later when they’re asleep.” He ignored their mom’s face as he headed back to his seat, and they all resumed eating their dinner.

“I have to admit I was worried before about our finances. We just recently started doing a little saving since the raise I got a few months back. Before that, it just hadn’t been really possible.” Her mom looked at her. “You know we would have done whatever necessary to get you to college, but this sure takes a load off." She paused but looked like she wanted to keep talking.

Instead, her dad continued. "You should be proud of yourself. This means you've earned your way there. Do you know how rare that is?" He looked at her mom. "We never would have been able to do that. This country has so many opportunities, so you can be whatever you can be." He paused again, staring right at Ariana's eyes. She made herself not look away. "We're so blessed to have kids who know that and take advantage of that. You're smart, Jimmy might be on his way to a scholarship for his basketball. You both work hard. "

Ariana looked at Jimmy, who smiled. She smiled back and took a deep breath, making sure to remember how this moment felt. She never wanted to forget it.

###

"Must be a bummer, huh? The whole Lucas slash UGA thing?" Mayra asked.

Ariana nodded.

"But you're still going to UGA, right?" They were in Mayra's room. Ever since Mayra had started driving herself around, they hadn't seen each other as much. So today, they had decided to hang out all day.

Jimmy had finally gone to take the test for his driver's permit with her dad this morning. It had been a couple of hours ago, and they still weren't back.

"Yep, I'm going."

"Well don't sound so excited there."

"I am. It's just really gonna suck." She had her arms wrapped around one of Mayra's pillows so it was covering her abdomen. There was a movie on TV, but they had both lost interest twenty minutes ago. Mayra was scrolling through something on her phone.

"No, it's not," Mayra said as she looked up. "And you better not be all mopey over there either. Meet new people, doesn't have to be guys, make new friends, join clubs, get involved, go out and have fun. I saw this thing on Twitter the other day. These next four years are gonna be the best of our lives. Don't waste them."

Ariana blinked and thought about that. She had a point. She remembered how excited she had been to leave for college and become a new person with a newfound freedom. Where had that gone? The longer she thought about it, the more she felt those feelings come back.

And like she kept saying, if she and Lucas were meant to be, their relationship would survive.

"Yeah, you're right," she said slowly.

"I know I am," Mayra laughed. "Just kidding. Your life is gonna be so cool because you'll be far away enough that nobody will know you so you can be whoever you want to be. But still close enough you can come and visit whenever. I, on the other hand, will be living at home because the college here doesn't have dorms, and I can't afford an apartment. Like half the people graduating are going there, so it's probably gonna be like high school all over again." Mayra rolled her eyes, put her phone down, and began flipping through the channels on her TV again.

Mayra had a point. This was going to be a fresh

start for her.

Just as she envisioned joining clubs, going to meetings, and maybe even going to a party with new friends, someone barged through the door.

She turned towards it.

Jimmy. With a driver's permit in his hands. He was out of breath.

Mayra laughed. "Did you just run all the way here?"

"Yeah," he said breathing heavily. "Maybe I should have driven, huh?"

He was wearing his basketball hoodie with his name and number on the back and the school mascot on the front.

"Anyway, guess what I got?" He jumped and landed on the bed next to them. "I passed with flying colors, a.k.a. a seventy."

"Oh, God," she and Mayra said at the same time. His arm was around Mayra, and he kissed her on the cheek.

"Who wants to go get a milkshake or something?" he said.

"No, thank you." Ariana got off of the bed and went over to the desk chair.

"Maybe later," Mayra said. "Besides, don't you have to have an adult with you?"

"In theory," Jimmy replied.

Ariana stared at him.

"So what are we watching?" Jimmy said, ignoring her look. He couldn't keep still. He kept moving his arms and legs around and then moving around on the bed. "Did I mention I had a huge coffee this morning to wake up? I think it's still having an effect on me."

###

"Man, I can't believe basketball season is over. This sucks. And we didn't even win the state championship," Jimmy said as he dribbled the ball around their driveway. He faked left then right even though no one was in front of him or blocking his way. Then he shot.

Swish. No surprise there.

"Second place in the state isn't bad, though." Ryan ran to get the ball. "What are we going to do with all our free time now?" he asked as he took a shot. Another swish.

Mayra and Ariana were sitting on some lawn chairs enjoying the sun. They had played a short game of two on two, but she and Mayra needed a break.

"Don't you have a girlfriend?" Mayra asked Ryan.

"No," Ryan said. He swung his head a little so his hair got out of his face. He was always doing that.

"So you guys want to play another round? We can switch teams if you want," Jimmy said.

"Nah," Mayra said. "Later."

"You said that like twenty minutes ago," Jimmy said, walking over to her.

"So?"

Ariana sighed and wished Lucas was there. But he was at work. He almost never got Saturday off.

Jimmy sat next to Mayra in another chair, but it was like there was nothing between those two. He kissed her on the cheek and had his hand on her back.

Mayra closed her eyes and smiled. Ryan kept

shooting.

Even if she missed Lucas, she liked seeing Jimmy and Mayra together. It was like they couldn't get enough of each other, like they were making up for lost time or something.

"Your mom still doesn't know you two are going out?" she asked Mayra.

Mayra opened her eyes. "Nope."

Ariana smiled and shook her head. Her parents didn't really know either. None of them had said anything, but Ariana knew they would figure out sooner or later. They always did.

"Then have our parents be all uptight and paranoid and not let us go out together anymore?" Mayra asked.

Jimmy didn't say anything. He got up and began dribbling again.

Ariana wondered how he felt going behind their parents' back. Not that it was the same thing as her and Carlos last year. That had been different. This was Mayra, who her parents knew well and trusted. She was a good person. Carlos had been different.

She got up and grabbed the ball when it bounced off the back board. She shot but missed.

"I just think you guys should say something." They stared at her. "I mean I'm not going to. That's your business, your call." She grabbed the ball again and kept dribbling. She shot again. This time it went in. "Sooner or later, though, they're going to find out, and it might not be pretty. You know how Mom and Dad can get." She looked at Jimmy, who was sitting now.

"We'll tell them," he said. "At the right time."

###

"Hey, you," Lucas said. It was after school. It was also Lucas's day off, and they had all lied to their parents to be together.

Ariana put her arms around him and buried her face in his chest. They were lying on his bed.

"So you told your parents what?" he asked.

"That I had to make up a test after school." She didn't want to leave the warmth of his body so her voice was kind of muffled.

"Do you really have a test to make up?"

"Not at all."

Lucas laughed. "Where's Jimmy? Wait. Let me guess. With Mayra?"

"Yep."

"At her house?"

"Yep." She tried not to think about what they were up to. Meanwhile, Lucas's mom and sisters were out visiting a relative or something. They wouldn't be back for a while.

"Do you think your parents are gonna find out?" She looked up at him and scooted up to look at him better.

"Nope. They're at work." She glanced at her phone. "My mom might be on her way home, but I'll get there a little after her and just pick up Jimmy on the way."

"Does that mean you have to leave soon?" he asked. His voice was a hoarse whisper.

She saw Lucas shift his gaze from her eyes to her mouth. Her upper body was kind of on top of him, and her thigh was against his. Then she saw him glance farther down than her face and raise his eyes back up to her eyes.

She had an idea of what he had been looking at, and it made her mind go a little crazy. She realized she was staring down at him, and now her mouth was slightly open. She closed her eyes as Lucas's face came up to meet her.

First, his lips pushed against hers softly, but she could feel his hands trembling as they held her waist. Ariana pulled back a centimeter and opened her eyes to look at Lucas. He did the same.

She had never seen him look like that. In the next second, she decided to close her eyes again and move her face until his mouth was on hers again. This time, she pulled on each of his lips. He responded, and then she could hear his heavy breathing. And she realized she was breathing heavily too. Her hands were around his neck and in his hair.

When she thought she couldn't feel any more good, she felt his tongue brush hers, and her mouth let out a groan before she could attempt to control herself. Then Lucas's hand moved from her waist to her butt and stopped on her upper thigh.

There it was again. His tongue on hers. She liked this. She moved her tongue into his mouth, and this time, it was Lucas who groaned.

He pulled on her thigh until she was completely on top of him. One hand grazed her butt, and the other creeped under her shirt. Not too fast. This was new territory for them, and she knew he would stop the instant she wanted.

She didn't want to stop, though. This felt right. It felt good.

If there was a guy she wanted to do this with, it

was Lucas.

She opened her eyes as his mouth moved to her neck. The sound of their breathing was turning her on even more. She looked down at Lucas's slightly curly hair before closing her eyes again.

Lucas's hand had reached the clasp of her bra, but he only gripped it. Didn't unclasp it.

She moved until they were facing each other again. She wanted to feel his mouth again, as good as the kisses on her neck felt.

Lucas looked at her and whispered, "Do you want to stop?"

Ariana didn't have to think to answer. "No."

Lucas kissed her again, like before, and it felt like she couldn't get enough of him. She wanted her skin to touch his. Any and all part of her skin to touch him.

With her shirt still on, Lucas unclasped her bra. She felt it detach from her body and felt the cool air on her chest.

Lucas's eyes met hers as his hand slowly came around to the front of her shirt. First, she felt his fingers brush against her abdomen. Then they were on her chest. Her chest wouldn't stop rising and falling from how hard she was breathing. Lucas began kissing her again, his hand awkwardly in between them.

He moved his hand to her upper back as he rolled with her until he was on top of her.

"Lucas," she whispered.

He stopped and looked at her. "Are you okay?

She made her breathing slow down. "I…am more than okay."

His mouth moved to her neck, and she finally wondered what time it was. That thought was lost as he moved back to her mouth.

Lucas used his knee to move her legs so his were in between hers. Then his hips grinded against hers, and she gasped. Lucas groaned as their hips touched.

Now she was trembling, and she wondered how it was possible for one person to do this to another, make someone feel this.

chapter twenty-one

Ariana wondered what time it was as Lucas kissed her.

"Lucas?" she whispered. "I think I have to go."

He stopped kissing her neck and took his hands off her hips. He kissed her on the mouth one last time before they checked their phones.

"Yeah, I think you're right."

"Crap." It was almost 5:00pm. Her mom was probably already home. "I have to go."

She got up, adjusted her clothes, and put on her shoes.

Lucas hugged her from behind before she could grab her book bag.

She turned around and hugged him back. "I'll call you later, okay?"

"Text me if you get in trouble or something. Sorry I kept yo—"

She kissed him before he could finish. "I love you. I'll call you later."

Lucas got up and put on his shoes. "Love you too. Come on. I'll walk you to your car."

A few minutes later, Ariana was on the road, but she could hardly keep her focus on it. She couldn't stop thinking about Lucas, not to mention his touch, his mouth on hers. On her body.

It had driven her crazy. In every way that was good. It was a good thing she was still on birth control because she really thought they were going to do it. In a way, she was glad they didn't. She wanted to wait a little longer and enjoy their relationship as much as possible before they got to that.

Then her stomach sank.

She still hadn't told him that she was definitely going to UGA. Her acceptance letter was due this week. She had to tell him. She would tell him. Soon. Her decision was pretty much made.

She bit her lip as she pulled into Mayra's driveway and Jimmy ran out the door and hopped in.

Jimmy didn't say anything as they headed down the street to their house, but his look said it all. She was a little late. Their mom was already home.

They headed inside. Ariana headed straight for their room as Jimmy announced they were home. She almost ran into her mom as she power walked down the hallway.

"Hey," she said.

"How was the test?" her mom asked.

"Oh. Good," she said, walking past her and adjusting her book bag on her shoulder.

"It must have been a long test. It's five o'clock," her mom called back as she went into the living room.

"Yeah," she yelled from her room. "I got stuck on some of the problems so I took my time."

She changed into some shorts and lay down.

She had completely forgotten to tell Lucas about

her scholarship. There was no question about it now. She wanted to go to UGA. She had found a way to go to UGA. She was going to UGA.

Which meant she and Lucas would no longer be together. Yeah, they'd do the long distance thing, but she thought about how hard that would be. They had to try. Right?

She got up and closed the door to her room. She had to get this out of the way and know how Lucas felt about all of this. It'd be the moment of truth.

She pulled out her phone and called Lucas.

It rang a few times before he finally picked up. "Yeah?" He sounded groggy.

"Oh sorry. I woke you up, didn't I?"

"It's okay. I fell asleep after you left."

"Sorry."

"No, it's okay. I'm awake. There's some stuff I have to do anyway." He sounded like he was getting up.

"Should I call you back?"

"No. It can wait."

"Are you sure?" Was she sure she wanted to have this conversation?

"Yes," he said drawing it out. "You okay? You didn't get in trouble, did you?

"No," she said glancing at her door and lowering her voice. "It's just...I have to tell you something."

Now she was rushing and talking too fast.

"I was going to tell you when I saw you today, but I swear I forgot. Um." She sighed.

"What's going on? Is everything okay?"

"Yeah. I just—I found out the other day I got a scholarship."

"Another one? That's awesome," he said. His sincerity made it that much harder to keep explaining.

"This one's kind of different. It changes things," she said. She looked blankly out the window. "It's forty thousand dollars."

"What? Are you serious?" He laughed a little

"Yeah. Ten thousand each year for four years." She couldn't decide if she should wait for him to do the math or just say it out loud.

She decided to wait a little bit longer. Just when she was about to explain what that meant, he spoke up.

"You can go to UGA," he said quietly.

"I—" she tried to say.

"I'm happy for you. Really," he said. The sincerity was still there, but not there was something else as well. Sadness.

"I'm sorry," she said. "I should have told you in person, but I didn't want you to think I was hiding this from you."

"No, it's okay," he said. "Thanks. For telling me." He sighed. "I mean, we kept saying that if it's meant to happen, it would happen, you know? It happened. This is where you're meant to be. I'm not going to stop you. I don't want to. I—I can't wait for you to go because I know this is your dream."

Tears threatened to escape from her eyes, and Ariana was kind of glad she was in her room instead of with him because she knew there'd be no way she could stop from crying if she was looking at him right now.

"We're not giving up, right?" she asked, trying to make her voice stay even.

"Right," he said. "I—I will always be here for you. If we're meant to be, then it'll happen. We'll get through it."

There was silence, and she focused on her breathing for a little bit.

Lucas spoke up again. "Are you excited? How did you find out? What did your parents say?"

"I got an email. Remember, it was that huge packet I had to fill out that the counselor gave me? She recommended me for it, and it paid off. My parents couldn't believe it either. They're glad they're not gonna go broke sending me to college."

"Yeah," he said. The smile seemed to be back on his face.

"What about you? Have you found out about your financial aid yet?"

"I should find out pretty soon, probably by the time we graduate in a few more weeks."

"Oh my gosh."

"What?"

"Graduation," she said, staring at the ceiling. "It's almost freakin' here."

###

Ariana and Jimmy got out of the car and headed inside. It was Thursday afternoon, which meant it was pretty much Friday.

Ariana yawned as she opened the front door and carried her bag to her room. Maybe she'd take a nap.

Both of her parents were in the kitchen. "Ya llegamos," she said with hardly a glance. She was brain fried.

It had been a busy week. She had stayed up really late finishing up a five-page paper for English and studying for her finals at the end of next week. Plus, one last project for DECA. After that, freedom. A few days after that, Jimmy would be out of school too, and they'd finally have summer.

"Jimmy!" she heard her mom yell from the kitchen.

She had been about to go ahead and lie down, but her stomach growled for a snack. Snack, then a nap.

As she headed out of her room, Jimmy was right ahead of her.

"What?" he said, padding into the living room in just his socks. He was already in gym shorts. That boy lived in gym shorts.

"Take a seat," his mom said. She was standing next to the couch where their dad was sitting. The TV had been turned off. Ariana walked past them and into the kitchen. She went straight to the cupboard where the bread was and popped some in the toaster.

"When were you going to tell us?" she heard her mom say. Her hand froze midway to the button for the toaster. She slowly turned around and padded over until she was just around the corner from the living room.

"Tell you what?" Jimmy asked. The stammer in his voice betrayed him.

"Are you really going to make us say it?" her mom asked.

She heard Jimmy sigh. "Mayra." Another pause. "How long have you known?"

"A little while. How long have you two been novios?"

"Who told you?" Jimmy asked.

Ariana peeked her head around the corner. Jimmy glanced at her, and she quickly pointed at her chest and shook her head quietly but violently. Jimmy looked back at his mom.

"I know you knew too, Ariana," her mom said loudly.

Crap, she thought. She walked into the living room.

"What do you have to say, Jimmy?" her dad asked. He was seated on the couch while their mom stood with her arms crossed.

Jimmy shrugged.

"Why didn't you just say something to us? We're your parents," her mom said, looking at her dad and back to them. "We're supposed to know what's going on in your lives."

"I was going to tell you—"

"When?"

"I don't know."

Her mom glared and pursed her lips.

"Soon. I really was. Ariana kept telling me to, but M—I wanted to wait." Now his arms were folded across his chest, and he kept looking around.

"Wait for what?" Her mom didn't lose a beat.

"Until Mayra was comfortable with everyone knowing."

Their mom guffawed. "I don't even know where to start. We're not everyone. We're your parents."

Her dad spoke up. "And if Mayra didn't want everyone to know, then you should have waited to become her boyfriend. All of this sneaking around does nobody any good."

"I know," Jimmy said. "I'm sorry."

"You're grounded for two weeks. No going out. No video games. Make sure you put the console in my room."

"What? Why?"

Ariana didn't know what to say. The same thing had happened to her last year. At least Jimmy was taking it better than she had.

"You know why. You guys go out making us think you two are friends when who knows what all of you are up to." She looked at Ariana who immediately looked away.

"We were sixteen and seventeen once," her dad continued. "We know the kinds of things that happen."

Jimmy walked down the hall into his room, probably to unplug his video game console. At least he got to keep his phone.

Ariana decided to head into the kitchen to finish making her snack. She was not sleepy anymore. She wondered what was going on at Mayra's house. Because if her parents knew, Mayra's mom had to know.

###

Ariana called Mayra after she scarfed down her snack, but she wasn't picking up.

A few seconds later, she got a text.

Cnt talk. Talking to mom on d fone. Call u later :/

Sounded like her mom wasn't finished. She was still curious about how all of their parents had found out about Jimmy and Mayra, though.

She got up and went to her desk to work on a project in the meantime.

Ten minutes later, her phone began to buzz. It

was Mayra calling. "Hey," she said.

Ariana had definitely heard Mayra happier. "What happened?" Ariana asked. "How'd our parents find out?"

"Um, do you really want to know?"

"Um, yeah, I want to know." She saved her project and closed her computer, looking out the window in the direction of Mayra's house.

"Well, my mom kind of found Jimmy in my room last night, like kinda late. We weren't doing anything except, you know, kissing, but she came home early from work for once in her life, and she absolutely freaked when she saw us."

Ariana's mouth fell open. "What?" She glanced at her door. It was closed, but that had been kind of loud. She had no idea Jimmy had snuck over. She guessed it probably wasn't the first time.

"Yeah, she told Jimmy to go home. Then she got all quiet, and then it was like a volcano exploded. And it just happened again. She told me she told your parents what happened, that they needed to know. So how bad did Jimmy get it?"

"Two weeks." Ariana still couldn't believe what she had heard.

"I got a month. I'm guessing my mom didn't tell her the whole story. But she said if we pulled something like that again, she would."

"You can't be serious."

"Believe me," Mayra said. "I wish this wasn't even happening. Just when I think things are going good, everything explodes in my face."

Ariana wanted to say how Mayra and Jimmy shouldn't have kept their relationship a secret in the first place, but she decided she wasn't the best person to be offering advice on that matter.

She had made the same mistake just last year.

###

Ariana rolled her eyes all during her English class. Wendy was in that class too, but she had left her relatively alone all semester after their incident last semester. The teacher had changed the seating and put them in opposite sides of the room.

She just got the usual dirty looks. But today she seemed to be in a really good mood, which meant Ariana was going to be in a bad one.

She wondered what exactly Lucas had seen in her besides the big boobs. That had to be it. Just the boobs. She rolled her eyes again and tried not to gag. She focused on the reading they were supposed to be doing instead.

"Okay. Let's get into small groups and discuss," the teacher said. Everyone started shifting their desks to get with their buddies, but the teacher spoke up again. "You know what? Let's switch it up. We've been in the same, stagnant groups all semester. Let's count off to five starting on this side of the room." Everyone groaned as he pointed to the side where Wendy was. They moved their desks back.

"One."

"Two."

The numbers reached Wendy. "Three," Wendy said with another eye roll. They kept going until it was Ariana's turn at the other side.

"Damn," she whispered under breath as the counting approached her. "Three," she said during her turn.

"Okay. Let's move," the teacher said, explaining where each group should meet and walked around as students moved to their spots.

She grabbed her binder, reading packet, and pencil and headed to the same place Wendy was headed.

Wendy looked her up and down as she approached. Ariana didn't break her stare. Wendy finally looked away as she reached a desk and sat down. Ariana did the same.

There were three other students already there. One was one of Wendy's friends. This is going to be interesting, she thought.

She looked at her packet, trying to find something to talk about for when the teacher came around. A guy in their group, Sam, began talking right away. Meanwhile, Wendy was already whispering with her friend.

"I give them another month. Maybe," she heard her say quietly. "And if he doesn't ditch her before she leaves, let's just say I don't think they'll last long anyway." Wendy glanced at her.

Ariana's jaw was tight and her hand squeezed her packet in her palm as she forced herself not to say something.

She knew they had to be talking about her and Lucas.

"I hear she hasn't put out either. So it's just a matter of time." Wendy glanced at her again. Her friend was smiling.

"What are you talking about?" she asked, not caring that the group was listening. She didn't break her stare away from Wendy.

"None of your business, sweetie," Wendy replied.

"I know you were talking about me. If you're as tough as you think you are, why don't you admit it?" The whole group was quiet now. Their half of the class started oohing. The teacher was on the other side of the room in an animated discussion with one of the groups.

Wendy looked around briefly before bringing her gaze back to her. She leaned forward. She wasn't in Ariana's face, but it sure felt like it. "Lucas is going to come back to me. Just watch. You're a distraction and nothing else. Do you really think he's going to wait for you when I'm going to be right here?"

Now the entire class was "oohing."

Ariana felt herself turn red. But she wasn't sure if it was out of embarrassment or anger. Maybe both.

She had no idea what to say to that, so she went with her impulses. There was no way she going to get pushed around by her. Before she knew it, she was out of her chair and in front of Wendy.

Wendy stood up too, the sound of her chair scraping the tile floor echoing throughout the room

Before she could do anything else, she heard the teacher yell, "Stop this instant. Get out of my class. Both of you. Now."

chapter twenty-two

Tears flooded Ariana's eyes as she fully realized what was going on.

She had gone through this last semester with Wendy. The principal had given her another chance and just given her ISS, but she remembered his warning about this kind of thing happening again. What if she got ISS again? Or got suspended this time? The deal had been not to get into trouble again or it would go on her record.

UGA would not be happy this kind of thing on her record. What if they changed their mind about her?

She closed the classroom door behind her and went to the opposite side of the door that Wendy was at.

She leaned back on the wall and closed her eyes, careful not to let any tears escape.

She crossed her arms across her chest and waited for the teacher to come out.

A minute of complete silence went by, and he was still inside the room.

She glanced at Wendy, who was on her phone.

She shook her head and stared in front of her.

"What is your problem?" she asked before she could stop herself. She looked at Wendy when she didn't immediately reply. She went on. "Can't you see that Lucas and I are happy? What kind of person are you that you're going to try to break us up?"

Before she could even take a breath after she was done talking, Wendy was already facing her. "He was mine first. He loves me, and I know we're going to be together again. It's just a matter of time," she said, dragging out her last three words.

Some short guy Ariana didn't know walked by with his student agenda in hand and stared until he disappeared around the corner.

"Don't you think that if he loved you, he would actually be with you?" Ariana said, almost laughing. Wendy had to be completely ridiculous, she thought.

"How do you know he isn't?"

At that moment, the door opened and the teacher came out with two yellow slips. He handed them each one.

"Principal's office. Now. And if you two decide to cause another spectacle on your way there, rest assured that you will not walk at graduation."

Ariana nodded and began walking. She heard the classroom door shut behind her. She tried to focus on taking steps forward instead of the fact that Wendy was right behind her.

###

"Another fight?" Jimmy asked at the end of the day. They were in the parking lot, leaning against their cars. Lucas had his arm around her.

"Did you get expelled? Because that's what I heard," Mayra said.

She shook her head. "Since it was really just an argument, the principal gave us ISS again. Two days this time." She looked up at Lucas, who was staring at the ground.

"But that's like almost all of our last week," Mayra said, her hands on her hips.

"I know. It means I can't skip on Senior Skip Day," she said.

"But that's like the best part of freakin' senior year," Mayra complained. Jimmy laughed.

"Don't worry," he said. "I'll skip with you."

She bumped her hip into his but smiled.

Ariana kept her arms crossed. How had her life come to this?

She looked up at Lucas again. He was being way too quiet.

Mayra suddenly grabbed Jimmy by the arm. "Come on. Let's go for a walk."

Even though Mayra was supposed to ride the bus because she was still grounded, she was cheating today since her mom was at work. She realized there was no way for her to find out she was still riding with Ariana and Jimmy. Unless Ariana's parents caught them. It was a risk they were willing to take, although Ariana had hesitated at first.

Now that Mayra and Jimmy were temporarily gone, she turned around so she was facing Lucas.

"What's going through your head?"

He sighed. "I don't know. I just don't know why you would let her get to you like that."

"Well, I couldn't let her think she can treat me like that," she said. "You should hear the things she says."

"I know. But you could have handled it better. Ignored her, I don't know."

Ariana kept her mouth closed instead of talking, but she spoke up as another question popped into her head. "Do you still talk to her?"

Lucas looked her in the eye. "Of course not. That's in the past. I have no reason to talk to her."

Ariana nodded. "She is so crazy. She thinks she's going to get back together with you."

"That is the last thing I would do. After we broke up, and she broke up with me, I got over it. But then she kept insisting we get back together. But I knew it was just not a good idea."

"Don't get offended or anything, but why would you go out with her in the first place? She's…you know how she is. Always involved in drama."

Lucas seemed to be staring off into space as he talked. "She wasn't always like that. She used to be different. That's why we eventually broke up. She began caring more about being popular and all that crap. It turned her into a different person."

Ariana thought about that.

She hugged Lucas, and he squeezed her back. "This is all going to be over soon, and we're going to miss it," he said. "But I'm happy because it means I'll get to spend more time with you, even if it means we're that much closer to you leaving."

A few minutes later, he said, "I wonder what your parents are going to say this time."

She sighed. "I can't tell them. I'm not gonna risk getting grounded or something and not be able to see you."

Lucas nodded but didn't say anything.

###

"Come on," Jimmy begged. "Let me drive. Just five minutes."

Ariana sighed and looked at him for a second. He was still supposedly grounded for another week. But their parents had agreed to let them go get something to eat and come right back since it was Friday night. As in they had to get something to go.

"Ugh. Fine." She pulled over into a gas station. "I need to get gas anyway. But you pump."

"Deal." She pulled into a spot and got out only to go the passenger side. She handed Jimmy a twenty her parents had given her for gas. He headed inside to pay.

Ariana closed the door behind her and lay back with her eyes closed. A minute later, she heard the beeps as Jimmy pushed the necessary buttons so he could get gas.

"So where we going?" Jimmy said, fastening his seat belt. Ariana did the same and sat up.

She shrugged. "I just want some fries. Maybe a smoothie."

"Burgers it is." Jimmy pulled out of the gas station and went a couple miles down the road to the local burger place.

Fifteen minutes later, they were headed home.

"So how are things with Lucas?" Jimmy asked with both hands on the wheel.

"Good," Ariana said. "How are things with Mayra?"

"Eh, could be better," he replied.

"Told you to tell Mom and Dad," she said. She kept her eyes on the road too. It was finally getting dark.

"Yeah, yeah," he replied, making a turn. "I could say the same thing about you and the whole fiasco at school."

Oops, she thought.

There were a few minutes of silence.

"Ready for graduation?" he said. "Less than a week left."

"Ready as I'll ever be," she said. She felt a pit in her stomach.

"Scared?" Jimmy asked with a quick look. "

"Yeah," she said. "It's really hitting me that I'm moving away. By myself. In a new place. That is damn scary."

"We'll come and visit, though. And you will too. I can't wait until I'm in college," he said.

"I bet. If you get a scholarship and play for a school, you'll always be on the road, meeting new people."

Jimmy nodded. "Just gotta keep it up. And not get injured in the next two years."

"Yeah, no pressure," Ariana said with a smile.

"Hey, did you ever hear from Carlos anymore?"

Ariana looked out the window, the smile gone from her face. "No. Why?"

"Just wondering. Making sure he never bothered you anymore."

They were on their street now.

"Nope. Don't really want to see or talk to him after…everything. He just wasn't good for me."

"Got that right."

As they turned the corner and came into view of their house, Jimmy turned off the headlights and slowed down in front of Mayra's house.

"What are you going?" Ariana said staring at Jimmy.

"Five minutes. I promise. I'll be right back," he said, taking off his seat belt.

"If mom and dad fi—" she began.

"They won't. Please. I need to see her really quick."

She sighed. "Okay. Three minutes."

Jimmy smiled and ran up Maya's driveway.

###

A few minutes later, she texted Mayra.

What was that about?

Ariana waited for it to send before putting her phone down on the kitchen table and getting her food out of the bag.

A couple of minutes later, her phone buzzed.

He missed me :)

Ariana smiled and finished eating. Then she went to her room, passing Jimmy in the living room. He was eating and watching a movie in there.

"More studying?" Jimmy asked.

"Not tonight. When are you gonna start studying for finals?" she asked without stopping. She'd study tomorrow night or Sunday. Whenever the senioritis ebbed off a bit.

"Eh," he replied.

Jimmy's senioritis had started two years early.

She went to her room and shut the door. She called Mayra as she lay down on her bed.

"Hey, what are you guys up to over there?" Mayra asked.

"Jimmy's watching a movie, and I'm in my room

hanging out," she replied.

"God, I'm so glad my mom didn't take my phone or I'd be going nuts by myself over here. After so many hours of cable, you just feel like puking everywhere."

"When is she giving you back your car keys?" Ariana said with a smile.

"After graduation next week. Riding the bus sucks. I'm literally the only senior on there."

Mayra's mom thought Jimmy and Mayra needed some time away from each other.

"Wow. Yeah, I don't envy you. Those freshmen must be all over you, huh?"

Mayra made retching sounds, which made Ariana bend over laughing.

"Hey, so was that the first time your mom ever caught you sneaking out? Or should I say sneaking someone in? I just thought about that."

"Yeah. Ruined my perfect record too."

"I bet." She lay back on her bed. She was starting to get kind of sleepy. Why did she always get sleepy early on Friday nights? She'd never understand that.

"So less than a week until graduation. Have you found a dress yet?" Mayra asked.

"Not yet. Doing some shopping tomorrow."

"Maybe I can come with you. My mom was supposed to take me. You know, since I can't drive, but turns out she has to cover some lady's shift. And she needs the money since I'll be starting college soon and the senior dues wiped the savings she'd started. The one good thing about community college is that it's not too expensive, so we should be able to pay for it if I get a part-time job this summer."

"That's good. But yeah, you can come with."

"Thanks. Just text me tomorrow," Mayra said.

"So are you excited about graduation?" Ariana asked.

"Hells yeah," Mayra replied. "I get my car back. I can go out. I can sleep in. No more homework or tests or projects."

"I know," she replied. "I can't wait."

"We can double date again."

"If our parents let us," she said. "Not sure they will now that there's a conflict of interest."

Mayra laughed. "We'll figure it out. We always do. Not to mention we'll both be eighteen and on the verge of going to college. I'll be working. You'll be getting ready to actually move out. They can't tell us what to do anymore."

"True."

There was a brief silence as Ariana imagined summer and beyond.

"So have you and Lucas done it yet?"

Ariana scoffed and looked around.

"You have, haven't you?"

"No," she said a little too loud.

"Maybe you're really telling the truth. Second base, minimum. Am I right?"

Ariana stuttered.

"I knew it!" Mayra said with a laugh.

"Mayra," Ariana said with a smile. She shook her head. "What about you and Jimmy, huh? Not that I really want to know, but you two haven't done it yet, right?"

"No way. Taking things slow, remember?

Especially right now."

"Good."

"What's that supposed to mean?" Mayra said with a laugh. "If we're together long enough, it probably will happen, you know."

"I know. Just give me more time to process that first. Not to mention you've only been going out—"

"Like over a month now."

"Wow. Seems like longer."

"Yep. You and Lucas are at like, what, seven months?"

"Almost."

"Things are getting serious, huh?"

"Yep." Ariana stared at her ceiling.

"Do you think you're gonna do it soon? Like after graduation? I thought for sure you'd do it at prom."

"Nah. Too cliché."

Mayra laughed. "God, prom sucked. Biggest waste of money, dress, and make up. Seriously, though, aren't you running out of time?"

They laughed, but Ariana hesitated. "We've gotten close, but it's still a little scary, so I think we're going to wait."

"Is Lucas a virgin too?"

Ariana fidgeted with the corner of the pillow case. "No."

"Oh. Well, make sure he uses a condom. I don't care if you're on birth control. You never know."

"Yes, ma'am," Ariana replied.

"Don't mean to be a downer over here, but do you think you guys will do it before you leave in August?"

"I don't know. It just depends. If it feels right,

you know? I've sent my confirmation letter, so there's no doubt now that I'm going to UGA. I just want us to make the most of the time we have left."

"But you two are doing long distance, right? You're not just breaking up after summer's over."

"No. Never. It's just gonna suck when I have to leave. Not seeing Lucas every day is going to kill me."

###

"I missed you, mall cafeteria," Jimmy said, his arms wide open like he wanted to give it a hug. They were at the mall.

He was still grounded, but her parents had agreed he could accompany Ariana and Lucas to the mall to hang out. Ever since the whole Jimmy/Mayra fiasco, they had been a bit stricter with her too. Jimmy still wasn't allowed to see Mayra on his own, though.

The mall would be closing in a few hours, but Lucas was gonna be out soon. So they were going to grab something to eat and watch a movie. The theater was open late tonight, and her parents had given them permission since Jimmy was there too.

"I'm so hungry right now," Jimmy said, looking around at all the tiny restaurants. "Where do y'all want to go?"

"I don't know. Why don't you find us a table while I go get Lucas? It won't take me long." She glanced at her phone for the time.

Jimmy nodded and they started walking in different directions.

She walked a minute and turned right to go into the clothing store Lucas worked in. He was walking out. He smiled as he walked in her direction.

"What's up?" he asked as they went in for a hug.

"How was work?" They began walking back to the cafeteria hand in hand. His hand was soft but strong, and Ariana liked how he held onto her firmly.

"Work was work. Where's Jimmy?" Lucas said.

"Getting us a table. So what movie do you want to watch?"

"I honestly don't care as long as it's not a chick flick. I'm thinking me and Jimmy would outvote you anyway."

Ariana laughed. "Action it is. You hungry?"

"Starving," replied.

"Another thing you two agree on." Now Lucas laughed.

A few minutes later, they were contemplating what to get.

"I think I want a couple of burgers and a milkshake," Jimmy said.

"I don't know," Lucas said staring at all the menus. "I could go for some egg rolls."

"And I want pizza," Ariana said. "I know. Let's each go to where we want, and we'll meet back here." She began walking and the other two did the same without another glance.

She got in line at the pizza place. She was wondering what kind of pizza she wanted when she heard someone behind her call her name.

For a split second, she thought it was Lucas. Maybe he had changed his mind.

A split second after that, her heart skipped a beat when she realized she recognized the voice. It wasn't Lucas.

Her breath caught, and she fought shivers as she turned around.

"Carlos."

chapter twenty-three

"How've you been?" he asked quietly. He was standing right behind her, not two feet from her. She looked up at him.

He looked different. Older.

And there was no smile on his face. But he smelled the same, his cologne bringing back memories.

"Fine and you?" she asked. She realized she had taken a step back.

Carlos glanced away, and Ariana didn't know what to say.

She heard him exhale, and she realized she needed to take a breath.

"I've been thinking a lot about you and what I would say to you if..." he started. "And now that you're here in front of me, I honestly don't know what to say."

He had a hand in each of his pockets.

She agreed with him. She still thought about him sometimes, wondered how his life had changed and where he might be.

"How is...everything?" she finally said.

He shrugged, shifting on his feet. "Do you

regret…everything?"

Ariana's mouth opened and closed again. What was she supposed to say to that? Her gut said yes. The last time she had talked to him…

"I thought so," he said. "I know I'm not worth crap."

"No," she said. "I mean, you—you've gone through a lot. Neither of us were ready. We both did stupid things."

He nodded.

She went on, her voice lowering. "We just weren't right for each other." This so wasn't going how she thought they would if they ever saw each other again. "The way things ended, I just wish—"

Then Lucas was beside her, then in front of her.

"You okay?" he asked. He was looking at Carlos, but she knew he was talking to her.

"Yeah," she managed, stepping to the side so she could see Carlos.

"What do you want?" Lucas asked Carlos.

Carlos gave a small laugh and turned around to leave.

Except Lucas grabbed his shoulder.

"Lucas, no—" she began.

"Get your hand off of me," Carlos said. Lucas was slightly taller, but Carlos had a completely different look on his face from just seconds before. Their faces were inches from each other.

Rage was the only word that came to Ariana's mind as she looked at Carlos' expression.

She put her hand on Lucas's arm. Then Jimmy was there. "Hey, what's going on?" Ariana noticed people were staring. The entire cafeteria had gone quiet.

Jimmy looked at her, and she gave him a pleading look. Jimmy got in between Lucas and Carlos.

"Come on, man," he said to Lucas. "Let's go."

Lucas and Carlos finally broke eye contact, and Carlos looked at Ariana one more time before leaving for good.

He bit his lip like he wanted to say something but couldn't.

Lucas finally turned around and put his arm around Ariana. The chatter in the cafeteria resumed, with tons of whispers all around them.

"What was that about?" Jimmy asked as they stood in line with Ariana for the pizza.

Ariana looked at Lucas, and Lucas looked at her.

"We ran into each other," she explained. She crossed her arms across her chest.

"Was he bothering you?" Lucas asked.

"No," she replied. She tried to read the menu above her, but no matter how many times her eyes looked at the words, she couldn't make out what she was reading.

It was finally her turn to order.

"What can I get for you?" the guy asked.

"Um, two slices of pepperoni, please, and a drink," she said.

A few minutes later, they were walking back to their table.

"We'll be right back, I guess," Jimmy said, as he and Lucas awkwardly walked off to order their food.

A few minutes later, they sat down with their food.

"You okay?" Jimmy asked as he bit into one of

his burgers.

She nodded and looked down at her pizza. She took a sip of her soda and tried to stop thinking about what Carlos had said.

And what he hadn't been able to say.

###

Jimmy walked ahead of Ariana and Lucas. The movie was over, which meant Lucas was probably going to talk about Carlos.

No more dark room with a loud movie playing to distract them. And she hadn't been able to get into it. She knew Lucas had noticed.

Probably Jimmy too since he was giving them their space. Which she didn't want.

Lucas slowed the pace. So did she, but she kept her head down.

"Hey," he said quietly. "What's going on?"

"Nothing," she said. He tried to stop in front of her, but she stepped around him and kept walking.

They had never gotten into an argument, and she didn't want to start now.

"I know this is about him. Do you not like how I handled it?"

She sighed and looked back at him. "Kinda."

Lucas looked around and back at her. "Sorry."

"Don't get mad. It's just that I was handling it. He was only talking. He wasn't trying to do anything."

Lucas just looked at her, his brows furrowed.

"You're not jealous or something, are you?" she asked.

"No. I just—it makes me sick thinking he might hurt you. I know what he did."

"I know. But like I said, I was handling it. If I felt

like I needed you, I would have let you know." She wanted to kick herself. That did not come out like she planned.

"Sorry. I should have let you two—" Lucas let his hands fall to his side as he turned around.

"What?" she asked, walking towards him. She noticed a couple of people their age walk past and look at them. She tried not to think about them. "Lucas."

"What?"

"Let's just forget about it. Before we know it, I'm going to be gone, and we're gonna wish we hadn't wasted our time arguing over something so dumb."

He took a deep breath. He turned around and hugged her. "I promise I'm not jealous. I just…don't want to lose you. You deserve so much better than him. I know I'm not perfect, but I—I would do anything for you."

"You are perfect," she said quietly.

###

"How do you feel?" Jimmy asked her.

Ariana looked down at her black graduation gown. Her hair was in beachy waves and her makeup was done. She held her cap in her hand, with two tassels, one for honor roll. Underneath, she was wearing a form-fitting black dress with a v-neck and short sleeves. It was a few inches above her knee, and she rounded out the look with black pumps with a dash of sparkle.

She looked hot. Underneath the gown anyway. She couldn't wait for Lucas to see her.

She wondered what Lucas looked like in a suit all dressed up.

"Awesome," she finally replied.

Jimmy, meanwhile, was in just-ironed slim-fitting black dress pants, a lavender dress shirt and patterned tie, and to top it off, a tight black vest.

"We both look hot today," he said, glancing in the mirror behind Ariana. He took his phone out and they posed for several minutes as they took selfies.

Jimmy put his phone back in his pocket. "Come on. Let's get going. I think Mom and Dad are ready too."

It was Friday night. Seniors hadn't gone to class today. They'd already taken all of their finals. So she hadn't seen Lucas yet. Mayra had swung by earlier but was probably heading to the ceremony about now too.

"Mayra just texted me she's on her way there with her mom," Jimmy said with his phone in his hand. He began tapping out a message before walking down the hallway. Ariana was right behind him.

Then she went back for her purse. She probably wouldn't need it, but she'd probably just leave it in the car in case.

She glanced at her phone. Yep, it was time to go. She had to be there early for rehearsal.

The two days of ISS had sucked big time, but she was so glad all that was over now.

High school was over now, she realized.

Good riddance, Wendy. See ya never, she thought. Her stomach still felt weird at the thought that she'd be gone and Lucas and Wendy would still be here, but she trusted Lucas one hundred percent.

She sighed. This graduation, this day, meant it was the end, the end of her life here.

No, she thought. The end here, a new beginning in Athens.

###

Ariana tried to take deep breaths as her row stood up and headed to the stage. She was in the very first row since she was an honors student and her last name started with an A.

She had to admit most of the speeches were pretty boring and took forever, but now it seemed like everything was happening in a blur.

The first person, Daniel Ackerman, was called. Applause. Second person was walking across the stage, a girl named Patricia Adwell. She heard a horn in the audience, and the line crept forward.

She walked up the steps to the stage. It was her turn.

"Ariana Aguilar."

This was it.

She focused on putting one foot in front of another as some distant noises reached her ears.

Her family screaming her name?

Was her back straight or hunched? Please don't trip, she thought as she neared the assistant principal with her diploma in her hand.

She had made it. She couldn't help it.

A huge smile broke onto her face as she accepted her diploma and glanced at the crowd.

She saw her family standing up, jumping up and down, and screaming for her. She continued walking until she was off the stage and back in her spot in the rows of graduating seniors.

She took a seat and turned around to wave at Mayra and Lucas. About fifteen minutes later, she watched Mayra's row a few rows down stand up and head to the stage. The line steadily kept moving until Mayra was on stage and her name was called. She put her diploma down to clap her hands and scream. She heard her family and Mayra's mom scream too. She smiled at Mayra as she walked past back to her seat.

She looked around and took it all in. She grabbed her phone from under her seat and snapped a couple of selfies, not caring how crazy she probably looked. She would never forget this.

A few minutes later, Lucas was on stage.

"Go Lucas!" she screamed, her hands cupping her mouth. She took a picture of him as he headed back to his seat and passed her.

He went over, grabbed her by the waist, and kissed her.

Ariana kissed him back, her hands around his neck.

Then he was gone, ushered by a teacher to his seat.

How had her smile gotten even bigger?

She sat back down and turned back to wave at Jimmy and her parents. They waved back.

Row after row of her peers went across that stage to receive the piece of paper they waited for four years to receive.

Ariana realized she had tears in her eyes as the last person walked across the stage, and the superintendent said something about making their high school degrees official.

They moved their tassels over to the other side, and the valedictorian came on stage.

"We did it!" she screamed, and everyone threw up

their caps.

As they filed out a minute later, she passed her parents, Jimmy, and Mayra's mom. Lucas's family was close too. They waved at her, and she smiled back but kept moving.

Outside the arena, graduates and family members filled the place like ants. There was a constant buzz, and the flash of cameras started. She walked around, looking for Mayra, Lucas, and all of their families.

Someone snatched her from behind.

"Jimmy," she said as she turned to see him.

"How does it feel to finally be free of high school?" he asked. Her parents were right behind him.

"Ah-mazing," she said as her mom came in for a tight hug. She hugged her dad next.

"Felicataciones, mija," her dad said.

Her mom kissed her on the cheek. She couldn't stop smiling, but at the same time tears threatened to take over. She had no idea she would feel so emotional.

She swallowed and looked around. "Thank you. Hey, do you guys see Mayra and Lucas?"

Jimmy scanned the crowd. "I think they're over there. Let's go, and we can take pictures," he said, putting his arm around her.

As she approached Mayra, they sped up until they were hugging.

"This is amazing," Mayra said.

All Ariana could do was hug her back. She turned to Lucas and kissed him on the cheek as they put their arms around each other.

"I love you" Lucas said in her ear. She saw his

mom and sisters walking towards them.

"I can't believe we made it," she replied.

###

That weekend, Ariana hugged Mayra and handed her a gift. "Happy birthday? How old are you now? Twenty-one?"

Mayra laughed as they pulled back. "I wish."

They were at all her house, her family and Mayra's mom. They had decided to celebrate graduation and Mayra's birthday together.

They were inside working on the food preparation so they could take it all outside and grill out. Her dad and Jimmy already had some fajitas on the grill, and all the women were in the kitchen finishing up the rice, refried beans, tortillas, pico de gallo, and salsa.

Ariana's mouth watered with the pico de gallo.

"I am so hungry right now," Ariana said, staring at all of the food.

"Me too," Mayra said, using her finger to grab some mashed beans from the edge of the pot.

"Let's start taking all of this stuff outside," she said.

"I'll be right back. I'm just going to change my shirt," Mayra's mom had said. She had actually been able to get the day off to do all of this.

Ariana grabbed the large bowl of pico de gallo while Mayra grabbed the rice. They went to the backyard, where a table and chairs were already set. The table cloth was coming off of the table with the breeze.

Jimmy saw and went over to put it back. They set all of their stuff down. She saw Mayra glance at

Jimmy as he headed back to the grill a few feet away.

"So is Lucas coming or not?"

"Nope. He has to work until nine tonight." They took a seat at the table for a minute, and let the breeze tease their hair and the sun touch their skin. "We're gonna be able to see each other a little bit more, but it also sucks because now he's working more hours."

Ariana's mom brought out more food before heading back in.

"So what's your mom think about you and Jimmy?" Ariana asked quietly.

Mayra looked at Jimmy again. He stood taller than Ariana's dad. He was flipping some meat while her dad grabbed a soda from the cooler nearby.

"She's never really gotten in my business before, but lately, she's been giving me lots of advice," she said, using air quotes. "I just listen and nod or whatever."

Ariana nodded. "So is she taking it better than you thought?"

Mayra shrugged. "We're not grounded anymore, so we can all go out again, but she's definitely careful. I don't know why, if it's me or him or what."

Ariana just looked at her, not knowing what to say.

"I mean, he's your brother. He's an amazing, good person. He deserves the best." Mayra looked down then at the table.

"He has it," Ariana said, speaking the thought that immediately came to mind.

Mayra smiled with her eyes and mouth, and it made Ariana smile too. Then Mayra leaned her head onto her shoulder.

"Hopefully your parents don't hate me now," she said.

"That's literally impossible. You know they love you to begin with, and now it's like you really are part of the family," Ariana said. "Imagine if we're sisters-in-law one day."

Mayra looked up at her. "Not sisters-in-law. Just sisters."

###

"I missed you," she told Lucas.

"Mmm," he said as he left a trail of kisses down her neck. "Me too."

Lucas finally gave her one more kiss on the mouth before settling back on the couch. They were at his house. His mom and sisters were grocery shopping, which she hadn't shared with her parents. Actually, his mom didn't really know she was here either.

"We need to stop doing this," she said, but she couldn't keep a smile off her face. "We're going to get caught one of these days."

"Maybe," Lucas said with a wink. "There's only a few more weeks of summer left, though, so hopefully not before then, right?"

She nodded and put her hands on his chest and swung a leg over him so she was kind of straddling him.

She looked down at him, and his mouth fell open a bit. She could see his Adam's apple. She wanted to kiss it.

Ariana bent down until her mouth was on his neck. She heard Lucas give a small groan, and his hands went to her hips. She kissed his neck a little longer and then moved to his mouth.

Lucas pulled away and looked her in the eyes. "Wanna go to my room?" he said quietly.

She hesitated, not sure about what he meant until after a couple seconds. She had told him about being on the pill, but they hadn't talked much beyond that except they would use protection whenever they were both ready.

"Sorry," he said quickly, sitting up and taking his hands off her waist. "We can stay here and —"

"No," she interrupted. Her heart beat so fast it was hard to catch her breath. "I want to."

Lucas looked like he wanted to say something but couldn't.

"Do you have a—" she asked.

He nodded, and they got up. He took her hand and led her to his room.

A minute later, they were on his bed, and she wondered what to do next. Lucas stroked her hair.

"Can I just say something before we…" he didn't finish.

She nodded.

"I don't want you to think that I'm saying this because we're about to do it. But I don't want to do it without you knowing this. "

Lucas took a deep breath and held her gaze.

"I love you so much." It was so quiet, Ariana wasn't sure she had heard it.

"I love you too, Lucas."

She smiled, and she saw Lucas smile for a moment before bringing his lips to hers.

chapter twenty-four

"Me and Lucas…" Ariana began a few days later.

"You did it," Mayra finished, looking up from her phone. They were on Mayra's bed. The TV was on, but they weren't watching it.

"Yeah," she confirmed.

"Oh my God," Mayra said, staring at her. "You finally lost your V card."

She ran to the window and peeked out.

"What are you doing?" Ariana said, laughing.

"Checking for tornadoes, hurricanes, and UFOs," she said, jumping back on the bed.

"Oh wow," Ariana said. "Really?"

"Really," Mayra said. "Nah, just kidding. Eighteen is a good age to lose it. Got all your stuff figured out. I don't even know if the right word is "lose it" because you chose to give it to someone you trust."

"True," Ariana said, thinking about that.

"So how was it?" Mayra said, chin resting on her hands and ready for all the juicy details.

"It was good," she began. "Not that Lucas wasn't, you know, but it just kinda hurt."

Mayra nodded and winked. "It'll be better next time."

A second passed, and Ariana got distracted thinking of what it had been like. Awesome. Kind of painful, but awesome.

"So only five weeks of summer left."

"I know," Ariana replied. "It sucks."

"We're gonna have to start registering soon for classes and buying books and all of that," Mayra went on. "Have you and Lucas been talking about all of that?"

"Some. We try not to. Just enjoy now."

Mayra made a face like she felt bad for them, but Ariana tried not to think about it.

"Have you guys talked about what would happen if you were to meet someone else?" she asked slowly.

Ariana shook her head.

"What would you guys do if one of you met someone else that you liked?"

Ariana shrugged and looked down. "I guess talk about it."

She tried not to think about Wendy. She trusted Lucas, but what if someone else came along?

###

Where was Lucas? Ariana had been waiting half an hour for him to arrive, but so far, nothing. No text. No call.

They were supposed to be meeting up to grab something to eat before he ran into work at the mall.

If he didn't get here right this minute, they weren't going to have time to eat at all.

Ariana paced and kept her growling stomach at bay. She had skipped lunch at her house and left to meet Lucas instead. And begged her parents to let her come alone. Her dad had finally agreed.

Ariana watched people walking into the fast food place. She hadn't even asked to go somewhere nice. Just somewhere they could grab something together before he had to get to work.

Ten minutes later, there still wasn't any sign of Lucas, and Ariana was ready to go home.

Just as she went to get back in her car, her phone began ringing.

No surprise there.

She swiped to answer and put the phone to her ear as she got in the car and closed the door.

She sighed and said, "Hey."

"Hey, I'm so sorry," Lucas said.

"Where are you?" Ariana said, hesitating to start her car but trying not to suffocate from the heat.

"I'm…barely leaving my house."

Ariana glanced at the clock on her dash. "There is no way you're going to make it here."

There was a brief pause before Lucas went on. "I know. I'm heading straight to work."

Ariana decided not to say anything.

"I'm sorry," Lucas said again. "My little sister got sick, and I had to take her to the doctor. My mom's car isn't working since last night, so we're having to share mine until we can get it fixed. I was gonna call you earlier, I swear, but there was throw up everywhere, and—"

"It's okay," Ariana said, turning on the car.

"Are you sure?"

"Yeah, I'm just gonna head home and eat there."

"All right. Maybe we can meet tomorrow? Oh, but I have to take my mom to work." Lucas sighed.

"It's okay. Just figure all that out first."

"Thanks. I hate that this happened. I really wanted to see you."

"Me too," Ariana said, pulling out of the restaurant and putting her phone on speaker. "I just feel like I haven't seen you in ages, and there's literally like two weeks before I have to leave."

"I promise you I will figure this out, and I'm going to spend some time with you. Monday is my day off, and I will make sure I get to see you."

"Okay. I just hate that this summer hasn't been what we thought it would be. It's kinda sucked. I mean, if we were going to be going to the same school in the fall, I honestly wouldn't care…" Ariana had to stop there to swallow hard and keep Lucas from hearing the tears in her eyes.

"I get you," Lucas said. "Believe me, I feel the same way."

"It's just not fair," Ariana said.

###

"Happy birthday," she whispered in Lucas's ear. It was a bittersweet day. She and Lucas were finally getting to see each other, but there was less than a week left until she had to leave for UGA.

She gave him a peck on the lips since his mom was there but gave him another squeeze before giving his mom a hug as well and then his sisters.

They finally went outside to talk and walk around. They began strolling down his street, hand in hand.

"You look good today," she said. He did. She tried not to stare too much, but Lucas looked hot in his cargo shorts and slim-fit t-shirt.

"You sayin' I don't look good every day?" he asked, a smile forming from the corner of his mouth.

"Uh," she said.

"You hesitated," Lucas said, acting offended.

Ariana laughed.

They began walking again and Ariana said, "Last week was so crazy. Even with your day off, I didn't get to see you."

"I know. Taking the car to the mechanic and getting it back took forever. And my mom needed to run errands before and after." He shook his head.

"I made sure to have Friday afternoon and Saturday morning off, though. I'm gonna need to work a crapload of hours after that, though, to help pay for the mechanic, but I don't care."

She'd be leaving Saturday. She had to be at orientation and her dorm by 2:00 p.m. And it'd take her almost two hours to get there.

Part of her had wanted Lucas to drive her, but she had decided it would be a hundred times more difficult to say good bye to him at UGA. And her parents and Jimmy had already offered, and it would be wrong to tell them no.

Ariana looked down and tried not to think about all of it.

"This is really gonna suck, huh?" Lucas asked, his hand holding up her chin. They were far enough away that his mom wouldn't be able to see them.

She nodded, not wanting to talk right now. She didn't want to cry in front of him.

She looked him in the eyes, and he came in for a kiss. A long one but sweet. Like they were telling each other how much they were going to miss each other.

A minute later, she said, "I don't have a gift for

you. I honestly didn't know what to get you. Sorry."

Lucas hugged her tight. "You've been the best present I could ever get. I just want you."

###

Ariana wheeled her suitcase to her car and adjusted the huge bag on her shoulder.

"I'll take that," Mayra said, grabbing the bag for her.

Ariana couldn't even bear to look at her best friend. "Thanks." Mayra had been just a couple houses down the street for almost as long as she could remember, and now she would be over a two hour drive away.

"You sure you have everything? Phone charger, toothbrush, ID?" her mom asked, walking behind her with another bag.

She nodded. Jimmy came out with a couple other bags. That was pretty much it, except for her folded up and packed bed sheets and her favorite desk lamp.

Jimmy went back in for them.

She looked at the back of her car, at all of the stuff sitting there. It looked wrong. It was supposed to be in her room, not out here.

This was really gonna suck.

And her dad wasn't here. He couldn't get off work, but they had hugged that morning. He'd given her some cash and an emergency credit card.

"Well, this is it, then," Mayra said, her arms falling to her sides.

Ariana finally met her eyes for a second, trying to keep the hurricane of emotions inside her at bay. "Good luck with your new job." She was gonna miss hearing Mayra talk about working at the local burger place.

Mayra came in for a hug, and Ariana put her arms around Mayra's neck, closing her eyes.

"This is gonna suck so bad, Mayra," she said quietly.

"I know," she replied. That was the first time she hadn't said how great UGA would be. "But you're gonna be so glad you did this. You're gonna come back a completely different person. Better. Just watch."

They pulled back, and Mayra gave her a smile. "Call me. Like every day. And I'll do the same. Keep me updated, okay?"

Ariana tried not to look at the tears starting to well up in Mayra's eyes because then her own tears might spill over.

All she could do was nod.

Mayra finally turned around and walked back to her house. Ariana watched her the entire time, aching for time to slow down just a little.

Then she saw Lucas's car pull up. He got out and headed up the driveway.

For the first time ever, she didn't see a smile on his face. An attempt at one, but not a genuine one.

And the look in his eyes…it killed her.

She met his eyes and walked toward him. She put her arms around his neck, not wanting to let go. But she did eventually.

"How do you feel?" he asked after saying hi to everyone. He took her hand and led her a few feet away while Jimmy and her mom went inside to grab their things so they could get going.

She checked her phone. "Okay, I guess. I have to

leave in a little bit."

They had had breakfast together early that morning, but Ariana had come back home to finish packing and Lucas had gone home to let her get her things done.

"Last night was fun," she went on. The movie had been good, but it had been hard to focus. After, though, was what she wouldn't forget. Ever.

She touched his shoulders, his neck, his face, trying to remember the feel of his warm skin from last night.

He put his arms around her waist, slipping them underneath her t-shirt. She felt his fingers press down on the small of her back as he put his forehead to hers. Their eyebrows touched, and Ariana got goosebumps. Lucas came in for a soft kiss. She deepened it, wanting more.

She heard her mom and Jimmy come back out of the house, and she put her arms around his neck as hard she could. Lucas squeezed her so hard she felt she couldn't breathe, maybe didn't want to.

She closed her eyes, committing Lucas's smell to memory.

"I love you so much," he whispered.

"I love you too."

"You'll be back before you know it, and I'll go up there. We will make this work. No matter what."

Ariana nodded, not letting go of him.

chapter twenty-five

Four weeks later, Ariana finally seemed to be getting her groove when it came to college.

She and Vanessa, her friend and roommate, arrived at the bus stop, and Ariana grabbed at the straps of her backpack, looking for the East/West bus. She needed to get back to her dorm. Lunch with her friends had been amazing, although she realized from her aching stomach she'd probably eaten too much. She'd walk back to her dorm if it weren't too far away. Maybe it was time to think about biking to class, she thought as she looked down at the love handle that was forming on either of her sides. Definitely. She smiled, though. She made a note to bring her bike next time she went home to see everyone.

She'd had a hard time adjusting to the college life at first but had finally made a handful of friends, which was crucial on such a huge campus.

She still remembered getting on the wrong bus the first day, even though she had done a complete walkthrough of her schedule the day before. Not fun walking in late to class at all. At least the professor hadn't made a big deal out of it, except for saying hi to her in front of the three hundred person lecture class.

"So do you have a ton of reading to do tonight?" Vanessa asked. They were both wearing strappy sandals and shorts with t-shirts. It was sweltering outside. Ariana couldn't wait to see the campus in the fall.

"Yep. You?"

"Tons. History is killing me."

Ariana nodded. "Me too."

"I'm so behind. I heard some people saying the readings aren't even on the tests."

"Really?" Ariana replied. "Don't know if we should risk it, though. We should see what the first test is like first."

"When is it again?"

"Like two weeks," Ariana said as the East/West bus pulled up. They got in line to get on.

"No freakin' way. Already?"

"Um, yeah," she replied, climbing the steps. She walked down the aisle and took one of two empty seats. She chose the one by the window. She liked to people watch. There were several dozen students milling about, walking to class or a dining hall, even the occasional professor or T.A. heading to the next class.

She wondered what Lucas was doing right now. She took a deep breath and focused on their last time together, besides saying goodbye. It was still too painful to think about that.

Next, she wondered about Jimmy and how his day had been. He was probably gearing up for basketball season with Ryan.

That was going to kill her not being able to go to most of his games. She had made a promise to him, though, to make it some of them. She had to.

Mayra. How was she holding up?

She hadn't talked to her in a few days, even though they'd said they'd talk or text every single day.

Same with Lucas.

It hadn't happened. Between their completely different class schedules, his work, her new friends and making time for studying, and Mayra's new job. It was impossible to keep up.

She had to call them tonight, though. Had to. And her parents. Although she could count on her mom to call every other day at least.

She sighed.

College was amazing. She never imagined it to be this fun meeting new people, studying together, going to the dining hall at two in the morning, and just learning.

But she also never thought it would be this hard leaving everyone behind.

###

"Whatcha thinking' about?" Vanessa asked.

Ariana kept her gaze out the window as they bumped along to their dorm.

"Who did you leave behind?" Ariana asked.

Vanessa had moved here too. From several hours away, though.

"An ex-boyfriend, who I don't miss," she emphasized. "And some friends. My family. I keep in touch, but I like it here a lot better." She could feel Vanessa's eyes on her. "Do you miss yours? Your family and friends?"

"Yeah. My boyfriend. My brother, my best friend. I didn't have a lot of friends in high school, but those three are just..."

Vanessa nodded and gave her a half hug as best as she could on the crowded, moving bus. They hadn't talked a lot about their loved ones before. Just the now.

"For me, it's my sister. She's older than me by two years and pregnant. It's hard being away from her and not seeing her cute belly grow."

Ariana turned to her and smiled. Vanessa was the first to go to college in her family too.

A few minutes later, she and Vanessa were going into their dorm room.

She set her stuff down on her desk and climbed the ladder up to her bed. She needed a few minutes of quiet with her eyes closed to process the day. Those classes were long, and she was still kind of full.

Vanessa headed off to shower. "Be back later."

"'Kay," she replied as Vanessa closed the door behind her.

She got up and grabbed her phone from her desk, her arm barely reaching it from on top of her books.

She looked at the time. 3:47 p.m.

Lucas would be out of class and heading home if she remembered correctly. She dialed.

Two rings later, "Hey, babe."

"Hey," she said with a smile. "I miss you."

She heard his sigh on the other end. "I miss you too."

"How was your day? Are you heading home or to work?"

"Home then work. It was good. Not too much homework and no tests on the radar yet. You?"

"Tons of reading to do and a test in two weeks. First one."

"I know you're gonna rock it. Because that's you do."

Ariana's heart skipped a beat. "I wish I could kiss you right now."

"I wish I could do more than kiss you right now."

Again with the heart skipping.

"Did you eat?" she asked, staring at the ceiling just inches from her face.

"Not yet."

"I did. At the dining hall. It was officially awesome. I think I've already gained the freshman fifteen."

"No way. Seriously?"

She laughed. "Maybe. Is that a problem?"

"Not at all. Just means there's more of you to love."

She could see him doing the wink he always did. "That's what I thought," she said, and he laughed.

She sighed. "When do I get to see you? This weekend?"

She had gone home a couple of weeks ago but had hardly seen him because of his work schedule.

"I have to work pretty much the entire weekend. This other girl has the flu or something so we're having to fill in her hours until she comes back."

"Okay. Not this weekend. Not next weekend because I'll have that test. I guess we can talk next week and see if maybe the next next weekend…"

She tried not to sound too hopeless there.

"Maybe I can come up there. I haven't gone yet. You could show me around."

"You really think they're going to give you the weekend off?" she said before he had hardly finished his sentence.

"Um, so not a weekend. Maybe weekend day? I'll ask at work."

She thought about the hassle it would be for him, his mom, and his sisters. He was supposed to help take care of them.

"It's okay. I can go there. We'll work it out."

"Okay. I love you. Hey, I have to go. I only have a few minutes to eat before I have to leave again for work. I'll talk to you later?"

"Yeah. Love you."

"Hey," he said right before she was about to hang up. "I miss you."

"I miss you too."

Next, she tried Mayra.

After calling three times and not getting an answer, she settled for sending a text instead.

Hey bestie. I miss you. Call me later.

She sighed, climbed down, and began the night's readings.

###

It was finally Christmas break. She was free, at least until January 3rd, when classes started back up.

Her final exams were finished and hopefully aced. She'd be able to check online in a week or two.

It was time to go home.

And she couldn't wait.

She had seen her family and Mayra a grand total of four times in the past almost five months. It had sucked.

She had seen Lucas a grand total of three times. That had sucked more.

Especially since they hadn't been talking much lately. It was as much her fault as it had been his.

As the semester had passed, they had talked less and less. School had gotten hard for both of them. Ariana's classes were really challenging, and she didn't want to settle for getting anything less than all As. Lucas, meanwhile, had seemed like a zombie last time she had seen him a month ago. She tried to remember the last time she spoke to him. It had to have been at least two weeks, and they hadn't talked more than a few minutes.

She had also missed almost all of Jimmy's basketball games. Mayra had sent her a few video clips, but it was nowhere near the same as being there to cheer him on. She was so excited that she was gonna be able to make it to his last game before he got out of school for Christmas break.

Ariana packed a few last things into a huge shoulder bag before looking around. Her charger. She unplugged it and shoved it into the bag. She had all of her toiletries and her pillow.

Vanessa came in. She set her keys down.

"Are you sure you don't want to come home with me a few days?" Ariana asked.

"Nah. A few days of quiet will do me good. And I have plans to hang out with Nick. No worries."

Vanessa wasn't going home right away. She had met a guy on campus. Someone in her chem class. Ariana had seen him on Twitter. He was pretty hot. And smart, from what Vanessa had told her. He had offered to tutor her, although it sounded like they had been doing more than tutoring lately.

Ariana hugged Vanessa, not letting go for a few seconds.

"Well, take care. Have fun but not too much fun."

They laughed.

"I promise I will. Or won't," she replied.

"Let me know if you need anything," Ariana said, emphasizing that last word. "I'll be back in a flash, or if you do decide you want to come spend time at my house, you're always welcome."

"Ditto," Vanessa said. "Stay safe. Text me."

Ariana nodded and grabbed her bag and phone. All her other stuff was already in her car downstairs.

She walked out and quietly let the door shut behind her, making herself slow down and enjoy the walk down.

###

A few hours later, Ariana was finally home. In her room. On her bed.

She hugged it and breathed in, closing her eyes. Seeing her parents and Jimmy had been just what her heart needed. It had proved impossible not to shed a few tears, especially when she saw how Jimmy had changed a little bit more since she had last seen him.

He still had one more week of school left, but Mayra and Lucas were supposedly already out of school like her.

Jimmy came into her room, jumped, and landed on her bed.

"Hey," she said with a smile.

"So you're coming to my game later, right?"

"Duh," she replied, making room for him. "I'm

already thinking of where I want to eat after."

He lay down beside her.

"So how are you and Mayra doing?" She studied his face for any hint of bad news. There wasn't any.

He stared at the ceiling. "We're doing pretty good, actually."

She thought for a minute. "You guys have been together almost a year, right?"

He nodded and looked at her. "Like eight months."

Lucas and Ariana had been together for over a year now.

They'd seen each other for a few hours a few days late on their one year anniversary two months ago. It had felt a little forced, and it was evident that Lucas had been really tired.

She hoped things would go better this time. She needed him. She remembered all the times they'd gone out last year, walking together, laughing. Things were so different now.

"How are things with Lucas?" Jimmy asked, finally breaking the silence.

She sighed. "Okay, I guess. Could be better. I'm just glad we'll spend more time together over the break."

"I bet you will," Jimmy said, putting his arm around her.

She tried to smile but decided to text Mayra instead. She at least needed to see her best friend tonight.

chapter twenty-six

A few days later, Ariana finally sees Lucas on his day off.

She had seen him the day after she had gotten back, but it hadn't gone that great.

Lucas had been in a rush as usual, this time to take his sisters to karate practice. They had taken a hit financially when his mom had lost her job, but he insisted on letting his sisters have a better childhood than what he'd had. His mom had found another job after a week or so, but she had to work more hours to make the same money she had made before, which already hadn't been enough.

Lucas was back to working full-time while going to school full-time and helping out at home.

Now she looked at the Lucas in front of her. He looked pale, his eyes had circles underneath them, and his head was in his hands.

She didn't know what to say. She just stared, wondering if he was so tired that he couldn't keep his eyes open or what.

"What can I do to help?" she asked, taking his hand.

He looked at her and blinked a few times.

"Nothing. It's okay. We're just getting through some tough times right now, but we'll get through it. We always do."

He seemed to be saying it more for himself than to her.

"Seriously," she went on. "I can take your sisters to their practices. I don't mind at all. I can even give you some money so you can cut back your hours for a while until you're on your feet again."

He looked at her and sighed. He shook his head. "I could never ask you to do something like that for me."

"Please, Lucas. I promise I don't mind. I don't have anything to do right now anyway, and I have savings—"

Lucas looked down. "I can't let you do that. These are my responsibilities. I can do it."

"Lucas—"

"Let's talk about something else. Please." His eyes still wouldn't meet hers.

###

"I need to tell you something," Lucas said a week later. They were in his car outside of his house. She had come over to see him, but they'd decided to get out of the house and grab some alone time.

Ariana glanced at him. He looked just as tired as the last time she had seen him, despite being on winter break.

"Lucas, has your mom seen how tired you are?"

"Ariana," he said, turning on the car. "Please."

She stopped and tried to figure out what was going on with him.

"I mean, you don't have class right now. How

come you're not getting enough sleep? I'm kinda worried here." Lucas went to put the car in drive, but his hand went back to the arm rest.

"I've been picking up some extra shifts at work. It's busy because of the holidays, and I need the extra money."

"Lucas, you need to take care of yourself first." Ariana turned her body towards him.

"I need to talk to you." Now he looked her right in the eye. Ariana felt a pang in her belly.

She waited for him to say whatever he wanted to say, but nothing came out of his mouth. Lucas looked back down, and his lips scrunched together.

Just as she was about to speak, he continued.

"I—I think we should take a break," he said, looking at her again.

Her mouth fell open before she could talk. "What?" she uttered.

"I'm sorry. Don't think I don't love you because I do. This is why I want to do this."

"That doesn't make any sense," she began. "If this is about how busy you are, I'm not pressuring you. We can work around it. I said I can help you. Let me help you."

It all came out so fast. Every thought that was flashing in her mind right now.

Lucas held her hand.

"I promise this is so hard and I don't want to do it, but we have to," he went on.

"I don't get it," she said, a couple of tears running down her face. She took her hand out of his and faced forward.

He scooted towards her. "You deserve better

than…this." He used his hands to indicate himself.

"I love you," she said, looking at him.

"I love you too," he said. "But you deserve a chance for these to be the best years of your life. Not waiting on me to show up all the time."

Ariana's chest convulsed as she finally let the tears come. She couldn't keep the sinking, crushing feeling in.

Lucas tried to hug her from his seat but only one arm reached around her.

"I'm sorry. I'm so sorry. I hate seeing you like this, but the more we try to make this work, the worse it's gonna to be. We're gonna regret trying to make this work.'

"No. I'm not," she said through the tears.

"Yes, you are," he said, looking at her. "I can see how much it hurts you that we can't have a normal relationship. You deserve someone who can give you that, and I can't give you that right now."

She tried to plead with him but couldn't get any words to come out. Just more tears.

She saw tears in Lucas's eyes, and he hugged her again before she could see them leave his eyes.

"I hate doing this to you. I almost wish I had never met you so we wouldn't be hurting so bad right now, but you're the best damn thing that's ever happened to me."

She felt him taking deep breaths as he tried to control his emotions.

"We don't have to do this. We can keep trying," she said.

He shook his head and pulled away. He wiped at his face. "This is what's best. I can't give you my best right now, and you can enjoy college, meet new people, and not be tied down by me."

She shook her head but began wiping away her own tears until they were gone.

She could see his eyes were red, and she wondered what she must look like right now. The tears wouldn't stop coming.

She thought about everything Lucas was saying right now. If this was what he wanted, how could she not give him that?

"If we're meant to be, then we'll get through this, right?"

She touched his face, and he nodded.

She nodded back. "Okay."

Lucas looked down and took a deep breath, and no matter how hard she tried, a few more tears ran down her cheeks.

Lucas looked back up at her.

He gazed her lips and came in for one last kiss.

She closed her eyes and tried to savor it, but it ended too soon. Lucas embraced her.

"I—"

He didn't finish his sentence.

"Bye," she whispered. She got out of his car and left.

###

"Oh my gosh, what happened?" Mayra didn't wait for Ariana to come to her but ran up to her instead.

Before Mayra's arms were around her, Ariana had already broken down. Her knees gave in as the tears returned.

She didn't even have time to think of how she had made it back to Mayra's house from Lucas's house.

"Come on. Let's go to my room," Mayra said, helping her up.

They walked together until Ariana was laying down on Mayra's bed.

She was full on crying now. She could not go home like this and let her parents and Jimmy find out that—

She cried harder into Mayra's pillow. Her chest ached for Lucas's arms around her.

"What happened?" Mayra asked. "Did you and Lucas…"

All Ariana could do was nod.

"Oh my God. I'm so sorry." After a second, "Why?"

Ariana tried to stop crying but couldn't. She was sure her eyes were swollen beyond recognition, and there was probably mascara all over Mayra's pillow by now.

She took a deep breath and tried to calm down, but the tears wouldn't go away.

She turned her head so Mayra could hear what she was going to say. "He just has so much going on. He said this is what's best for us." She felt her chest about to convulse again as she went on.

She broke down again and sunk her face back into the pillow. Mayra hugged her best as she could.

Mayra rubbed her friend's back as Ariana said through the pillow, "What am I gonna do?"

Her chest continued to heave, and Mayra shushed her.

Several minutes passed by until Ariana's body finally got tired of crying. Only dry sobs escaped from her body. She felt numb and stared at the wall of Mayra's bedroom. She hugged the pillow under her, trying to imagine it was Lucas.

It wasn't, and somehow, more tears filled her eyes and streamed down her face.

"You're strong. You're going to get through this."

She thought of Christmas without Lucas and his silly, sweet sisters.

She thought of the first day she met Lucas in Spanish class, when their eyes first met, their first kiss. The first time she tasted his lips. She wished her entire body hurt instead of feeling her heart break.

She stared at the gold bracelet he had given her for her birthday over a year ago.

How the hell was she going to go on without Lucas?

###

"So how was your Christmas and New Year's and everything? Did you and the boyfriend finally get some alone time?" Vanessa winked at her as they unpacked their things back in their dorm.

She and Lucas hadn't even spoken after… deciding to call it quits. It had been almost a month. She supposed that, after everything, they just weren't meant to be. She glanced at her bare wrist. She'd finally taken the bracelet off before leaving for Athens, but she hadn't had the heart to leave it behind or throw it away. Instead, she had stashed it away. For now.

Vanessa waited for her to say something. Ariana swallowed the lump in her throat and blinked several times.

Time to rip off the bandaid, then.

"We broke up," she said with hardly a glance at her roommate. She focused instead on unpacking the semester's textbooks. She'd busied herself with ordering them over the break and getting a head start on reading them. Reading other books, like fiction, reminded her too much of Lucas and what they'd had, and she just wasn't ready to face that.

Vanessa stayed silent, and Ariana decided to pretend she didn't care. She didn't. She took another glance at her, and Vanessa finally spoke up.

"Um, are you okay?"

She gave her a small smile and nodded. "I will be."

Vanessa came and gave her a hug, and the tears showed up before she had a chance to prepare. She gave Vanessa the smallest push away to give her the hint that she needed to be alone.

Vanessa went back to putting away her clothes, but her eyes remained on Ariana.

Ariana turned around and took a deep breath, forcing the hot tears back inside of her.

She had to get through this. Had to. Coming to UGA had been her dream. Still was. She wasn't about to ruin that.

The next four years of her life would mean something. Maybe they would suck if the rip inside her didn't eventually heal. She didn't know about that yet. But she would do what she came here to do. Graduate with a degree and make herself and her family proud.

chapter twenty-seven

Three and a half years later

Ariana got out of her car and headed inside to meet Jimmy and Mayra. They were going strong as ever. If anyone was meant to be, it was those two.

She wondered what they looked like. She hadn't seen them or her family since Christmas because of her internship, and now it was May. She was done with college. All she had left was graduation in a few days, and they'd all be driving up to Athens together for that.

Ariana took her time walking from the parking lot to the restaurant entrance. People milled all around. It was Friday night, and it was full. She maneuvered through the crowd and wondered if Mayra and Jimmy had made a reservation. Her parents wouldn't be there since they were still at work, but she'd get to see them later.

And all the time now. She was moving back home to look for a job. She had a degree in International Business with a minor in Chinese. She'd definitely kept herself busy the last few years.

It had been the only way to cope with losing

Lucas. They had talked a few times after they had broken up, but eventually, like all things, their friendship had also come to an end not long after. For a while, she had wondered if Wendy had gotten what she wanted after all that time, but from what Mayra had heard, she'd moved on to obsessing over someone else. As far as Carlos, Mayra had only seen him from afar once their second year of college.

Ariana had dated a couple of times, but no one had felt like the one, so she had gone back to focusing on school.

Her mind wandered to what she always thought of when she was back home.

Lucas.

She wondered how life had gone for him. Mayra saw him sometimes, but they hadn't really remained friends either.

Last time she heard, probably a year or more ago, Lucas had finally moved on and was dating someone else.

She took a deep breath and decided not to think about Lucas anymore.

This was a night for celebration with the people who would never leave her life.

Jimmy and Mayra. Mayra was graduating too. Jimmy had a couple years to go, but soon enough, he'd be graduating, maybe going pro with his basketball.

She climbed up the steps, keeping her head down as she found her way through the crowd of people.

Someone opened the door for her, and she turned around to smile and thank whoever it was.

Instead, Ariana froze at the face staring back at

her.

"Ariana."

She moved out of the way to let other people in and out and turned back to him.

"Lucas."

She swept her hair out of her eyes and quickly looked him up and down. He was in a black suit and tie.

Damn. He looked good. Not like she remembered him. He looked happy. Rested.

"What are you doing here?" he asked. She thought she saw him checking her out too, and she smoothed down her dress and hoped her hair looked okay. She hadn't had that much time to get ready after getting here from Athens.

"I'm meeting Mayra and Jimmy for dinner. We're celebrating."

"Graduation?" he asked.

She nodded.

"Us too." He indicated behind him, and she saw his family seated outside. His mom and sisters. His mom stood up and came over. His sisters followed after her.

They looked so grown up.

"Are they in middle school now?"

He nodded. "That's right."

"Como estas?" his mom said, coming in for a hug.

"Bien. Y usted?" she replied.

"Good," she said. His mom looked older, with more wrinkles, but less stressed.

She smiled. His sisters looked beautiful in purple and blue dresses and with their hair done. They had a little bit of makeup on.

"Look at you two," she said quietly at them.

"Hi, Ariana," one of them said. The other sister looked too shy to say anything. "Are you here to eat with us too?"

"Oh, uh—" she began. What was she supposed to say to that?

"We'd love it if you could," Lucas said, looking at her. His mom smiled and nodded. "No pressure, though," he added.

She froze then nodded. "Um, let me get Jimmy and Mayra. They're around here too. Yeah, I'll be right back," she said with a quick smile. She went inside and looked for those two.

What were the odds, she thought. This was so awkward, but she couldn't tell them no. She'd have to sit through this dinner with Lucas.

And his girlfriend.

Tomorrow, she'd be back to living life without him.

"Hey, you," Mayra said, coming up to her. Jimmy was right behind her. The stubble covering the bottom part of his face made him look so grown up.

"You two look hot," she said, momentarily forgetting her run-in with Lucas and her family.

"You too," Mayra said.

She went to hug Jimmy. He squeezed her hard, and it was too much. Tears flowed down her face.

"I missed you so much," she whispered as best she could in his ear, but it was impossible to reach him.

"I missed you too," he said, kissing her cheek. "How are you?"

It was a loaded question. School, herself, Lucas.

"I'm good," she said, convincing herself at least, and remembering what had just happened a few minutes before.

"Um, guess what?" She turned to face them both. "I, uh, ran into Lucas and his family, and now we're eating with them. If that's okay, I mean."

Jimmy looked puzzled, and Mayra made a face like "whoa."

"We just happened to run into each other, and one of his sisters thought I was meeting them for dinner too, and I thought it was rude to say no when they invited me. So yeah. We're eating with them. Is that okay with you guys?" Everything was coming out way too fast, and Ariana's heart was beating erratically, and she had no idea what to even do with her hands.

"If it's okay with you," Jimmy said immediately.

She nodded. "I'll live, I guess. I pretty much said yes, and it'd be even more awkward to go back and say no."

"I was about to say," Mayra began. "That was fast."

Ariana shook her head. "Definitely not. And you said he had a girlfriend, remember?"

She nodded. "I'll go tell the hostess," Mayra said before walking off.

"This should be interesting," Jimmy said.

###

Ariana peeked at her phone again under the table.

"Do you have to be somewhere?" Lucas asked quietly. He was seated right beside her.

"Oh no. Sorry," she replied, putting her phone

back in her purse. She didn't know what to say so she kept her mouth shut and looked down at her plate.

Everyone was finishing up eating, so she hoped they'd get up to leave soon. Luckily, his girlfriend hadn't showed up.

It had been fun catching up with his family, but she just wanted to get home. She thought she was over Lucas, and she almost was, but there was a small part of her that still hurt for what they'd lost.

She had no idea how Lucas felt, but she didn't want to find out. She just wanted to get outta there.

"Here you go," the waitress said. "It's been a pleasure havin' ya." She handed each group their checks.

She took Jimmy and Mayra's check. "I got this, guys." She hadn't made much money on her paid internship, but she had managed to save a little pile of cash.

Jimmy began to protest, but she stopped him. "I said I got it."

"Thanks, bestie," Mayra said from the other side of Jimmy.

"No problem."

A few minutes later, they were all walking out. She sighed in relief. She just wanted to go home, hang out with Jimmy and Mayra a bit, and crash. Tomorrow, she'd start job hunting and hopefully soon, apartment hunting.

She couldn't wait to have her own place and a decent paycheck. College life had been fun, but she was ready to move on to the next part of her life.

"It was nice seeing you guys," she told Lucas, his mom, and his sisters. "Take care."

They came in one for one last hug, and they began walking to their car on the opposite side of the parking lot. It was just Jimmy, Mayra, and her now.

"We're on that side too, actually," Mayra said, nodding in the direction Lucas and his family had just walked off to.

"Oh, I'm over here. You guys want to meet up in a few minutes?" Ariana asked.

Jimmy and Mayra looked at each other and nodded. "My house?" Mayra asked.

"See you there." She turned to walk towards her car. A minute later, she was getting in when she heard footsteps approaching quickly. She turned, expecting Jimmy or Mayra.

Only it wasn't Jimmy.

It was Lucas.

"Hey," he said. "Can I...talk to you for a minute?"

She nodded. "What do you want to talk about?"

She wondered whether she should close her car door or leave it open. How long was this going to take?

He came a few steps closer, until he was just two feet from her.

Whoa, she thought. Too close. Her heart began to speed up.

"I know it's been almost four years," Lucas began. "And you probably think I'm an asshole for what happened and you probably hated seeing me tonight and having to eat with us—"

"I don't hate you," she interrupted.

"What?"

"I don't hate you," she repeated. "Was it awkward

seeing you again? Hell yeah." They laughed. Awkwardly. "But I don't hate you."

He stayed silent for a few seconds before going on.

"What I'm trying to say is…I've never been able to stop thinking about you. And the more time passes, the more I'm sure I made the biggest mistake of my life letting you go four years ago."

She couldn't believe what he was saying. "Wait. Don't you have a girlfriend or something?"

"No," he said. "I did. Briefly, but it didn't work out. Wait. Do you have a boyfriend? I guess I should have asked that first, huh?"

She couldn't help but laugh. "Yes, you should have asked. No, I don't have one."

She tried to go back to getting into her car.

"So can we, I don't know, start over?" he continued. "Be friends again? Be more than friends?"

Ariana's breath caught, and she turned to look at him again. Her face felt hot.

"I have to know something first," she said quietly. She took a step towards him.

"I know I couldn't give you what you deserved last time. You deserved better. You still do. I can give you that now. I will do whatever it takes to make you the happiest woman in the world. I promise."

"You know I love your family," she said. "But you shouldn't have to put them aside for me. They need you."

"They'll always need me," he said. Her heart sank a little. "Not as much as before, though. My mom got her papers this year. She has a license now. She already has a better job. I wouldn't be here right now if I didn't know I could give all of myself to you."

"Wow," she said with a smile. "I'm happy for you. And your mom. And I don't know what to say. Maybe this is too fast."

He took her hands. "What do you want to say?"

She met his gaze and paused to look at him a few seconds. "I'm not saying yes to being your girlfriend just yet. But yes, I want to give us another chance."

Lucas smiled, and it made her smile. Maybe this could work. Either way, she had to know.

"What did you want to know?" he asked. "Earlier."

She paused, wondering how to say what she wanted to say. "I wanted to know for sure that I still had feelings for you."

Lucas's mouth fell open a little, and she took the opportunity to take the last step towards him and kiss him. His hands went right to her hips.

He gave a tiny groan in his throat as her lips moved against hers.

She pulled back a couple inches, trying to focus on her breathing.

Yep. She definitely still felt something. She stared at his mouth, his eyes.

"So when can I take you out on a date?" Lucas whispered.

###

A few minutes later, Ariana was finally buckling her seat belt and turning on her car.

What had just happened? She had not expected things to go that way, but they had, and she realized she did not have a problem with it.

Maybe Lucas was the one. No one else had felt

like the one, like Lucas. She wasn't sure yet, but she'd find out.

She made herself stop smiling at least a little, but it was impossible. She was smiling like an idiot right now.

She had Lucas's new phone number saved in her phone, he had hers, and he was going to wine and dine her.

Before she went to pull out of her parking space, her phone buzzed. She wondered if it was Lucas. That was fast.

But it wasn't Lucas this time. It was Mayra.

Let me guess. Going out with Lucas?

How did she know? She sent her three question marks followed by three exclamation marks.

Saw Lucas heading back in your direction ;) BTW, Jimmy says if he breaks your heart again, he's kicking his ass.

Author's Note

As always, I just want to take a moment to say **thank you**. My writing isn't possible without you.

The story continues, this time with Jimmy and Mayra, in *All In*, book 2 of the Changing Hearts series.

Find all the download links at yeseniavargas.com/all-in/

Jimmy has big dreams...

Jimmy's captain of the varsity basketball team, and he's going steady with the girl he's loved since he was a kid.

But he wants a college basketball scholarship more than anything. The odds are overwhelmingly against him, though, and then there's the fact that he's probably just not good enough to play college ball.

And he's willing to do anything to make them come true...
But he doesn't expect something completely out of his control to mess up everything he's been working for since he made varsity freshman year.

He must practice harder than ever if he wants a half decent chance of getting noticed by scouts during senior year.

Jimmy will do anything for that chance at college ball. He just never realized that would mean pushing the girl he loves away or watching his best friend spiral into someone he doesn't recognize.

But he might lose it all for nothing...
Sometimes, dreams require big sacrifices. But is it a sacrifice he should make? Or has he already lost everything?

Download this book at yeseniavargas.com/all-in/

If you want to know when the rest of the books

in this series will be released, make sure you sign up for my mailing list. You'll also have access to **free review copies** of my future books and **VIP reader giveaways.**

Sign up at http://madmimi.com/signups/152177/join.

One more thing. **An honest review helps other readers find my books, which allows me to keep writing them.**

If you can take a couple of minutes to write an honest review, it would mean the world to me. Thank you in advance for your honest review of Without You.

Yesenia

Acknowledgements

A huge thanks to my family and best friend for their amazing support throughout the production of this book. My best friend, Zendy, is there with me through it all. Shoutout to my little girl for reminding me that sometimes I need to take a step back and just enjoy the little moments with her. She's my life.

My editor, Brenda, has continued to be amazing, especially for catching inconsistencies and typos that slipped by even when I read this book over and over again.

Last but not least, a HUGE SHOUTOUT to my biggest fan, Kendra Ayers, who does not relent in cheering on Ariana, Mayra, and Jimmy and expressed her utmost support every step of the way. More thanks to everyone who signed up for advanced review copies and posted their honest reviews.

I appreciate each and every person who helped me on this journey and played a part in writing and publishing Unending Love. Thanks so much.

About the Author

In my pretty much nonexistent free time, I love to read (preferably on my Kindle), write, edit other writers' books, binge-watch Netflix, attempt to stay active, and spend time with family. I live with my husband and daughter in Georgia.

If you'd like to see what I'm up to or where I hang out online, check out my website: http://yeseniavargas.com/